Drusilla Modjeska was born in 1946. She has lived in Australia since 1971. *The Orchard* won the Australian Booksellers Award, the NSW Premier's Award and the Kibble Literary Prize. Her other books include *Exiles at Home* (1981), *Poppy* (1990) and, as editor, *Sisters* (1993). She is currently working on a book about Australian women artists. She lives in Sydney.

The Orchard
DRUSILLA MODJESKA

Published in Great Britain by The Women's Press Ltd, 1997
A member of the Namara Group
34 Great Sutton Street, London EC1V 0DX

First published in Australia by Pan Macmillan Australia Pty Ltd, 1994

British Library Cataloguing-in-Publication Data
A catalogue record for this book is available from the British Library

ISBN 0 7043 4514 5

Printed and bound in Great Britain by
Caledonian International

Contents

Acknowledgements

This book was written with the assistance of a fellowship from the Literature Board of the Australia Council, and also with the assistance of a residency at Varuna Writers' Centre granted by the Eleanor Dark Foundation. Much of the book was written in two short bursts at Varuna, in the studio where Eleanor Dark herself once worked, looking out into the orchard, and the garden she planted. Inside the house Rhonda Flottman and Peter Bishop were excellent hosts; in the garden Kate McConnell was a patient source of conversation and information.

While I take full responsibility for the views expressed here I would like to thank the Sydney Jung and Feminism Group for its discussion of the story of 'The Handless Maiden' which began the process of thought and meditation that has ended with *The Orchard*. In particular I thank Alison Clark, Marie Tulip and Leslie Devereaux.

I would also like to thank Helen Garner and, at Pan Macmillan, Judith Lukin-Amundsen and Hilary McPhee.

The wound and the eye are one and the same.
James Hillman

'I' is only a convenient term for somebody
who has no real being.
Virginia Woolf

The
Verandah

*e*ttie is famous for her neck. She says it grew two inches, just like that, in 1925, the year she turned twelve and the loopy girl next door buried the baby in her mother's vegetable garden. The baby was premature, and the loopy girl fat, which is why no one knew she was pregnant. But surely, at seven months, someone, even in a household comprised entirely of men, should have noticed. Ettie's mother, who kept an eye on the girl and taught her how to prune the fruit trees that grew behind the house, should have noticed. Instead she found the dead baby, tiny bloodsmeared creature, the next morning when she was working the long rows of vegetables which fed the family in their exile on Sydney's northern edge. She found the girl in next door's shed. She led her through the fence, away from the doleful gaze of the uncle who hadn't yet shuffled out onto the verandah for his morning smoke, and into her own warm and orderly kitchen.

Ettie was at the table totting up the week's takings from her vegetable round. The girl, who could not be induced to drink the tea Ettie's mother poured for her, seemed unable to speak. The jerky lines of words that usually came from her in a rush had disintegrated into a random babble from which neither Ettie nor her mother could prize an inkling of meaning. Questions resulted in a torrent of noise but no sense. At lunchtime Ettie's mother sent out for the police. In 1925, when this happened, the only possibilities for a girl like that were the courts or the lunatic asylum. Either way it was the police who would have to take her away.

When Ettie tells this story, although I have no reason not to believe it is true, it's sometimes hard to distinguish from the fairy tales she uses to illustrate her life. When I imagine the world in which she lived as a girl all that time ago, I do so through the lens of history. But Ettie herself doesn't see the past through a plate-glass window separating then from now. She sees the past more as a dream, and in that dream all of us are linked, and it doesn't matter that children on Sydney's northern outskirts once walked to school in old boots or bare feet, and now are driven in Saabs and Volvos, for there are passages that every one of us must traverse on our entry into life. It is the journey of the soul that marks us, Ettie says. Or not. And for that journey the past has as much meaning as the present, and legend is as potent as the truest of stories.

Ettie says that when her mother found the dead baby, her hair went grey over night. Literally, she says. Her mother found the baby, handed over the loopy girl, and when she woke up the next morning her Slavic hair, coarse and dark, had turned steel grey and white. During the day she still worked the long rows of vegetables which Ettie took round the neighbourhood to sell. In the evenings Ettie's mother told stories from Middle Europe where her family once lived, and it was from her that Ettie first heard the tale of the princess with the silver hands, which, by and by, I shall tell you.

.   .   .   .

Although in old age Ettie has lost some of her height, her neck has lost none of its magnificence. But when her neck first shot up from her body, Ettie was disoriented and felt herself a little weak. Its sudden growth had affected the nerves that run through the upper vertebrae into her arms. At least that's Ettie's theory; and no better explanation has been offered by doctors from that day to this for the periodic tremble that afflicts her hands, a kind of numb weakness that spreads down from the shoulder. This tremble has not been incapacitating, but it has had consequences. She soon learned that if her arms were well exercised, then the tremble came less often, and less severely. It is this, Ettie says, that made her a gardener. Otherwise she might well have been a painter. The tremble itself didn't stop her painting, it was only ever intermittent, and by the time she was taking classes during the thirties, months would pass between episodes. On trembly days she offered herself as a model to those of her fellow students who were creating themselves in the image of the reproductions of Picasso and Modigliani that were pinned to the studio wall. The characteristic lift of her neck can be seen in early works of certain artists collected in the archives of our galleries; when these student works are shown, it is as the first indication of her fame as well as theirs, though of course at the time, when she posed for them, no one knew what was to come. She was innocent, both of the future, and of her own powers.

And then, in 1937 not long before the war, she fell in love with Jock and the balance of her days shifted to his George Street studio. There she spent more time on the couch so Jock could paint that splendid neck, than on the canvases she'd lugged across the street for herself. Lying for her lover, absorbing his tribute, and listening for Helena's step on the stairs, she relinquished innocence and justified the betrayal of her first ambition and of Helena, her friend, Jock's wife, by the canvases – his, not hers – that piled against the studio wall.

During those years before the war, Ettie rode the evening train back to the peasant smell of earth and cut vegetables. At weekends she took the basket of cabbages and pears along the uncurbed streets, selling to the neighbours, or exchanging fruit for eggs, or a jar of jam. She lived one life in her mother's house with its shrines and legends, and another in the studio with Jock where the talk was of free love and modern art. These worlds she travelled between, along a mere few miles of railway track, might as well have been separated by oceans, hemispheres, mountain ranges. When the war came and the life that opened around her in the studio snapped shut with the swell of her belly, the tremble that eddied along her arms was like a signal from the world she'd left, a reminder that though the future beckoned, the past held a warning.

. . .

My friend Louise says it was Ettie who taught her that
the past need not always be appeased; from her she
learned to embrace it as a dream, allowing the narratives and rich images of memory into the clatter and
uncertainty of the present. In this it was fortuitous that
she met Ettie so soon after Gerhard, Ettie's husband,
the one who gave her neck its real fame, died. The year
was 1974. It was Louise's first research job, and her
appointment was with Gerhard to whom she'd written,
not because he was married to Ettie, though of course
she knew that from the portraits, or even because of his
reputation, but because he had once been a refugee.
She had written, the time had been confirmed, and
when she heard of Gerhard's death she was already in
Sydney. She rang to cancel, but Ettie said no, come
anyway, life must continue. So on the appointed day
Louise caught the train to the mountains and walked
down the track to the house. She came through the
gate, knocked on the wide-open door, and was greeted
by silence. She went round to the other side of the
house and looked out over the escarpment to the valley
that tumbles into a blue-green canopy of forest gums.
The doors onto the verandah were open, she could see
a book and a teapot on the table beside a chair. She
walked along the wall towards the orchard and found
Ettie tying back the espalier pear that had escaped in
the spring winds.

'I thought you were an apparition,' Ettie said, taking
off her gardening gloves. 'I had quite forgotten.'

Louise was not embarrassed by the forgetfulness of
the widow or by the absence of the artist. For her it
was not strange to speak of the dead; she had been born

into the presence of their ghosts and knew how to protect herself against their wayward influences.

The stories that Ettie told that afternoon were as much from her own life as they were from Gerhard's. She told Louise, my friend, that she had had to leave Australia just before the war and although the circumstances of her departure were veiled, Louise understood that a child was involved and that Ettie's sacrifice was necessary to save the child. This she told as a prelude to the shock of her return after the war when she felt as much a refugee as those she worked among. She told the story of Gerhard's ship and the children who stumbled off it, none of them his, and none of them hers, and how they'd met first in the customs shed where she was gathering up the children, and then later at a party in Kings Cross. This was what Louise had travelled from Melbourne to hear – the story of his arrival – but when it came she didn't take out her list of carefully prepared questions, absorbing instead the scroll of talk that moved backwards and forwards across the years of Ettie's life with the richness of a complex palette: Jock and the George Street studio, this house in the mountains, her old mother with her vegetable garden, and the story of the loopy girl, and how her neck had grown.

Later Ettie said Louise was like a good angel appearing in the garden with her adorable black pigtail and almond clear eyes. These days Louise wears her hair in a loose braid, but then she still pulled the plaits tight after the custom of her ancestors. Although the first of her family had come here with the gold rush, Louise, who'd grown up in a country town, relegated to the kitchen of its only restaurant, felt herself as much a foreigner as Gerhard fresh off the boat; more, her creamy-brown face an island in a sea of freckled red. For her the welcome of that verandah was a balm; as was this still, receptive girl for Ettie, willing where many are afraid, to receive the words that rose from the grief of the widow.

Louise's memory of that day is itself like a dream: those open doors, the orchard laden with blossom, the woman dressed in gardening clothes, tea on the verandah that faces into the drop of the valley. When they walked through the house looking at the paintings, some of them Jock's, most of them Gerhard's, Louise knew that the bare boards of those rooms, the large table in the kitchen, would become as familiar as anywhere she would live. As indeed they have. For Louise, Ettie was the mentor who would show her the way, not into ambition or fortune but into the shape of her own life. For Ettie this girl was one aspect of the daughter she'd lost. Clara is the other, but of course then, in 1974, Clara was still a child.

When Louise married Don, Ettie was at the wedding. When Louise and Don moved to Sydney, Ettie was among their visitors. When Louise's first boy was born, Ettie cut flowers from her garden and caught the train down to the hospital. And that is where I met her, beside Louise's bed in a large airy room in which the cries of babies echoed sweetly and the smell of milky nappies floated in the air. At that first meeting I noticed the tremble in Ettie's hands, and I held the vase still as she arranged the flowers.

· · ·

There are some who say that Ettie's garden is a work of art. When they do, they are usually referring to Ettie's shift of allegiance from painting to gardening that came, finally and completely, with the war, and the birth of the child she gave to Helena; but it's a commonplace she greets with a frisson of unkindness, and such people are lucky if they're asked again. To call a garden a work of art, Ettie says, exposes ignorance both of gardens and of art. She says that if there is a connection then painting is a kind of gardening, not the other way round. Yet these tactless guests might be forgiven their clumsiness. Ettie reads Gertrude Jekyll's colour theory for pleasure, and her garden is poised and composed. Even in its wildest parts, where it tumbles into the gully, or along the top of the escarpment where laburnums meet banksias, and the moody oriades entwine in the maples, its shape seems coaxed to Ettie's plan. But she says in gardens, where everything is real, the uncontrollable forces of weather and season have the upper hand. The wall garden may seem a pure example of mannerism with its espalier pear, its geometric beds of herbs and lavender, its gravel paths and low box hedges, but that wall, the wall that makes it all possible, was built first and foremost to break the wind that comes gusting up from the valley. Control is always temporary, Ettie says. Provisional, contingent. Wind can change direction; walls cannot. Plants can grow over bricks; frosts are not deterred. Which paint changes its colour from week to week, from month to month? Which composition rearranges itself within a year?

'But,' I say to Ettie's retreating back, 'gardens, like paintings, always mean something else.' She might sniff, but walking the pathways through Ettie's garden, taking whichever direction appeals, with no compulsion to travel first here, then there, following paths with their twists and turns, sudden vistas, hidden corners, it is as if one traces the course of one's own interior life, meandering through its dark corners and spectacular views, its dangers and comforts, its loves and withdrawals.

The track down to Ettie's place is steep and rocky; tourists sometimes take it by mistake thinking it's a way into the valley. When that happens Ettie opens the gate for them to turn round, and points the way back to the road that runs out on the spur where there's a car park, a lookout and steps down to the falls. For the rest Ettie's house is tucked away out of sight, a world unto itself, a sanctuary, an adytum. That's what draws people. That, and the garden. Or, perhaps I should say the garden is the sanctuary, the adytum Ettie's bedroom where nobody goes, only Alec when he's invited, and the girl Clara.

. . .

On visits to Ettie's, one can go a whole day barely seeing her, just a glimpse of her wheelbarrow, or the sound of her boots as she comes in through the kitchen door for the next brew of tea. She likes to quote Gertrude Jekyll that a lady in the garden should be prepared for any contingency, and in particular for inclement weather. Ettie is not caught short by heat, or wind, or sudden squalls. And while she works outside with only birds and rustling creatures for company, her visitor can lie undisturbed, given over to the half-world of her verandah. Having grown up in a country where there were no such passageways between garden and house, with beds hauled out and plants growing in, the verandah has become for me an enchanted place. Neither in nor out, it holds both possibilities and excludes neither. On that verandah with its spiders and even an occasional snake, it's as if for a moment the cry and shudder of life gives way to musings that come, rolling and inconclusive, from a secretly held part of oneself. Dreaming and only half attentive, looking through strands of jasmine and wisteria that loop like curls on a great beauty's neck, towards the escarpment, it's as if, from the vantage point of a verandah bed, that great expanse of sky rolls in over us from the very edge of existence.

On other days Ettie invites her visitors to follow her down into the gully where the pond needs clearing, or to the orchard where there's pruning to be done. If I am there alone, I always go with her; but when Clara is there, I stay quietly on the verandah. 'I need a strong pair of hands,' Ettie says, and Clara sighs and lifts herself from her chair. It is then that Ettie becomes fabulist and rhetorician, telling the stories that are her real intention for rousing the girl from her reverie; not stories from her adult life, those are kept for the evenings, for Alec, the last, or should I say the most recent of her lovers, and for Louise and for me; she tells the girl the tales her Polish mother told her as they worked their way along the rows of vegetables that kept the family through the twenties, through the depression, right up to the war. She tells the girl fables about princesses with silver hands, stories of orchards laden with fruit, stories of good kings and forgetful messengers. Tangled in these tales, brought from old Europe, is the story of the loopy girl and the trees of which Ettie's mother took charge, teaching the girl to prune, filling the baskets with fruit that afterwards, after the girl had gone, Ettie would hawk around the neighbourhood. Tales of the girl's uncle, who existed in the half-light of a verandah that had become a dumping ground and storeroom, and shuffled as if he were an old man, the senses blasted out of him in another, earlier war on the other side of the world, not far from the disputed territory of Poland from which Ettie's mother had escaped, just in time. All these stories Ettie tells Clara.

But there is one story she does not tell Clara.

As a consequence Clara does not know that she is Ettie's grandchild. Very few people know the story that began with Jock in the George Street studio, long in the past, and comes into the present in the form of Clara. This is a story Louise and I are told as a secret. It is a burden that Ettie does not want handed on to another generation. What she means is that she does not want Clara burdened; and there is nothing any of us can do to dissuade her. The secret becomes ours, and she trusts us with it; the burden also.

. . .

From my position on the verandah, shaded, and yet open, from which I can see while not being seen, I watch Clara and Ettie in the garden. I watch as Ettie clears the border that runs along the path from the verandah to the edge of the escarpment. Her kneeling shape is silhouetted against the sky. Clara, standing, looms above her, tall and angular to Ettie's rounded crouch. When Ettie looks up to speak to the girl, this secret granddaughter, the long stalk of her neck folds out from her body and pushes the knob of her head up into the air. Their dark shapes are like caricatures, hardly people at all, and in that tableau against the rush of clouds, for a moment it is as if they exist only in the secret that binds me to them both. Then Clara turns and walks back along the path towards me, her spiky hair catching the breeze, and she becomes herself again, and I remember with a stab of nostalgia the silky hair, a pale brown, not quite red, not quite blonde, that hung down her back during the years of her teens, and Helena's heartbreak when it came off. Helena, who brought Clara up, a second child born of another, had created the girl in the image of her name: old-fashioned dresses, shoes with strap and button.

When the hair came off, Helena blamed Ettie. Ettie had indeed come down on the train to see Clara, but though there are few she'd do that for, her concern had nothing to do with her hair. Clara had written saying she wanted to live on her own. She wanted to leave Helena's house in the suburbs and move into the city. She asked Ettie if she could take the flat with its large windows that look out onto a shaded street at the edge of Kings Cross, just as the hill crests and runs down into Woolloomooloo. That Clara hadn't said anything to Helena was tactless, perhaps even cruel, but Clara was eighteen, a mere girl, and she knew that by leaving she would hurt the grandmother she had known as mother.

The hair, which came off that morning, was incidental. As it happens, Clara says, Ettie didn't comment on it at all. When they parted she ran her weathered old hand through it, fluffing it up (Clara felt a slight tremble) and said, *you look like a proud tall emu.*

. . .

I was on the verandah watching Clara and Ettie out-
lined against the clouds, and thinking of the history that
binds them, because the day before, Clara had arrived
unexpectedly in a rage. It was a Saturday. Louise's boys
were with Don, and she and I, visiting for the weekend,
were lazing on the verandah when Clara's car come
thumping down the track.

'Have you seen the paper?' she said, banging open
the door.

At that time Tom, Clara's first love, her first lover,
had a column in the Saturday papers, the sort of column that is designed to attract notice, the sort of column
people turn to eagerly with their Saturday morning coffee. Indeed Ettie, Louise and I had been among those
who'd turned to it that very morning, and had read
Tom's reflections on an exhibition of women's art
which went by the tile of *Hands, Windows and Doorways*.
Clara and Tom had been to its opening together and
afterwards, lying side by side in the flat that was once
Ettie's, they talked about the symbols of power and
sexuality; they talked about the reality of power and
sexuality; there was nothing, it seemed to Clara, of
which they could not talk. To her it was as if at last
their understanding of the world, their hopes for themselves, coincided. As they lay together, she spoke of her
work on women's self-portraiture, and when she said
this research was an endeavour as much of the heart as
of the mind, it seemed that at last he understood her.

There were many expressions she used that night,
and from them Tom was to draw the phrases, the ideas
that filled his column – about hands, about windows,
about *the icons of feminine agency*. That was Clara's phrase,
and Tom was to use it. She told him the story of

Artemisia Gentileschi, the seventeenth-century artist who was raped as a girl and went on to create some of the century's finest work. That too he was to use. But that night Clara spoke with the urgency of self-revelation, thinking nothing of where her words would end, whose purpose they would serve, only that she shared them with her lover, that she shared them with the man with whom perhaps, after all, she could have a child.

Artemisia Gentileschi, Clara told Tom, was raped in her father's studio. When Agostino Tassi arrived in Rome from Florence in 1611 to work in Orazio Gentileschi's studio and teach the young Artemisia architectural perspective, it was a position of trust he assumed. He used it against her one afternoon in the May of that year when he found her in the studio alone with a woman lodger. He dismissed the lodger and raped his pupil, his host's daughter. Some months later Orazio Gentileschi, Artemisia's father, brought the case before the papal court where the records still survive.

At the trial a torture called the sibille was used on Artemisia to test whether she spoke the truth. The sibille was a device made up of a series of metal bands which were clamped over the fingers and pulled tight with strings. The pain was acute, and the damage could range from bruising to broken bones. This was used on the hands of a girl who was not yet nineteen, and already known for her fine control of canvas and composition. In her case the injuries appear to have been temporary. As the first version of her *Judith Slaying Holofernes* was begun in the year of the trial, she was clearly not kept from the easel for long. Just over a decade later a drawing by the French artist Pierre Dumonstier le

Neveu shows a strong hand with a deep furrow across the palm, raised with a fine brush held between forefinger and thumb. The scarring, if there was any, does not show.

The sibille was not used on the hands of Agostino Tassi whose fabrications of Artemisia's sexual misconduct were, even by the court's own admission, a great deal more fanciful than Artemisia's measured account of the knee on the bed between her legs, the hand at her mouth, the breaking of the hymen, the blood in her pudenda (the word she used), the knife she picked up afterwards.

The conceit of le Neveu's drawing is that the beauty of Artemisia's hand is magnified by the beauty it creates. A masculine compliment, Clara said, that drains her of all but the simplest of meanings. In Artemisia's self-portrait, dated 1630, nearly twenty years after the rape, she raises her hand to the blank canvas in a gesture that will bring herself into being; what she was to discover from the canvas was more than mere beauty, the illusion of which is easily made. For the woman who survives the sibille, Clara said, and Tom was to repeat, the journey to self-discovery is made on terms only she can inscribe.

Although the trial is a cause célèbre in art history, and although Tom had taken the same undergraduate course as Clara in Italian Renaissance, the name of Artemisia Gentileschi came to him as if for the first time that night. He sat up, switched on the light, and took notes as Clara spoke. When Tom turned the light off that night, and turned back to Clara, he knew his column would be one of his best, and she, in her vanity, mistook his gratitude for a deepened understanding of herself. The week passed peacefully. She spent it in the gallery while he wrote the column. He didn't show her a draft; that in itself didn't surprise her, he was always pressing against deadlines, although after the event she took it as an indication of his guilt. So that Saturday morning she read her words served back to her without forewarning. She was alone at the time, sitting at the table in the kitchen of the flat that had once been Ettie's. Tom had gone out. Leaving the page open on the table, her coffee half drunk, toast untouched – signs Tom saw with the first intimations of anxiety – Clara got in the car and drove up to the mountains, where Ettie, Louise and I had read the column over breakfast.

'That sounds like Clara,' Ettie had said when we came to the disputed paragraph. '*The convoluted struggle for a woman to see herself as the primary term.*'

'A complicated way of putting it,' I said.

'She means she's struggling to know who she is,' Ettie said.

'Then isn't it time you told her the truth,' Louise said. But Ettie was not to be drawn, and as the day was to shift into a direction none of us expected, that particular wrangle, that conundrum, was left hanging, where it always does, in the air around us.

. . .

'I mean it's a fact, isn't it,' Tom said when he arrived that evening and Alec poured him a strengthening whisky. 'Artemisia Gentileschi. I could have looked her up in a book.'

'If you'd looked her up,' Clara said, 'you might have spelt her name right.'

'It isn't the facts,' Ettie said, 'that Clara minds. She would have given you those. She did. It's that you took her ideas as if they were yours.'

'They came out of a conversation,' Tom said

'*I went to the exhibition on a cold night splattered with rain,*' Clara quoted. '*I went.*'

'Well I could hardly say I went with my girl friend,' Tom said.

'You could have said, *I went with a woman who said . . .* And seeing as we had the rain splattering on the pavement we could have had a conversation in a coffee shop.'

'But we had it in bed,' he said.

'You can change the location,' she said.

'I give up,' Tom said.

'Oh dear,' Alec said, reaching for the decanter as if it fell to him, as Ettie's lover, to mediate this dispute.

'Look, I'm sorry,' Tom said. 'I wouldn't do anything to upset you. Honest. It didn't occur to me.'

'That's probaby the point, dear boy,' Alec said. 'I don't think we chaps understand how women feel about their thoughts.'

'I suppose,' Ettie said, 'you could call it an advance that a man will turn on the lights and take notes as a woman speaks. I never knew a man who'd do that.'

'Some advance,' Clara said, 'if it turns up in the weekend papers as his words.'

'Don't be angry,' Tom said. 'In future I'll show you everything in draft. Would that help?'

'I'm not angry,' Clara said. 'I'm disappointed.'

And in that disappointment began her emotional education. And in the wake of her emotional education came Tom's.

.   .   .   .

As I watched Clara and Ettie that afternoon, protected by the shade of the verandah from the glare of the sun that illuminated them, it was as if, just for that moment, past and future stood outside each other and unsettled my own present. I saw myself as a young woman proud with grief, and I saw myself strain towards the peace, or calm, of age. It was a moment in which the complexities of my life were poised between both possibilities, as brightly lit as the silhouetted figures I observed. From my vantage point between them, in the borderline of becoming between youth and age, it was the shape of a woman's life that I considered: the long struggle that some name love, and others a more individual becoming, although it may be that to achieve one is to achieve the other in that journey towards the centre of her own life.

It is from my position between Clara and Ettie, with one hand reaching back and the other stretching forward, that I offer the three pieces that form the centre of this book. If I had to name them I would call them essays, for although they contain as much story as fact, and nudge towards fiction, they proceed with the spreading movement, horizontal and meandering, that the essay – a porous, conversational, sometimes moody creature – makes its own.

When I think of a way to describe my pleasure in this form of writing, my enchantment with it, a way of thinking to suit a stage of life that straddles and is between, the image which swims up is of Ettie's bedroom, that inner sanctum no one, except Clara, would dare to enter without invitation. The room, large, with two french windows, is sparely furnished: a wide bed, a table on which are books that have overflowed from

the shelves, a glass decanter of water, two framed
photographs (one of Jock as a young man, the other of
Helena holding a baby wrapped up tight for the journey
back to Australia), and a bowl of roses.

The walls are a kind of tapestry of her life: photographs, plans for the garden, stories Clara wrote when
she was a child, Gerhard's self-portrait of arrival. On
the wall between the windows that look east onto a
verandah and beyond that to an orchard that glows red
in the dawn, is the only painting Ettie has admitted to
as her own. Painted at the end of 1938 in the George
Street studio during a southerly buster, it is a gouache
of an eye tethered by fine threads, each of them reaching down to a flower, or a plant, that is clinging to its
hold in the earth.

From the ceiling hangs an angel with outstretched
wings and furious lips, which Alec found in Indonesia,
where he went to woo the stubborn Ettie. It flies above
the bed, guarding this enchanted room like one of
Rilke's *almost deadly birds of the soul*.

The
Adultery
Factor

Clara

Clara says secrets should always be told. She said it quite emphatically. She said how else do you know who you are, or where you are. At the time I didn't think anything of it, for Clara's young and prone to moralisms; it's only now that I see the irony of her certainty, and that night as the first probe at a secret that cannot be told. In that probing, like a tongue worrying a tooth, I bear some responsibility. For reasons of my own I encouraged the conversation, even prolonged it, thinking not of the story of which Clara is the distant result, only of the story Louise told.

We were at Ettie's again that night, up in the mountains, and at the end of dinner, when we might as easily have drifted off to bed, Louise told a story about a man, a wife and a mistress. She once knew the mistress, quite well as it happens, and had just that week run into the man; they'd talked in the street, and on the spur of the moment had gone into a cafe for lunch. It was then that he told her the story, as if justification was required, as if there was something that needed to be explained, as if Louise, by the mere fact of lunch, had insisted on it.

And out it all came, a tale of passion and hope, a tale of that deep familiarity of habit which is another form of love; two stories bound together by the secrets, the lies, the definitions that none of them – neither man, nor wife, nor mistress – escaped.

Clara's response to the story was that the very act of adultery brings with it bad faith, bad taste, personal weakness. At twenty-six, she is young enough to believe she will never give in to compromise, and old enough to know she probably will; as a consequence she had no sympathy for any of the three in the story Louise told. She said that if they'd faced the truth, they wouldn't be in the mess they are in now. Simple.

Ettie agreed that the lies hadn't helped, but truth, she said, would never be amenable to rules for any occasion. She said there were secrets that in honour we must keep, others that in compassion we should tell. The failing of this generation, she said, meaning Louise's and mine, the generation in the story, is that we no longer know how to discriminate; we seem unable either to live within the forms that marriage and the family give to us, or make the break and live outside them. When the forms held, Ettie said, whatever the cost, there was a moral code, or at least the recognition that when passion didn't fit the form, all the players had responsibilities to bear. These days nothing seems to hold, everyone speaks too much and says too little. These days, she said, everyone wants something for nothing:

love without risk, sex without hurt, safety without boredom.

Alec, who had a certain sympathy for the man, said that the temptation for all of us is to keep secret events in our lives that will affect those on whom we depend, for we fear their reaction, their retaliation, should we tell them the truth. Or else, just as bad, we blurt out our guilts as if we could off-load the burden onto those we've already injured. He said it's no longer considered an art, a human achievement, to know when to speak, and when to remain silent.

'Was it ever?' Ettie said.

It's not only in cases of adultery that Ettie sees the moral failing of which she complains. She wants to know if we're prepared for the answers we will be asked to give when the young turn to us, as one day they will, with questions we won't have anticipated. Although she said all this that night and I remember it clearly, I didn't attend to this question, and I didn't anticipate Clara's. But I am getting ahead of myself before I've begun. Clara ends this essay; she doesn't begin it. What she has to say is the result, not the cause of it. It begins with reflections that had nothing to do with her; none of us, except perhaps Ettie, had her in mind at all.

My only other memory of that night is of candlelight that threw strange shadows upwards onto our faces, and onto the portrait behind where Ettie sat: the pastel of a reclining Ettie that Jock did those years ago in the George Street studio; 1938 it must have been, maybe 1937, before the war, before the pregnancy. In that unaccustomed light I saw Ettie's painted face, preserved across the years, as innocent and curiously empty. I had seen that portrait many times, but never as I saw it that night. Although there was something about the eyes that teased me, if I hadn't known the woman into which that face had grown, I would have had no interest in it at all.

'The fate of a woman,' Ettie said, getting up from the table to say goodnight, 'won't change until she sees herself neither as wife nor as mistress. That is the challenge that is made of us. To some it is made young, to others it comes late.'

The Story

It was midsummer when it began. Several years ago now, when the city overflowed with visitors. In the late afternoon heat people stirred from sleep and pushed back their shutters. In the shaded room the man and the woman lay side by side and the quiet murmuring of their voices barely disturbed the room's somnolent air. They lay still, their heads turned towards each other, their arms resting against each other, their fingers linked, each with a leg bent in towards the other; they were close enough to breathe the sweetly familiar odours that had become the focus, quite suddenly, of their night dreams and daytime hopes.

The man was telling the woman stories from his childhood, and she was weaving her own story into the anecdotes he chose as a way of showing himself to her. Sentences ebbed and flowed between them, paragraphs slid gracefully from one voice to another. Such harmony, they felt. Such understanding. *It's as if there's nothing I can't say*, said one to the other, *it's as if I've known you all my life*. Their amazement amazed them, they doubted that ever, anywhere, either had felt so received, so held, so accepted. They planned a future which, just for that moment, both of them believed. Even the week in Siena. For him the room in which they lay was a miracle of regeneration. He admired the prints on the wall, the notes by the telephone, even the beads looped over the edge of the mirror. For her it took fresh life, this room that displayed her as she displayed herself to the one she'd taken to her heart as well as her bed; it took on new meaning by the very fact of his presence. In this exchange, they exchanged breath, they exchanged secrets, they exchanged the juices and fluids of their bodies. They were happy. Happy was indeed what they were.

It was the woman who looked at the clock. She turned her head and looked.

'It's gone five,' she said.

'I must go,' he said.

'I know,' she said, gathering herself in from his touch, pulling away with the slightest movement of her head, lifting her hand from the curl of his fingers.

'It won't always be like this,' he said. 'I promise.'

'Don't make me wait too long,' she said, wrapping herself in a sarong patterned with monkeys and tree creatures. As she stood, the air in the darkened room stirred.

The woman went out onto the verandah. Heat, noise, brightness, greeted her. The texture of the air, still soupy, was no longer dense, no longer laden. She could smell its grittiness, as if the wind had brought the dust of the inland all the way to the beach. The man followed her, his eyes lowered against the light. He was tying his tie. He stood behind her and circled her with his arms. She gave no indication of response. He moved his hands to her breasts. She leaned her head back and rested it on his shoulder.

'Don't,' she said. 'Not when you have to leave.'

'I want to be sure you'll remember me,' he said.

'I will,' she said.

In the taxi crossing the city to the house where his wife and children waited, the man felt a curious sense of nothing. A sensation of wellbeing: still, empty, emptied out. It was an emptiness, a release of all feeling, that he recognised in himself as a deep and secret pleasure. He leaned against the plastic seat, he felt it hot through his suit, and watched the flicker of familiar streets, the late afternoon parade of people returning to the welcome that awaited them at home.

His wife opened the door to the house that had been bought in both their names.

'You're late,' she said. 'Can't you even remember when you've promised your daughter a swim.'

'I'm sorry,' the man said and bent to kiss her. She turned her head from him, and at once regretted it, turning back to receive the kiss that had been withdrawn as deftly as it had fleetingly been offered. The air in the hall at that moment was slightly acrid; motes of dust caught in the still bronze light that came through the glass panels in the front door. Above them a child wailed. 'You're always late. It's not fair.'

'Come on,' the man said, shouting up the stairs. 'There's still time. A quick dip before dinner.'

'It's much too late,' his wife said, picking up a bowl of dead roses with a sigh. 'She's got homework to do.'

'We'll be back in an hour,' the man said, running up the stairs to change. Water was what he needed. Water, and the company of a daughter.

Confession

Fifty years ago Virginia Woolf said that *before a woman can write exactly as she wishes to write, she has many difficulties to face.*[1] I am not thinking of material difficulties when I quote her, but of the emotional and psychological impediments that change more slowly. How can a woman (how can I?) write exactly as she wants about a love affair, her own or anyone else's, when there are other people whose lives will be affected by what she says? How can she write about a love affair when the world of criticism and opinion favours a man's facts, or his myths, over a woman's romance, her fantasies, her gossip? When a man writes, or speaks, of love, it is to affirm his right to a narrative in which his sexual destiny and his right to tell the tale are in happy partnership. When a woman writes of love, it is a risky business, for her agency with the pen contradicts her prescribed destiny as a woman. Where one requires that she take the initiative and act, the other invites her to wait, and to receive. Every woman knows that when a man's desires, his domestic needs, his romantic pride are at issue, her story is likely to be run off the rails. It's not just her version against his; it's the legitimacy of the story itself that's at stake. If a woman writes of love, and in doing so speaks her mind, breaks the restraints, the constraints of definitions and names that are ever-present to her – wife of, mistress of – if she bursts out into anger, or a shadowy ambivalence, or into grief, it's considered an unseemly act: embarrassing, slightly pitiful. Her critics, the critics, will accuse her, the woman who writes in this way, of confession. As if the 'I' on the page should have known better than to let slip a messy reminder of the body that holds the pen. As if there weren't in any case gaps and fissures between that 'I', that body, that pen. As if confession was a transparent term.

When Louise told this story, it was not her story that she told. She was confessing nothing. But telling the story the man had told her evoked fragments and glimpses, feelings and thoughts that lay dormant, half conscious in her, and in us her listeners. She told it, and we listened, through the lens of our own experience. As she gave an account of a love affair that was offered to her as an answer, questions rose from it and transformed it, so that it became a departure point for other stories, counter-stories. Maybe the critics are right after all, and the act of telling can evoke confession in a woman; but where they, the critics, mean to imply that all she does is kneel in the dark and confess her sins, a list of failings she already knows, what she does in writing, in telling, is to search, sifting through the many versions and possibilities to find the shape and truth of her life, the story she doesn't yet know, the image and narrative she struggles to bring, like her self, into being.

The Story 2

As the months of that summer passed, the man and the mistress met – or at least spoke – every day. Every weekday, that is. They spent afternoons in bed, mornings on the phone. They squeezed their work into already crowded evenings and weekends. At first they were careful, meeting at her house and avoiding the streets. Then they became reckless, as if they needed the gaze of the world to confirm the pleasure they took in each other. During the day they met in cafes; at night they went out to restaurants and bars. The man was proud to be seen with the woman, his mistress; that is to say he was proud when he saw her with the eyes of the strangers they moved among. On those few occasions when they ran into someone he knew, he was embarrassed, and deeply ashamed. Sometimes he did not even introduce her, and she stood awkward and sullen while the pleasantries that were exchanged excluded her. Afterwards she refused to take his arm: she said he treated her like a mistress, like a whore, like a convenience. When they ran into her friends, it was his turn to squirm as their eyebrows raised in the question that could not be answered. A note of wretchedness crept into the joy that had so recently come to them undiluted; or so it had seemed.

In the cafes and bars where they sat, the woman would say things like *no one has made love to me as you do*, believing as she did that she'd found freedom to express the longings she'd reined in all her life; and he would reply *it's as if a light goes on when I'm with you*. Where once that was enough, now she began to insist, why should she not, *then we should be together, surely we should be together*. And he, demurring, took fright. *I wish I'd met you twenty years ago*, he said. *Well you didn't*, she said. *And what are you going to do about it?*

We don't want to listen to more: to the adjectives flipping around in the air above them as if their luxuriousness, their snappy sharpness, their sexy confidence, could change the squat solidity of the noun that bound them. In cafes the woman could play temptress and libertine; in bed there was only the present; but when the door clicked closed behind him that noun cracked like a whip. She was left in an empty house. There was no one to cook dinner with her. No one to share the Saturday papers. No one to plan Christmas holidays.

Was she envious? Was she sad? Or was she resentful? Resigned? She went to the shelf and took down a book. What else could she do?

Reading Habits

Louise says women read less for comfort than for research. She says that in her own case reading has given shape to her life. She says reading saved her when she was a child, the third born to the family that worked the Chinese restaurant in a small country town in northern Victoria. In the fifties the town had no high school. A bus drove the kids the thirty miles to the next town, but only until the school certificate. After that she was saved by the teacher who persuaded the mayor to fund her travel another thirty miles to a town with a school from which she could matriculate. The mayor was won over, the teacher said, by the list of the books which Louise, who was then still Lily Lou, had read. She was fifteen at the time, and the list ran to several pages. She was the first child from her family, and the first girl from the town, to go to university. Melbourne University. That's why she says books saved her. They got her to university; they married her to Don; they stepped her out of a world of tables and orders, customers and deliveries, and into a life of study and thought, papers and lectures. Even with children, there were always books by her side. They saved her then; and they saved her years later when Don went, leaving her alone in a house which, in his absence, became a place of draughts and book dust and empty desks. While the children played dungeons and dragons, she lit the fire, wrapped herself in a shawl and read her way through a long winter.

That's when she first read *Anna Karenin*. She said that from the perspective of the wife it wasn't much help: there it was laid out for her, the speed with which men tire of their wives. And the inevitability of their boredom. Had she been like Dolly, making the most of it, resenting her husband, settling for a half-life of security and convention? Would she have acted as Anna did? Could she? But then, while disappointed sometimes, she wasn't repulsed by Don, and she wasn't bored. On the contrary, almost to the end she would have said she loved him. That's the word she would have used. So, during that winter of loneliness, when she was a wife without a husband, Louise found no comfort in *Anna Karenin*; and she was unmoved by the fate of Anna herself. Now, as adultery is the subject of our talk, she is reading it again.

Ettie won't read it again. She read it fifty years ago, in London, during the war, where she was stranded after the birth of the child she bore to Jock and gave to Helena. She read it while waiting for the German invasion. She says that if you take the bare bones of Anna Karenin's story you can learn a harsh truth about the relations between men and women. The complex dance between Vronsky and Anna could only end in death, Ettie says, for although we name it passion, every step can kill: a dance in which domination and submission exhaust their possibilities. Vronsky's desire is driven by the need to conquer Anna. The tragedy of it, Ettie says, is that Anna's desire exactly matches his; she longs to be conquered. The paradox of her desire is that it evokes at one and the same time the need for independence and the longing to submit. But when Anna has acted, when she has thrown off the husband whose control she resents, when she has given herself over, body and soul, to her lover, when she has made that great gesture, her capacity both for independence and for submission has used itself up. It is a move that cannot be made again. Conquered, there is no longer any need for her to be conquered. Once she has sacrificed everything that has meant structure and security, how, as mistress who has become as familiar as wife, can she keep the conquering Vronsky? *Like this*, she asks Dolly, with her arms curved across her lovely breast? That breast no longer offers a challenge, no longer promises satisfaction. When he tires of the dance and she cannot revive him, the final steps lead to his withdrawal, and to her death. That's Anna Karenin, you might say; but Ettie's point is that any woman who places herself in the role of mistress and remains there ultimately faces death. If it's not a literal death, she says, suicide or pills, then it'll be the death of her soul.

'That's a bleak rendition,' Louise said.

'Indeed,' Ettie said.

Ettie dwelt on it, that blunt lesson, during the years of the blitz when she was separated from home and country, lover and child, hauling bodies and fragments and casualties out of the rubble and into her ambulance, reading Jock's letters in the hostel at night, looking at the photos of the child who was taking her first steps in a garden under the antipodean sun while she was stranded in a city where bombs rained down. That's why she won't re-read *Anna Karenin*.

'In Tzarist Russia,' Louise said, 'what else could a woman be but wife or mistress.'

'There are plenty of Anna Karenins in Sydney right now,' Ettie said. 'They're just harder to spot.'

Stella Bowen

Clara is not interested in Anna Karenin. She's not interested in the masochism of women; she's interested in their art. She says she'd rather talk about Stella Bowen than Anna Karenin. For her research Clara will travel between cities to see a single letter, to glimpse a diary, a snatch of interview. Stella Bowen, although one of the best portrait artists of her generation, is not easy to research. Her story tends to vanish into the more famous narratives that surround her. Who was she? I could tell you that she was born in Adelaide in 1895; I could tell you that she was one of the best women modernists; that she was an official artist for the Australian War Memorial during World War II; that she painted Edith Sitwell's hands. But none of these descriptions will place her as it will when I tell you she was the 'wife' in that affair Jean Rhys had with Ford Madox Ford and wrote about in her novel, *Quartet*.

Stella Bowen grew up in provincial Adelaide. In 1914, after her mother's death, she persuaded the trustees of the estate to allow her a year in Europe; this they did, but their condition that she return at the end of the year was swept aside by the war she felt herself a bene-ficiary of. She enrolled at the Westminster School of

Art, where she was taught by Sickert, and by the time she met Ford Madox Ford in 1917 she was already moving in avant-garde literary London. *To me he was quite simply the most enthralling person I had ever met.*[2] This from a young woman who knew Ezra Pound, May Sinclair, Wyndham Lewis, Arthur Waley. But she didn't marry Ford. She couldn't; he had failed in his suit for divorce that had been splashed across the British papers while she was still a girl in Adelaide. But she accepted an offer of domestic partnership from a man twenty years her senior, and she bore his child. Their union was, she wrote, *an excellent bargain on both sides . . . What I got out of it, was a remarkable and liberal education, administered in ideal circumstances. I got an emotional education too, of course, but that was easier. One might get that from almost anyone! But to have the run of a mind of that calibre . . .*[3]

Their union lasted nine years, and it dissolved in Paris after Ford's affair with Jean Rhys. The affair precipitated the separation, but did not, in itself, cause it. Stella Bowen had by then already discovered the lack of symmetry in a partnership between a man who did not doubt the greatness of his writing, and a woman who was struggling to name herself as an artist. During their time together, the domestic routine was organised entirely to suit his work: even whispering was not permitted while he was at his desk. Although he recognised, and even encouraged her talent, he resisted any change to a routine which suited him that it might better suit her. By the time Jean Rhys arrived in Paris, Stella Bowen had already begun the thinking that was to lift her *from the atmosphere of a stuffy room into the fresh night air.*[4]

But first there were the months of humiliation and

rejection while Ford was in love with Jean Rhys. There were no secrets about this liaison. One could say that he did her this honour; or that doubting neither his right to the dalliance, nor her loyalty in the face of it, he didn't think to protect her. And so there were the meals she had to sit through while his attentions danced over her rival; there were the nights she slept alone while Ford visited the other; there were the days when in front of her easel she couldn't clear her head of Ford and his drama; and there were the days when she didn't get to her easel at all. And there was the mess to clear up afterwards. Ford, she wrote, *had a genius for creating confusion and a nervous horror of having to deal with the results.*[5] For him the episode was but a *'pic de tempéte'*, and in his view there was nothing to prevent a return to their usual routine. But he was wrong; the desire for freedom had already made its mark in Stella Bowen and she was not far off her best work.

Why are people allowed – and women encouraged – to stake their lives, careers, economic position, and hopes of happiness on love? she wrote in her memoirs. *Why did not my god-fathers and godmothers in my baptism, and my copybooks at school, and my mother when she tried to explain the facts of life, all tell me, 'You must stand alone?'*[6]

For Clara the unfolding of Stella Bowen's life, which she traces through libraries and galleries, has become a task of discovery. But while Clara praises Stella Bowen as an artist who made herself over as a woman who was neither wife nor mistress, Ettie reminds her that, artist or not, she had first to experience herself as both.

'She lived in a time and place where it was possible to step outside those definitions,' I say.

'Jean Rhys had her writing,' Louise says, 'and look

what happened to her. Thrown over when Ford Madox Ford tired of her. Pensioned off into a cheap hotel room.'

'If we can believe her account of it,' I say. 'It is after all, a novel.'

'The truth you are all resisting,' Ettie said, 'is that some women do not survive. They never lift themselves out of their submission.'

The Story 3

Christmas that year wasn't so good. The man and his wife took the children to the beach, but even there, in a house at the end of a track that led down to a rocky cove, the children were fractious, his wife irritable. On Boxing Day, when finally the children were asleep, the woman, his wife, asked the man if anything was the matter. She even asked the fatal question: was there someone else? And he, caught short, fearing the consequences, lied. In a long practised gesture of comfort he put his arms around her; in a reflex of relief she leaned in, rested her head on his chest and gave into the tears she had not shed all summer. That night they slept close together, husband and wife, but in the morning it was again as it had been. The man was absent-minded, devoting himself to the children and taking mysterious walks alone. He climbed the headland by the steepest path as if that might settle the thoughts that warred in him: thoughts he could not name as feelings and knew only as a turmoil of impossibility. He felt like a train on two tracks. He walked into the township and pressed coins into the pay phone just to hear his mistress' voice. *I don't know why I did it*, he said. *I don't know why*.

When the family returned to the city, the absences began again, the late nights, the unexplained silences. There was sweat and effort about everything they did. Then, one afternoon the man rang his wife to say he'd be working late. Immediately, and without doubt, she knew that what he told her was not true, but she could not bring herself to admit what she knew. So she told herself that after all they were for the family, those extra hours of work, but because everything she told herself ran counter to all that she knew and denied that she knew, she short-circuited herself, took an aspirin, her head still ached, poured herself a scotch and fell asleep on the couch. Dull misery, a sort of blankness that had begun to affect her spirits, turned into sleep.

The children shook her. She pushed them away. Their dinner was uncooked, their homework undone. They felt, even if they did not name, the distress that shimmered unspoken in the air around them. They knew, as only children do, the cause. They sheet home the blame. The boy rang the office. His father was still there. It was not yet seven.

'Mum's asleep again and we can't wake her up,' he said.

'She's tired, I expect,' his father replied. 'Why don't you give her half an hour and make her a cup of tea?'

'We want you to come home,' his son said. 'We're hungry.'

'But darling,' the man said, 'I'm working.'

'Can't you work at home,' the child said. He wept. 'Please,' he said. 'We're scared.'

And his fear communicated itself to his father, as

father's did to son. A good father, you might say, would care for his son and go home. Which is what the man did. Alarmed and guilty, he made the necessary phone call, spoke roughly to the woman he would have taken to bed, and rang for a cab. Coming through the door of the house he shared with his wife, he heard her talking on the phone. On the stairs he found his son, waiting.

He opened the living-room door. 'I'm back,' he said to his wife.

She looked up from the sofa. 'I thought you were working,' she said.

'The kids rang,' he said. 'They were hungry and frightened. Why haven't you got the food on?'

'Don't speak to me about food,' she shouted, angry at last, holding the receiver away from her face. 'If you're that concerned, put it on yourself. I'm on the phone.'

'I've given up an important night's work because of this,' the man said looking around at the mess: school bags, shoes, magazines, teacups, papers.

'Big deal,' she said. 'I gave up my degree *for five years*.'

He picked up a dirty glass, a plate with a half-eaten sandwich on it, and went into the kitchen.

'Why don't you and Mummy love each other any more?' the boy, following him, asked.

'Of course we love each other,' his father said, banging open the saucepan drawer.

Did he lie? Or did he, in a sense tell the truth? And she, what did she tell?

Making Him Jealous

Louise says that when she was deep in the shadow of marriage, dedicated not only to the reality of her own small brood, but to the edifice of the family itself, she took to reading the advice in women's magazines. She confesses this with a gesture of self-irony; a shrug which lifts her hands to show us her empty palms. At first she read the magazines in doctors' waiting rooms, or surreptitiously at the newsagents'. Then she paid good money and took them home with her. She did as she was advised. She bought new clothes; she fed the children early so that she could light candles when she ate with Don; she left books on marriage and love, even erotic poetry, in places where they would be seen not as a rebuke but as the gentlest of invitations. But nothing broke through his distracted courtesy at home, his occasional bouts of irritation, his unexplained absences. So Louise took further advice. *Make Him Jealous*, the magazines proclaimed. *We guarantee it will work.*

Early in the marriage, during the rocky seventies, she'd had a few flirtations, nothing much, a smooch in the park, hands lingering over stack service in the library. She hadn't wanted more; she wasn't even sure that she wanted that much; Don was plenty for her, and the excitement of friends, of reading, of thought, made up for the flat patches that came between them. Then there were the children and she had even less inclination; and much less time. She wasn't troubled by the occasional flicker of attraction that occurred somewhere on the edges of her awareness, like a jolt of memory or a line of song. Love affairs belonged to the same past as all-night parties, bed-sits with candles on the mantelpiece, nights sleeping on the beach. Once, at the children's school fête, she had the much more troubling thought that she should have married the man who was rostered on to the kindergarten stall for the same afternoon. An affair didn't occur to her. She knew women who did have affairs, married women like herself, but she couldn't see that they were happy, these women, with more demands to juggle, more sources of anxiety and doubt. She knew one woman who had a man in another city, a man she rarely saw, but whose presence shone in her life, a beacon that lit the gloom of the present. That, she thought, might be a solution of sorts: a fantasy with a sufficient tinge of reality to ground it in real life. But she'd prefer her real life to regain its tinge of fantasy. And so, with guilty fascination, she read the article on *How to make your man jealous*. Arousing the jealousy of men is a dicey business, the magazine warned; but to arouse their suspicions is only fair. It is often quite effective to allow a man to doubt the certainty of your affections. Louise had seen more than one wife control her husband by directing a bored sort of weariness at him. But it wasn't what she wanted either. She didn't want to have to resort to strategies and tactics, *managing her man*. She wanted, quite simply, the ease and openness she and Don had once known.

To see if it'd jolt him into remembering, she took the article's advice and tried flirting with men on occasions when Don was also present, paying them more than usual attention, inclining her head towards them, her hand fluttering on another's arm; but far from being jealous, Don seemed not to notice. So she went a step further and arranged an elaborate hoax. She told him, affecting the casualness that is affected by the guilty, that she was going to stay the night with a friend (which was in fact true) and proceeded to spend the day doing her hair, washing her best silk underwear, dressing carefully, giving him a whiff of the perfume (L'Air du Temps) she'd bought only the week before. She even arranged for her friend to ring in the afternoon and, getting Don, to sound surprised, which he then did not, when he reminded her that Louise was preparing for an evening with her. When she got home the next morning the children complained that their father had spent the evening on the telephone. *He was talking for hours*, they said. *Hours and hours*.

The Story 4

The man and the mistress only ever spent one night together. He had a free weekend while his wife took the children on a camp with the wives of his colleagues. They went south. So the man and the woman, his mistress, drove north into the wine-growing area where they'd been told there were old pubs with courtyard restaurants run by city chefs, smart guesthouses, quiet retreats. What they hadn't been told was that the weekend they'd chosen was a wine festival – and every room was booked. At the third hotel the woman on the desk pursed her lips as if she knew the secret they brought trailing into her lobby. They returned to the car and drove another twenty miles. And another after that. In the quiet capsule of the car they drove through shallow valleys with vineyards on either side, through townships alive with music and dancers; they drove over shaded streams and through stands of eucalypts. At last, as darkness leaked into the sky, they found a room in a motel on the highway back to Sydney. They bought pizzas at the truck stop next door and ate them in their room. Through the wall they could hear the dull moan of a television and a coarse rhythmic grunt that never resolved itself, dying down only to start up again, on and on, always at the same tempo: dispirited and dispiriting. They took the pizza boxes out to the bins and walked along the highway in the dark, watching themselves illuminated in the rush of passing trucks.

When they returned the next morning to the mistress' empty house, the small leather bag she held over one shoulder knocked against the vase on a shelf in the hall. As the vase hit the boards and cracked open, so did she. For the first time disappointment and frustration burst into anger. As if the man had made the vase break. As if he should have known when he'd given it to her that it was an awkward shape, too wide for a shelf, too round for flowers: less a vase than a pitcher which, had she been a woman who scrubbed clothes on stones, or rinsed her sheets in clear river water, she'd have filled with milk and carried high on her shoulder. It should never have been an object for contemplation to be placed on a shelf beside the bird from Bathurst Island and letters waiting to be posted. Inappropriate in every way.

The man said it was okay, vases broke, he'd buy her another. He put on the kettle and buttered toast while she swept up the shattered shards of clay.

'It's all wrong,' she said. 'Everything's wrong.'

'Be patient,' he said.

Clara and Louise

It is my secret opinion that Clara is falling out of love with Tom; and that Louise is falling in love with Akim. Clara would deny this; Louise probably doesn't yet know it. But that is what I see. Watching them together, Clara and Louise give an unexpected impression of physical similarity, which, viewing them separately, is of course impossible. Louise is one of those women who can appear dreamy, with slow, certain movements, as if someone has just woken her from a long absorbed thought, or a dream perhaps, a daydream, a thoughtful meditation; but at the moment it's as if her senses are all on alert. Clara, thin and angular, is usually jerky, moving fast through the world, filling the air around her with urgency; but in her current mood she has slowed to meet the sorrow that is seeping over her. Now when Clara and Louise walk together, instead of an impossible compromise, they are adjusted to each other's pace, as Louise's capacity for slowness meets Clara's restlessness in a graceful lope.

Louise, at forty-five, still wears her hair in a long plait, but where once her mother pulled it tight so it stuck out, a wiry pigtail, now she twines it into a loose braid that hangs down her back with strands of grey and white looped through the black. Her fringe, once a clear line across an uncreased forehead, is still a glossy black when combed from the crown of her head, revealing her silvery secret only when it lifts in the wind, or is disturbed by the fingers that run through it. Her face, a cream-brown oval that is smooth in repose, creases when she smiles. It is then that her years show. Alec says that if we lived in a world that could value them, such lines would be prized as a map of a woman's life; a record of the stories she trails behind her, the stories she is poised to step into. Louise thinks Alec is being gallant when he says this, and accepts it as nothing more than one of his old-fashioned compliments; but I think he is encouraging her to take the leap, to see the offer Akim is surely making: that open hand, that edge of smile.

Clara, who once had a braid herself, has cut her hair so short that the angular bones of her skull show through the shadowy fuzz that is left. She had it cut on impulse, came home, saw herself in the mirror, and wept. Tom found her standing on the bathmat with a glass of whisky in her hand, still staring at the mirror.

'It will grow,' Tom said. 'Give it time.'

But Clara has had enough of waiting. Time is not what she wants to give; not to Tom, not to anyone. She feels oppressed by time, flattened out by the weight of the past, held back from the future. With her hair gone she finds herself caught in the shallows of an uncharacteristic depression. Although even as a child there was a slight stance of the tragic about her, this is the first time I have known her without the drive Helena used to call impulsive. She is anxious and, in the midst of plans that change daily, self-doubting and resentful, as if there is something life holds which is being withheld from her.

Of Ettie she asks what happened to Helena's papers, and whether there are any of Jock's paintings in the attic in the mountains. Of me she asks my opinion on the value of history as if she wants to know the reason for her own research. Is she investigating history to bring it into the present, to shape her own life; or is she trapping herself into the past with its secrets and silences, its tug to the grave? Of Louise she asks what it's been like living alone for so many years, without lovers, without sex, without someone in her bed. Was she afraid? Was she bored?

So when Louise gave Clara the dress, an exchange

that might otherwise have been casual became an occasion of grief. The dress was in a bundle of clothes Louise no longer wears, and she offered Clara a choice of the best before the rest went into the mission bin. It was a short dress with a low neck, made of a woven silk and patterned in deep reds, and blues as dark as black. It was a dress that could no longer accommodate Louise's changing curves, and though once a favourite, she registered only the slightest twang of regret when she put it in the pile. But when she saw Clara twirl across the room in it, inviting our admiration, it was as if Louise saw her youth walk away, lost and irretrievable. The moment passed and now Louise says it's comforting to see the dress on one who wears it with grace. But at that moment, when she made the gift, and Clara made the choice, she felt her life rush away from her and the future grow dry.

For me, watching this exchange, it was not as if the future had walked away from Louise, but quite the reverse, it was as if Louise was walking into the future, shedding the trappings of youth, the short skirt tight across the hips, the display that youth uses to catch the attention of which the world has plenty to spare. In that gesture I saw Louise grow into herself, and I saw Clara not as the inheritor of an off-cast youth but the receiver of a hard won wisdom. I saw the fluidity of their similarity, and the flux of their difference. In that exchange of a dress I saw steps made, different and similar both, in the coming of age of two women.

Then why is it so hard to leap, with our hands free, into the future?

The Dance of Domination

It's all very well for Stella Bowen to say we should, as girls, have been taught to stand alone, we should have been taught the dangers of pinning happiness on the vagaries of love. But while we live in a culture in which our deepest desires are formed in the family, while our hopes for intimacy and personal satisfaction are hooked to the romantic dyad, a great deal more than teaching is required. *Level headedness*, Marie-Louise von Franz says, *and commonsense self-observation and reflection . . . a certain wisdom and humaneness.* These sensible attributes are called for because the drama of love is never sensible, but dangerous and alluring; and because the romantic figures and projections originating in our own psyches, *always want to seduce us away from reality into rapture or pull us down into an inner world of fantasy.* It's not a matter of refusing love, or passion; on the contrary the task of maturity is to experience it fully, so that we can understand this powerful realm through the capacity of both heart and mind. *Whoever cannot surrender to this experience has never lived*, she says; *whoever founders in it has understood nothing.*[7]

Stella Bowen went into the relationship with Ford Madox Ford believing that happiness was *a kind of present that one person could bestow on another*[8] and left it understanding *that there can be no such thing as 'belonging' to another person (for in the last resort you must be responsible for yourself, just as you must prepare to die alone) . . .* This is what she means by gaining an emotional education. *How trite it sounds, how not worth mentioning. But what a discovery it makes!*[9]

But in order to gain this education, she had first to experience the dance of domination, that play of submission and control that is acted out in the most ordinary of daily manoeuvres between lovers, and which is thrown into exaggerated relief in the drama of adultery.[10] Jean Rhys' account of her affair with Ford casts Stella Bowen as the self-seeking, self-satisfied wife. Jean Rhys casts herself as victim as much to the rival woman as to the man. Indeed the novel produces more tension in the hatred between wife and mistress than in the love, if that's what it is, between either woman and the man. The mistress' wish to smash a wine bottle over the wife's head is more convincing than her love for the husband. The two become entwined. *Little wheels in her head turned perpetually. I love him. I want him. I hate her. And he's a swine. He's out to hurt me. What shall I do? I love him. I want him. I hate her.*[11] If *Quartet* has any value at all, it is as a representation of an extreme form of the masochistic position in the dance of domination.

Ford Madox Ford did not write of the affair, but he wrote a great deal about adultery. *The Good Soldier*, which was first published in 1915, follows the emotional fate of an adulterous man. That it is narrated by an innocent is all the more revealing. One man describes another, and reading the novel it is tempting to cast both as aspects of Ford Madox Ford himself: the man who enjoys the conquest of women, and the man with the nervous horror of emotional mess. In *Quartet* the man has a curious naivety as he articulates his self-absorbed needs. In *The Good Soldier*, the philanderer acts blindly, following impulse without thought, or reason, and without understanding the consequences.

The man is eventually destroyed; and the women are left with the mess.

In the 'dedicatory letter' addressed to Stella Bowen as the preface to the 1927 re-publication of *The Good Soldier*, Ford writes: *what I am now I owe to you*. He would never have returned to writing after the war, he says, had it not been for her support and belief in him. And although *the seas now divide us*, he hoped the re-publication of the novel *may give you some pleasure with the illusion that you are hearing familiar – and very devoted – tones*.[12] Stella Bowen and Ford Madox Ford had separated the year before; Ford was writing the dedication from New York where he was living with the next woman. There is no record of Stella Bowen's response to this extraordinary exercise in evasion and sentimentality.

In her memoirs she wrote that he was a man *who needed to exercise his sentimental talents from time to time upon a new object. It keeps him young. It refreshes his ego. It restores his belief in his power*.[13] She recognised that she was the *new object* when Ford needed *a new lease of after-the-war-life*. She also recognised that with him she could never be fully equal, either as partner or as artist, for if she was she would then have been of little use to him.[14] I doubt if the 'dedicatory letter' would have impressed her.

In this dance of domination, agency is given to the masculine, and passivity to the feminine. This doesn't mean necessarily, or simply, that men are active and women passive (consider all those men who go into bondage parlours to get whipped), although it's no secret that men tend to assume the universal position (even under the lash), the first person active, as if it were theirs alone. When a man desires, the object of his attention, whether or not she (or he) reciprocates, is forced into the drama of that desire. It doesn't mean men always win, far from it, although they rarely understand why they lose; but it does mean that in affairs of the heart men assume the right to act, and the worth of their own agency. *When we love another 'as an object'*, Thomas Merton says, *we refuse, or fail, to pass over into the realm of his own spiritual reality, his personal identity.*[15]

That Stella Bowen comes out of this story better than Jean Rhys is not because she was wife. There is nothing of intrinsic value in being a wife rather than a mistress. That Stella Bowen comes out of this story better than Jean Rhys is because she learned from it the nature of the dance in which she was engaged and stepped outside her own complicity in an objectified role. So when she says we should learn to stand alone, she doesn't just mean because men let us down, though often they do, but that to develop this capacity is an integral part of our quest to become fully ourselves. Jean Rhys foundered in her own victim pleasures; she was underhand and manipulative. For Stella Bowen the adulterous drama was an impetus towards the redefinition of herself as neither wife nor mistress. Her story is more disturbing to the master narrative, and less well known than a novel which casts the woman as failed object more effectively than any man could have done for her. When it comes to the celebration of feminine masochism, Jean Rhys has (in that regard) created a character to rival Emma Bovary.

Jean Rhys went on to write three more novels in praise of the wronged woman. She was caught in a cycle of repetition that didn't show any sign of shifting until *The Wide Sargasso Sea* in 1966, which, if nothing else, does it rather better. Stella Bowen on the other hand, within a few years of leaving Ford, had established herself as an artist. In the portraits from which she made a living, she entered the private world of her subjects; in her large compositions, those oblique angles on gardens and groups at tables under trees, she brought the public and the intimate into an expansive moment of co-existence. *I painted various interiors, which always turned out to be pictures of windows. I loved painting windows and I loved painting hands.*[16] It wasn't just that leaving Ford freed her to do the work she would have done anyway; but that the emotional education she gained during those nine years changed the perspective of her heart, and of her eye.

This is what Ettie means when she says that the fate of a woman won't change until she can see herself as neither wife nor mistress.

The Adultery Factor

Years ago I taught an adult education course. My enrolments were healthy and on the first night all but one student turned up. The second class was also full, more or less; and then it went off steeply with five absences in the third, and seven in the fourth week. I was mortified. What had I done wrong? Was I not interesting enough? Clever enough? Funny enough? Perhaps I was too feminist, too confrontational? (It was back in the days when one was.) I went to the office to confess my failure.

'Oh that's normal,' the administrator said. 'It always happens.'

'Why?' I said. 'Why would so many people pay up and then abandon the class so soon?'

'Lots of reasons,' he said. 'They find it doesn't suit them after all, it clashes with something they hadn't anticipated, they change to a class that friends are taking. And then there's the adultery factor.'

'The *what*?'

'Well,' he said, 'quite a lot of people enrol in classes like ours in order to get legitimate time with their lovers. They come to a couple of classes to get the hang of things so they can talk convincingly to their spouses about it.'

'How do you know?' I asked.

'We catch them out sometimes,' he said. 'Not intentionally. Say if a teacher's sick and we ring round to tell the students or to change the time or something, and we get onto their spouse. For instance we might ring the next morning and this cold voice will say *but she was there last night*.'

'That's depressing,' I said. 'Teaching as a decoy.'

'Not always,' he said. 'We had a judge and his associate who enrolled in Italian for Beginners. They did very well and went on to work their way through all our Italian classes. When they'd done the most advanced, they came to ask if we could put on another, and in the course of making this request, and us explaining there wasn't the demand, it came out that they did the classes in order to be together! It was their shared life. I suggested French but one of them spoke it already, and they didn't seem interested in Indonesian.'

'What happened to them?' I asked.

'I don't know,' he said. 'I see her name in the paper occasionally, she's prominent in the ACTU, but that's all. I'd have liked to have been able to help.'

Ettie Says

Ettie says it has long been her opinion that a woman has come into her maturity when she's prepared to admit that she does not like *Madame Bovary*. Ettie is certainly in her maturity. She has just turned eighty. This is an achievement of which she is proud. Not that she sets store by mere chronology; longevity in itself, she says, doesn't necessarily prove a thing. It's the shape of a life that matters. To celebrate the shape of her eighty years, she took a train down to Sydney, booked into a small, smart hotel near the harbour and invited Alec and Clara to dinner.

When I heard that these were the birthday arrangements, I thought that at last she'd tell Clara the truth, give her the account of her origins that hums in the air around them. But no, Alec reported, nothing was said, and if that's how Ettie wants it, it's fine with him, don't nag. But he had nagged, if that's the word for it, as much as Louise and I had done, only a month before when we were in the mountains on the same weekend. I'd gone up on the train early in the week and was lying on the verandah overlooking the precipice of the escarpment reading *Madame Bovary* when Louise's car came bumping down the track on Friday afternoon. Alec clambered out in his shorts nursing a tiny Japanese maple in an old tin can.

'It takes a hundred years to grow,' he said as he gave it to Ettie.

'Surely you don't expect me to be around that long,' she said.

'I expect you to be remembered at least that long,' he said, kissing her powdery, tissue-paper face.

While they tottered off around the garden, bickering and boasting, Louise came and sat on the verandah with me, drinking green tea from the small round porcelain cups she'd given Ettie, and looking up into the spider webs that hung from the corners like lace.

'When does Akim get back?' I asked her. He was in New Zealand building a house.

'Next week,' she said.

'How do you feel?'

'I think I'm scared half to death,' she said, going out for a broom to knock down the cobwebs. 'I'm scared it'll tip me back into all those old longings. I mean I feel them already, pressing on us with the first kiss.'

It was in the evening when the house drew in around us that Ettie made her remark about *Madame Bovary*. Alec said, scrunching up his face as if with the effort of remembering, that Emma Bovary was an accurate account of the masculine psyche if not the feminine. I said it was an exercise in misogyny. He said it was a brilliant portrayal of the use men make of women, or would, given free rein: their fear and fascination turned into control. Men make the mistake, he said, of thinking that by possessing women, they can possess their own longings and memories. He is a man who likes to talk about sex and love as if, finally, he's got it all worked out. He said the paradox men face is that once they possess a woman, if that's all they want, there's no longer any reason to possess her. They sort of empty out, he said. A very painful business. He said he was almost sixty before he realised this. He smiled at Ettie as if he were handing her a trophy. She, knowing the story, appeared not to notice.

'No wonder there's so much adultery,' I said.

'Is it any different?' Louise asked.

'If you mean does it happen more,' Alec said, 'probably not.'

'Of course it's different,' Ettie said getting up to stack the dishes. 'These days with your easy ways about sex, you think you can tame it, control it by acting on every impulse. Well, men have always thought that. But now women do too. We didn't. We never thought that. You resist the force of love whatever you may say, in and out of bed. We didn't. And we accepted the consequence. We had to, that was how the world was. We didn't have the choice, and in some ways I'm glad of it.'

'There, there, old girl,' Alec said. Ettie can go a bad colour.

'You sit there philosophising, you silly old goat,' Ettie said, 'as if a last-minute recantation will save your soul. Sixty years of irresponsibility and suddenly you're the guru. It'd never have happened, this change of yours, if Moira hadn't left and this time not come back. Be honest.'

'Well,' Alec said.

'Well, nothing,' she said. 'Some of us didn't have the luxury of sixty years to make the shift.'

'Some people never do it at all,' he said.

'So?' she said.

'You women understand about change,' he said. 'It's in your bodies.'

'What nonsense,' Ettie said. 'It's in our lives. And it's in yours too, if you had the wit to see it.'

Piling the plates and clattering, she made a glancing reference to the story that lives so strongly in her, though it is rarely told: the story of the child that was born to her and Jock and given to Helena. She has told it to me only once. I remember her voice, calm and quiet, as she described the pact that the two women would go to London together, so that Helena could return with the baby as if it were hers. She told me of the long voyage, of the nights in the boarding house waiting for a baby, and for a war. The agreement was that Ettie would stay on for a decent interval, after which she would return as a cherished aunt; war or no war, Helena insisted on that bargain. *A decent interval* is the phrase Ettie used. It made her laugh again, a short glassy laugh, as she stood at the sink, her rough old hands glossy from the washing up water. '*A decent interval*,' she said. 'In 1939 a decent interval meant six years. More.' She didn't see the child whom Helena named Dorothy until she, the child, was almost seven years old. She'd seen Helena off on the boat from Southampton when the baby was a month old. But the image that stayed with her, imprinted on her memory for days, weeks, years to come, was not the baby wrapped tight in her shawl, but the glint of triumph as Helena lifted one arm, holding the child close with the other, and waved goodbye.

And now there is Clara, who sometimes I think Ettie loves best in the world, as if she has collected the interest on all that was diverted and made impossible when that ship pulled out from the quay. Clara who was born to Dorothy and, if Ettie has her way, will never know that she owes her existence not to Jock and Helena, the only child of their only child, but to a brief passion, the adulterous union between Jock and Ettie.

'Last time Clara came,' Ettie said coming back to the table with coffee and a bottle of brandy, 'I had a sudden urge to tell her.'

'Why didn't you?' Louise said.

'After all this time,' she said, 'why muddy the water?'

'The water's already muddy,' I said.

'Mud settles,' she said, as quick as a flash, and I thought of the pool in the gully, of which she is so proud, its surface still as glass, and the slight movements across the bottom made by the creatures that live in the mud.

'You should tell her,' Louise said. 'She adores you. She'd want to know. It's a wonderful story in its way, and it might help her.'

'Better than someone telling her after you've gone,' Alec said.

'There's no reason not to,' I said. 'Helena is dead. So is Jock.'

'It's not to protect Helena and Jock that I don't tell,' Ettie said. 'I wouldn't do them the injustice. What happened was part of their lives, and like it or not they had that responsibility. But to tell Clara would be to burden her with our mistakes, to make her live her whole life in that shadow. When I wanted to tell her it wasn't for her sake, it was for mine. It was the vanity of an old woman who wanted to die seeing love acknowledged in her grandchild's eyes.'

The Story 5

The mistress never saw the house to which the man belonged by right. She saw the family in the street, and that, mercifully, was only once. She was in his suburb, driving through, on a route she sometimes had to take, expecting always to see him, though it was only on this occasion that she did. Was that him, the man bending towards the girl? Was that the man who bent to her in the house he'd come to enter as his own? He stood up and turned to face her way; but his eyes, not quite focused, were looking past the car in which she sat, and in which, on more than one occasion, they had made what is commonly called love. And the woman with him, was that her, the wife, the rival she thought of daily? The man took a bill from his wallet and handed it to the woman, his wife; the same wallet from which he took the credit cards that paid for the meals he ate with her, the mistress, and for their one motel.

'I'm an expensive fuck,' she told him.

'I can afford it,' he'd said.

For her, a woman who was used to paying her own way, it was a treat that he paid, that he booked the restaurants, that he held open the door, offered to drive, took charge. She was quick to accept these attentions as part of his courtship, and their erotic exchange; she didn't think, she didn't realise, that for his wife it was one of the mechanisms of her dependency, and his control; as a consequence she didn't see that it was also bedded into her own dependence, her own lack of control. Unlike his wife she, the mistress, did not have to ask for the money she carried in her own purse. She didn't have to ask for a cheque when she needed a new coat. She, the mistress, misread the man's capacity to pay as an indication of his care for her, and it wasn't until well into the affair that she realised that for him it was merely accustomed behaviour, nothing more.

What did she, the mistress, feel that steamy afternoon when she saw the man in the street with his family: a happy scene, domestic, ordinary, repeated, no doubt, many times. She felt closed out. She felt denied and dishonoured. She wished that her eye had the power to turn him to stone. It wasn't jealousy she felt, not that exactly; she calculated quite finely what she had. What took her by surprise was the pain of seeing herself unrecognised and unseen. It was this that she resented. She resented that she could not be seen, that the structure of the situation rendered her invisible. It made her feel lesser, as if by not being seen in her relation with him she was not seen at all. She became transparent, a shade; the car as flimsy as a carriage, as inconsequential as a pumpkin. When she got home even the kitchen table seemed insubstantial, as if it would disappear at a touch; the life she inhabited lost shape, credibility, certainty; it seemed to peel, or melt, at the edges. For the first time she felt the urge to tell his wife. A small hand-grenade in the form of an envelope dropped into the letter box of that smug family home. She could, she thought, send a copy of the letter the man had sent her two years before. *I want to know what I am when I'm with you*, he'd written. And even if, as it turned out, he hadn't lived up to the intentions he'd laid before her – to leave, to get a house, to settle the children, to tell his wife – and even if she'd blown it by giving in on the whiff of a promise and becoming his lover anyway, still that letter would do something. It'd certainly make her visible.

'a snare and a downfall'

What is it we hope to see in the eyes of our lovers? What do we want our lovers to see? Our ideal self reflected back in love? A glory we wouldn't recognise as our own if we stood alone? Is the cruel truth that we seek in love not a loved other but our own heightened selves? Narcissus fell into the pond and drowned, drawn by the beauty of his own reflection. It was a punishment made to fit the crime, for Narcissus, absorbed in himself, had never been able to recognise love when it was offered. Unable to recognise the reality of another, he mistook his own shadow for love. It is a modern disorder, that narcissistic shadow, *a snare and a downfall*.[17]

We live in a culture that daily encourages us to find our identity in that reflection of another, to experience ourselves as most real when we are in love. We live in a culture that encourages us to see ourselves as others see us. To become an object in the regard of others means that others become objects to us; and so too do we to ourselves. No wonder we are all in pursuit of control: to make sure that object is ours. No wonder submission is so delightful: we are reminded of ourselves by the control we allow another to exercise over us.

These days the discarded mistress doesn't weep on the hotel bed where she's been dumped by the man in a final pay-off. She goes to the gym. She works out until her body is a reasonable replica of the body of a woman ten, or twenty, years younger than her. Like the frightened wife she keeps the cosmetic industry in good profit. She even considers the scalpel. What is pitiful about such women with their old faces is not their age but their determination to remain young as if that alone would guarantee their renewed currency in a world which trades in people, and the factor of their sex. Is the suburban nightmare of humiliation and conquest that is acted out in the drama of adultery so different from the S & M clubs that at least offer their wares as they are? Are repressed forces which in bondage houses are given the crudest of expression and paid for in money, taking in the family a suburban form, so that like the suburbs themselves even our pleasures, our losses, our betrayals take a shallow and conventional form, decorated though they are with the rhetoric of love? Is what we see in both these cases – suburban adultery and S & M – decadence without imagination? There's more imagination in the gay culture with its masquerade and ritual that occasion more titillated voyeurism than disapproval. In that sexual grotesque, domination is an honest perversion compared to the empty cruelties of adultery where humiliation and objectification are enacted but never acknowledged, giving, as far as I can see, very little pleasure to anyone. *Death, like a final orgasm, like a full night, waits for the end of the play.*[18]

The indignity meted out to those women who look to the scalpel and the gym as they cling to youth, is that it can never work. Why would a man who wants a girl (fresh and lovely as girls are) choose a substitute princess? No woman can win that way. And what woman worth her salt wants a man who wants a girl? With a shift in the viewing lens from the firmness of the breast to the fullness of the being, it may not seem as if everything ends with the arrival of the first lines on our face. On the contrary, it could be that with age it's all just beginning; for it takes time to come into one's own life, to know one's strengths and capacities, to develop the flexibility that allows not the domination of others, or ourselves, but a mutuality that trusts those we love with the truth about ourselves. *Love is only possible between persons as persons*, Thomas Merton says. *That is to say, if I love you, I must love you as a person and not as a thing.*[19]

Think about it. It's not as easy as it sounds.

Airborne Conversations

On a plane from Melbourne to Sydney last year, the computer sat me next to a man roughly my age: Australian professional class, university educated, casually well dressed, reading the *Guardian Weekly*. What put him out of the ordinary, or at least I thought so at first, was that he was travelling with a child, a girl, about seven or eight years old. I'd already caught the man out in a minor diddle over change from his wine: that is to say I noticed, and he saw that I noticed. So you can imagine his discomfort when I put down my book (*Anna Karenin* as it happens) and listened (one can't help but listen on planes) to this conversation with his daughter. It was the name of his hotel that caught my attention; he was explaining that when they got to Sydney they'd go to the hotel – one, as it happens, that I know quite well, though not for reasons you might suspect – so he could leave his bags before taking the child on to Grandma's.

'Why can't you stay at Grandma's too?' the child asked.

'Because I've got to work late,' the man said.

'What sort of work?'

'You know,' he said. 'I've told you. I've got meetings, and paperwork to do.'

'People don't have meetings at night,' she said. 'Why can't you do the papers at Grandma's?'

He reiterated a position which never changed; all the way to Sydney it never changed: he had papers to read, and meetings, and these activities had to take place at the hotel.

'You don't like it at Grandma's,' the child said.

'Of course I do,' the man said.

'You're going to see that friend Mummy doesn't like,' she said.

'I told you,' he said. 'I've got work to do.'

'What?' she said. 'I can't hear you.'

'I can't talk any louder,' her father said, his eyes flickering towards me. 'We're on a plane.'

'Talk louder,' the child said.

'Would you like a swim at the hotel?' he asked. 'We could both have a swim.'

'You don't like it at Grandma's, do you?' she said.

'Of course I like it at Grandma's,' he said.

'I don't like her either,' the child said.

'Who?' the man said, surprised. 'Grandma?'

'No,' she said. 'Your friend. The one Mummy doesn't like.'

'I'm working tonight,' the man said. 'I've told you. I'm working.'

'I can't hear,' she said. 'Talk louder.'

'We're on a plane,' her father said.

'There's no rule about not talking loudly on planes,' the girl said.

'Wouldn't you like a swim?' her father asked. 'And a cake? We could have a cake too.'

'No,' she said. 'I want you to come to Grandma's.'

Powerful though such a man may be, and early as a girl must learn it, he could not meet the eye of the unknown woman who sat quietly beside him with a book in her lap.

Alec Says

Alec says a lot. I clamber up the steep stairs of the tower where he lives at the top of his son's house. From the window seat I can see across the harbour through the trees to the fish markets, the back of the bridge, the container docks. Alec sits in the battered leather chair which was all that he salvaged from the house where he and Moira lived for thirty years. He pours tea from a Brown Betty teapot.

'Why didn't you take more furniture?' I ask, gesturing to the booklined but Spartan room.

'Couldn't face it,' he says. 'The kids took most of it. They were getting married. Thought it was important.'

Alec says women make the mistake of thinking men are powerful. He says we think that because they exercise a warped sort of sexual agency they are powerful in themselves. On the contrary, he says, men are driven, poor sops.

'You can't plead testosterone for ever,' I say.

'That's not it, girl,' he says. 'You'll never understand. Now *listen*.'

'I didn't come for a lecture,' I say, but I smile as I do, for of course I have, or I wouldn't have come; he chuckles and bobs his head up and down, his baby-fine hair shining like a soft-focus halo. In the still of the afternoon light I listen, trying to remember the details, the cadences of his voice, picking from the river of words the moments that will explain whatever it is I can't grasp about men and the disappointments and misunderstandings that rise so easily between us.

'For all those years,' Alec says, 'I used to congratulate myself for forgiving Moira. I forgave her tearfulness, her resentfulness, her plain ordinariness and the fact that there were times when it bored me. I considered myself a good husband. I would never have left her. When she left, it was Ettie who asked me point blank who was I to forgive. She didn't mean because of my women, at least I don't think she did. She meant I was setting myself up as a tin-pot god, I was turning Moira into more and more of an object. Ha! But the joke was on me. When she had that affair, oh years ago now, just after the war it must have been – I still don't like that bloke as a matter of fact, he's in a home the old toad, I knew no good would come of him – I thought nothing worse could happen. There was no greater betrayal. Little did I know. I was gallivanting all over the country, always with a pretty author on my arm – well that's what publishers do, or they did then, I don't know what they do now that they're mostly women, a cast-iron excuse – and anyway I knew Moira knew I'd always come back, and I did. I did. She was the anchor, really, it only ever made sense when she was there. And all those years when I thought she was there, my wife, stoking the home fires, raising the kids, all that time she was planning her retreat. Well not literally, I don't mean that. But there she was back at university doing her MA and writing her own book. It never occurred to me for a moment that it'd be published. The Parramatta Female Factory didn't strike me as a publishable subject, not for a minute. I suppose female convicts might have, but I hadn't put two and two together and remember we're talking twenty years ago, more: that sort of thing hadn't filtered through to someone like me, let alone the marketing chaps. The truth is, dear girl, a man doesn't expect his wife to get up and write a book. He doesn't expect her to get up and leave. And I can tell you when she does it's the most terrible shock. I used to think that if she'd gone off with some bloke I'd understand, though Ettie says she doubts it and I have to admit it was years before I felt civil when she did. And that was after we were divorced. He's not a bad bloke. We have a drink sometimes and talk about Moira. He misses her, poor bastard. I think he really knew her. I never did. In my better moments I can be pleased for her. I am, yes, really, I'd say I am.

'What you girls don't understand,' Alec says, 'is the power a man feels when he persuades a woman to open up to him. It's like nothing else on earth. It's as if in that moment he is reunited with heaven, he's a god, she's the finest creature there ever was, there's nothing but sky and ocean. What men don't understand is that they can repeat that sensation endlessly, or as endlessly as they can manage, but it will never stay with them, it will never make them a god. As fast as it comes, it goes. Try again and there's an empty sucking feeling. Look down and there's a woman asking something of you, god knows what, but the chances are you can't give it; and the mere fact of her asking stills the ocean, blocks the sky. Suddenly it's sordid, like being in a brothel, exciting and sickening, a wad of notes, an obsequious madam and a bad smell coming up under the eau de Cologne.

'Looking back,' Alec says, 'I wanted to know Moira. I chose a fine wife. But I didn't know that's what I wanted and even if I had I wouldn't have known how to set about it, I wouldn't have known where to begin. I was frightened, I didn't know myself. I didn't know what she'd ask. Battening her down, battened me down,

I battened down the past. It worked. It worked fine. But it's not what you'd call a life. When she left I was in a shocking state. Ettie took me up to the mountains but she only let me stay a week, and that's as long as I've ever stayed, she says she needs to be on her own. She wouldn't take me, not for years she wouldn't take me. Heal yourself, she used to say, and I'll see what I think of your scars. I try to explain all this to my son. I hear him down there trying to please the family, trying to please the girls, well they're almost women now, telling them what he thinks will keep them quiet, and am I the only one who knows what he's up to? I caught him in the botanical gardens with a rather smart little number, a lawyer she must have been, all dressed up in black. But then I know what goes on downstairs while he's away, I'm here all day. Does she think I'm blind? I'm just an old man up here in the tower, what would I know. I'll tell you what I know: I know that sometimes we have to wait to the end of our lives before we know the first thing about its shape, its meaning. These days people think they can buy anything and if they can't they ought to be able to. What they don't know is that there are times in every person's life when what they need is nothing. I don't mean poverty, I don't mean that, that's a terrible cruelty and it's time we did something about it, we could if we put our minds to it; what I mean is a spiritual nothing, a time of darkness and nothing, of being alone with the emptiness and the fear and the tears and the loss; that's the way to the only riches it's worth our while trying for. You can't take a woman with you when you go.

'I'm an old man, dear girl, but I still appreciate a shapely pair of legs and you certainly have that. Shall I pour you another cup of tea? A whisky perhaps?'

The Story 6

It occurred to both the women at about the same time that the way things were it was probably worse being with the man than it would be being alone. But for one the implications of this realisation were considerably more frightening than they were for the other. Getting out of it was rather more complicated for one than for the other.

The mistress complained to her friends; she refused to see the man for several weeks, even for months at a time; she went out a lot. And although nothing satisfied her, although everything seemed shallow and pointless, she didn't let on to the man. As far as he knew she was out and about enjoying herself. This time it was he who saw her in the street with someone else. That the man she was with was of no significance, at least not in the way the man assumed, didn't matter at all. When she saw that the man, her lover, had seen her, she let her hand rest, casually, momentarily, on the arm of the one with whom she was crossing the road. The man, her lover, felt the sharp stab of a feeling he hadn't named since the children arrived, and now probably no longer could. Panic? Jealousy? Fear? It was a sensation he did not like. He felt like a train on two tracks, and he could feel the rails diverge beneath him.

At home his wife's face was set in lines of determination. She had discussed the situation at counselling; she suggested to her husband that they go together. There's a lot to consider, she said. The children. The house. Lawyers. The man felt control slip from him and as it did he realised it had never really been his, a sort of illusion that always held the seeds of exactly this.

The girl, his daughter, came home from school with a bad report. He, her father, made an appointment with the headmistress; and he agreed to the appointment that his wife made with the counsellor. He felt himself trapped in the needs of others, responsible, burdened, lost. He tried to regain control by the strange move of taking his son to meet his mistress. Afterwards, when he thought about it, he could see it was an attempt to curb the divergence, but as soon as he walked into the cafe he knew his mistake. He saw the look of panic, even dislike, that flickered across his mistress' face as the boy rocked his chair, louder and louder, faster, spilling teas and coffees, spilling his milkshake, disturbing the adjacent tables, making conversation impossible, ensuring that desire evaporated, sides were taken, positions acknowledged. From the window of the cafe, the mistress watched as the man took the boy by the hand and set off down the street. The boy skipped. The mistress did not.

For the Children

When I hear of people remaining together *for the children*, I immediately smell a rat. I suspect cowardice, and a double punishment in that virtue. I know it from my own experience. The child grows up in an atmosphere of distress made all the worse by denials, and by the reassurances that pass between tight lips. Nothing matches. The child senses the collapse, she feels it with her body, while all the time being assured of the security that is daily slipping away. The harder she clings, the further it seems to slip; the more she fears, the more she is reassured; the greater the reassurance the greater the doubt that opens beneath it. And so the child still lives with the distress she is said to be avoiding by the sacrifice of the parents, and is in addition taught to doubt both her own responses and the good faith of those who gave her life.

Clara says growing up with Jock and Helena was boring. Dead boring. She says she doesn't suppose it damaged her, the boredom of it, a lot of kids must have that. What she couldn't bear was the boredom between them, between Jock and Helena. As a child she longed for someone to launch out, to launch off, to throw caution to the winds, to show that the world was comprised not, or not only, of the next meal, the next round of homework, but of risk and daring, moments of dazzling beauty.

Louise says it's all very well if you don't have children, but when you do you're already in a state of guilty anxiety. Parents rarely think they've done enough and when their children meet the blows and wounds of life they can see only that they've failed. It was the thought of the children, she said, that kept her marriage the structure, the stricture, it became. It wasn't until after Don left that she began to see there were gifts a parent could give a child other than the unquestioning security of convention and marriage.

Alec says look at his kids. Are they such a success to be laid at the door of the *intact family*? He says they were raised to expect security and they cling to it even as it dissolves around them. He taught them nothing, he says, about how to live. On the radio, Alec says, and he should know for he listens a lot, when divorce and the breakdown of marriage are discussed, one rarely hears the word *change*. There's talk of change in the economy, there's nothing else as we're warned that jobs, pensions, free education and subsidised health care are no longer certainties we can rely on. Alec says it's the change itself we're encouraged to fear; and the fear undercuts the debates, the policies, the possibilities we're being asked to consider. So great is the fear, one rarely hears it said of personal life that the only certainty of which we can all be sure is that of change. Instead, he says, we're taught to cling, cling, cling. No, he says mournfully, he did a bad job. He should have taught them to move with change when it comes, to stretch and grow. To understand the flux of their own emotions. That way, he says, they might have had a chance of understanding someone else, to love without fear. Well, maybe they'll get there anyway, he says.

Louise didn't consider any of this until those years alone when she had the boys to raise with a father only for holidays and weekends. It was during those years that she thought again of her own childhood. Her plight hadn't been boredom, that suburban luxury. She had grown up with a gritty realism that only then, nearly twenty years after her parents' deaths, she came to see as training in a practice for living. She grew up watching while her mother, as the saying goes, worked her fingers to the bone. She wore them to the bone in the restaurant the family worked but did not own; Louise's father cooked, her mother (and once her grandmother) chopped and peeled, scrubbed and cleaned; her aunt, and then her brothers, served. Twice a year the rich man who owned the restaurant drove up from Melbourne, a fat puffy-faced man accompanied by his son in an English-style cap, and parked his dark blue Rover in the lane where the deliveries were made. He walked through the restaurant, putting his finger in the noodles, poking his nose into cupboards, climbing the stairs, complaining of the condition of the woodwork as if a family could live somewhere for years, five children and not a scuff mark. He chucked Louise under the chin.

'Lily Lou,' he said. A clever girl who should be sent down to Melbourne. 'I could use a girl like you.'

'Her teacher is making arrangements, sir,' her mother said.

'Ah yes,' the rich man said, taking a pound note from his wallet.

Louise tells two versions of this story. She might say, and often does, that she was saved by a list of books. This is the Australian version of her life: the rise from shop to school to university. But these days she might equally say that books are merely an exercise for the mind. What saved her, though she was slow to realise it, was that her parents' lives demonstrated the law of impermanence. The daily grind might seem permanent enough to Australian eyes, but the lesson Louise learned was to distinguish the illusion of routine from the reality of change. With Western eyes she saw the unchanging routine; with Eastern eyes she saw daily evidence to the contrary. She saw the vegetables arrive, she saw them chopped, she saw them cooked. She saw her mother labour, she saw her rest. She saw her grandmother die, she saw her raise her eyes, and face the movement of life into death. All this she saw, and she glimpsed its significance as she faced the abyss that opened before her, and before her children.

Lying Awake

When the man described to Louise the confusion of his feelings as he let himself into the house late at night, she asked him what his wife was doing.

'She was in bed,' he said

'Was she asleep?' Louise asked. 'Or awake?'

'Asleep I think,' he said. 'I often wasn't home until late.'

'Was she always asleep?' Louise asked.

'I shouldn't think so,' the man said. 'No, not always.'

What was she thinking as she lay awake waiting for his return? What fantasies of revenge did she indulge during the hours she couldn't sleep? These were questions Louise did not ask. They were questions she did not need to ask. She remembers exactly what it was like to wait in a quiet house with every sense turned towards the soft click of a door. Did she dream of murder, or execution, perhaps, like Elizabeth I ordering Essex to the tower? Louise remembers the satisfying shock of that story. Did she want to see him beg? Or did she dread, like the equivocating Elizabeth, that to chop off his head would break her heart? She remembers wanting Don hurt, and she remembers wanting him hers. No, perhaps not that. She wanted things as they were; she wanted, like the wife in the story the man tells her, the comfort of family life. But that was not what she had. She tried to face the reality. She tried telling herself she'd be better alone. She considered the prospect rationally, sensibly. She thought about the women she knew who lived alone, and remembered that there had been times when she had almost envied them. But none of these sensible thoughts stilled the dread, the dreadful fear of growing old alone, no, not that, of going mad from the clamour in her own head. Now she says it saved her life being faced with that clamour, coming to realise it wouldn't send her mad, stilling it, knowing it. But then, still afraid, gripped with dread, she lay in bed and listened, as the wife in the story does, as the man, her husband, opens the front door, walks along the hallway to the kitchen, runs the tap. She listens as he opens the back door and stands in the cool air pulling off the tie he's recently retied. Does she know that he thinks of the one whose breath still fills him? Does she know the sombre burden he carries, ensnared by two women, and satisfying neither? Does she care? She waits, hardly breathing, listening to his movements with more intensity than she does to the shallow beating of her own heart. She listens as he comes up the stairs, not wearily, but with a springy step, and she thinks *he's pleased to be home*, but at the top of the stairs, instead of coming in to her, he turns along the landing, past the children and into the bathroom. She listens to the hiss of the shower and while he stands under that stream of steaming water she feels coldness creep in around her knees, her ankle joints, a sort of heavy coldness, and though it is still summer she pulls on a T-shirt and finds the blanket folded at the end of the bed. She does not ask herself the question that is waiting not to be answered. She listens not to the pressure that is building in her head, white noise, but to the sharp click of water in the pipes as the shower turns off. She listens as the bathroom door opens, she smells her own shampoo, she waits as he creeps along the landing, past the children, without opening their doors, and quietly pushes open hers. She lies still in the dark as he lifts the sheets and gets in beside her.

'Are you awake?' he says.

'Yes,' she says. 'I couldn't sleep.'

'You shouldn't wait for me,' he says. 'You know how it is.'

'I wasn't waiting,' she says. 'It's just that I couldn't sleep.'

'It's glorious outside,' he says. 'I was thinking coming home how this summer's gone on and on. We should take the kids somewhere before it ends,' thereby betraying both women in the bifurcated life he presents as one.

Fantasies of Revenge

Artemisia Gentileschi knew what it meant to cut off a man's head, the strength it would take, the determination. Judith and her maid lean in towards their ghastly task, Holofernes' blood spatters their clothes, their arms are braced, their faces a study in concentration. There is no virtuous denial in their task. It is not relished exactly, but nor is it stepped back from. A woman's survival might depend on such a task, and on this occasion clearly does. Judith has her knee braced on the bed for further leverage. She is a woman of middle age, with nothing of the seductress, or the noble widow, or the innocent about her. She knows what she is doing, and could well do it again. Abra, the maid, a young woman with a striking resemblance to the Artemisia of a later self-portrait, uses the strength of her body to hold Holofernes down while Judith takes off his head. Such is the position of the sword that Abra is in direct line above it. Her arms are spotted with blood. In

Artemisia's second version of *Judith Slaying Holofernes*, neither of Abra's hands are visible; in the first only one can be seen. There is nothing damaged about Judith's hands. One grasps a hunk of his hair, pulling his head back, while the other forces the sword through his neck.

By the time Artemisia Gentileschi came to it, this bloodthirsty topic was a well established trope of religious narrative art: the virtuous Jewish widow saves the city from attack by slaying Holofernes, the bestial enemy commander; she seduces him into inviting her into his tent where, with her maid (usually depicted as an ancient crone), she overturns his evil intentions and calmly decapitates him. Many versions of the story pre-date Artemisia's, most of them hinting at the bloody moment which is captured either just before as the sword is raised, or afterwards as the women escape with the head. Even Caravaggio, who paints the gory moment of death in a composition that is a dress-rehearsal for Artemisia's, is squeamish when it comes to the strength that Judith must have needed to hack off a man's head. She stands well back as the blood spurts from his severed neck. It would not have been shocking *in itself* for Artemisia to have chosen this topic, indeed from the trial records it seems that a Judith series was already under way in her father's studio; but the power of her composition bursts into the present almost four centuries later not so much as the vengeance of Judith, as the brilliance of Artemisia.

Artemisia Gentileschi painted this bloody scene not once but twice. The second, the more famous Uffizi version, is dated 1620. The first version dates to 1612, the year of the trial at which she, and not her accused rapist, had her hands fitted with the sibille. Reading the trial records,[20] the painting springs into brilliant relief. Her evidence is assured and calmly determined. It is vivid with detail, and confident of a narrative which pitted her ability with image against his capacity for deceit.

On the day of the rape Agostino Tassi came into the studio of Artemisia's father while she was working. *When he found me painting,* she told the court, *he said: 'Not so much painting, not so much painting,' and he grabbed the palette and brushes from my hands and threw them around.* After he'd sent Tuzi, the woman who lodged with Artemisia, out of the room, Agostino took her hand and said: *'Let's walk together a while, because I hate sitting down.' While we walked two or three times around the room I told him that I was feeling ill and I thought I had a fever. He replied: 'I have more of a fever than you do.' After we had walked around two or three times . . . when we were in front of the bedroom door, he pushed me in and locked the door. He then threw me onto the edge of the bed, pushing me with a hand on my breast, and he put a knee between my thighs to prevent me from closing them.* Artemisia knew the strength of a man, and what it is to be pinned against a bed. After he'd raped her, and let her up, she testified, *I went to the table drawer and took a knife and moved toward Agostino saying: 'I'd like to kill you with this knife because you have dishonored me.' He opened his coat and said: 'Here I am,' and I threw the knife at him and he shielded himself; otherwise I would have hurt him and might easily have killed him. However, I wounded him slightly on the chest and some blood came out, only a little since I had barely touched him with the point of the knife. And the said Agostino then fastened his coat. I was crying and suffering over the wrong he had done me, and to pacify me, he said: 'Give me your hand, I promise to marry you as soon as I get out of the labyrinth I am in.'*[21]

Did Agostino Tassi marry Artemisia Gentileschi? Of course not. He had another wife whom, incidentally, he was accused (in passing) at the trial of murdering. Would Artemisia have wanted such a man? She was an artist of formidable talent; but the world of art was not stepped into just like that if you were a woman in seventeenth-century Rome.

A Man's Dreams

Back in Sydney, at the end of the twentieth century, the man in our story falls asleep before his wife. He, after all, though troubled, is sex-sated. He's never seen Artemisia's *Judith Slaying Holofernes*. He saw Caravaggio's version in a recent touring exhibition; it disturbed him at the time, but he has not thought of it since. It is not his own blood of which he dreams. Indeed he does not dream of blood at all. His dreams are clipped and dry: stakes driven into hard ground, ships propped askew on empty blocks.

His wife remembers the Caravaggio, but it is no more real to her, even as a fantasy, than Elizabeth ordering Essex to the Tower had been to Louise. It's not revenge a wife wants, Louise says, not exactly. What she wants is salvation, and for that the wife turns to the man, her husband, sleeping beside her. She lies still, and when sleep comes, she, the wife in our story, finds herself immobilised once more in a dream she's had off and on throughout the marriage. In the dream she wears a harness as children did many years ago when she was small, only the reins are long: yards and yards of them. In some dreams she soars high in the sky in her little harness and she can just make out her father standing far below her in the park. At other times she is snagged in branches and caught around tree trunks, and she can hear her father's voice calling to her. In this dream, on this night, she is standing on a rock at the end of a very deep, very beautiful lake, and the reins hang down loosely to the ground below where a man, perhaps her husband – his features are indistinct – is resting; and although all she needs to do is release the harness which is clipped quite simply between her shoulder blades like an angel's wings, and slip the straps over her arms, she doesn't. She waits on her rock filled with the desire to jump into the water, and a terror that wakes her with a start.

Beside her, her husband turns and dreams of tunnels threatening darkness, of buildings with rotten foundations, of women lined up, row upon row of them, waiting and wanting.

Tom Asks

Tom rings one afternoon and comes banging on my door. He is all noise and uncertainty, thundering up the steps, disturbing the air as he comes along the hall.

'Is Clara having an affair?' he asks, without preliminary niceties.

'Goodness Tom,' I said, 'isn't that a question you should ask her?'

'She says she's not,' he said. 'But I don't believe her. She's strange. Sort of distracted. Not like she used to be. I know I've upset her in the past, but I've always been faithful. She knows that, but sometimes I think she doesn't care. I don't understand her at all. Do you mind if I talk?'

'Go ahead,' I said. 'Though I may not be able to answer you.'

'I don't want the sort of lives you people have had,' Tom said. 'Sorry. I don't mean to be rude. I mean I think we've learned something. All your marriages, and lovers, and the mess of it. Clara knows I adore her, I thought she wanted a baby, for us to be a proper family, but she's distant, all the time distant. She used to be soft, so willing somehow. It's as if now I have to persuade her. Not sex. I don't mean crudely. I mean to talk, to do all the things we used to do, the fun. I try to tell her everything, I know she hates secrets, but it's hard to tell everything about your work. I mean there are some things that are just too complex. And involve other people. And I don't have much time. It's cut and thrust in at the paper, I can tell you. Not everyone gets ahead.'

'Perhaps,' I said, 'she's preoccupied about other things, and it has nothing to do with you. Have you tried asking if there's anything else bothering her?'

'Of course I ask,' he said. 'Every week I ask her how her work's going, what her supervisor says, what she's reading. She's vague. She tells me in bits and pieces, but I learn more when I hear her on the phone talking to other people, than I do when she talks to me.'

'Maybe there's something else,' I said. 'Something that's not to do with her work.'

'I doubt it,' he said. 'I mean, I do know her.'

'Of course you do,' I said, comforting, dissembling. 'You know she's thinking of going to Europe next year?'

'Yes,' I said. 'I'll probably be there at the same time myself.'

'Well, why?' he said.

'To see what she can find out about Stella Bowen for one thing,' I said. 'You know that. And she needs a break after all this work.'

'Are you sure there's not someone else?'

'Ask her, Tom,' I said. 'Ask her yourself.'

'I'll never understand women,' he said. 'Just when you think you're getting somewhere they slip away. She used to be so, well, so loving. You know. She used to tell me everything. Too much probably. It was more than I could listen to. Maybe Ettie knows.'

'Ettie's in Melbourne,' I said. 'You can't ask her. What about Alec?'

'Alec is no help,' Tom said. 'He saw me having lunch with a journalist the other week. A woman, you know. I mean it was all pretty much above board, it didn't even occur to me what Alec would think. But he's convinced I'm sleeping with her. Oh it's hopeless. He's so certain that that's what everyone really wants, he can't see that it isn't. Your generation was sex mad.'

'I'm hardly Alec's age,' I said.

'Well you know what I mean,' he said. 'You lived through the sixties.'

'Seventies,' I said. Tom, I remind myself, was born in 1964.

'I've never meant to hurt her,' he said. 'When I have it's been unintentional. Truly. And now I'm trying to make it all up to her, I don't seem to get anywhere. It doesn't feel like it should.'

'What should it feel like?'

'We ought to be happy.' Tom said. 'Oughtn't we?'

Happy Couples

The answer I didn't give Tom is that there are indeed happy couples, even happy families, but I would say that it is not they that are all alike. It is the unhappiness of couples that seems to me predictable as they do battle over control; it is the occasions of their happiness that are to be found after their own fashion. When one sees happiness between a man and a woman who have travelled beyond the state of *being in love*, and beyond the war zone, it is a blessing to be in their company. Paradoxically it is not so different, this blessing, from the happiness of those who have learned to live full lives without partners though not without connections and intimacies (by which I do not – necessarily – mean sex). Happiness is perhaps the wrong word. It is the quality of being fully oneself, not at rest so much as defining one's own terms, not to impose them on others but as a basis of mutual connection – and not only with a spouse. Individuation is closer to the quality I mean, a more hardly wrought and painful process than the rose-covered cottage the word *happiness* conjures up, and that Tom can feel slip from his grasp; though to achieve it, even to begin to achieve it is, surely, a source of the fullest pleasure. It requires the ability to see others as sovereign as oneself; it takes great presence of mind, Ettie would say, raising hands that still occasionally tremble, and great strength.

I didn't say any of this to Tom because, at that time, it couldn't have answered his question. Living with Clara, he saw that she was unhappy, but seeing, he could understand only the effect of her unhappiness on himself. What other answer would I have given? Clara was not having an affair. At least not that I knew of, though I knew it was possible, even likely, that the time would come when she would. If she were to, she'd probably tell him, it's become a point of honour with her, that sort of honesty. But what was there to tell him in the meantime, when he was gripped by the fear of the cuckold? That she doubted that he was, after all, the man with whom she could have children? That she wanted a year in Europe, but when she contemplated leaving for so long, she was afraid of losing him? That she didn't want to cut her ties even while she felt bound by them? These were the infidelities, the betrayals, that cramped her one by one; this the unhappiness that Tom felt but could not understand.

'You've always set so much store by telling the truth,' I say to Clara.

'I don't know what the truth is,' she says. 'It's not like there's a statement. He wants something definite, and all I have are thoughts.'

The Story Ends

When the end came, it came fast, and in the most predictable of ways. The man's cousin, a woman with suspiciously blonde hair and a liking for bright clothes, saw him lunching with the woman, his mistress, in a restaurant at Bondi. They, the man and the mistress, were at a table on the verandah. Aware only of the brightness in which they sat, they paid no attention to the group of women who sat in the shadow of the room behind them. Their feet, the man's cousin told his wife, were *entwined beneath the table, plain for anyone to see.*

'Are you in love with her?' his wife wept, gasping against the fear that burst on her with the force of a ruptured dam.

'How could you?' she said as she stood limp and sodden in the door of the study where he was making up a bed. 'Don't you ever think about me? About the children?'

'It's over,' her husband said, afraid of the unnamed possibilities that lay ahead, for him, for the children, for her. 'I promise you it's over. It was only a momentary affair. Never serious. I promise.'

'That's what men always say,' his wife said slamming her, once their, bedroom door. The children, wide awake, sat up in their beds. The boy felt a hot flood of pee on his legs; the girl began to retch. The man, their father, changed sheets, soothed brows, held small hands until at last the children slept. He, in his make-shift bed, lay in the still dark, consoling himself with the thought of the disasters he had averted, the rages and tears, the loneliness, the battles, the cost. He thought of the long years stretching ahead, as the years had stretched behind, with days so alike they all became the same. He thought of the one who had made each day clear and bright: unpredictable, exciting. He felt like two trains heading for each other on the same track.

The next afternoon the man, whose breath tasted sour in his mouth, rang the woman, his mistress. He told her he couldn't make dinner. He said he was sorry. He said the french doors that had been put into the dining room had left a lot of rubble.

'You're standing me up for rubble?' his mistress said. 'For *rubble*?'

'I can't just leave it,' he said.

'Why not?' she said.

'The children,' he said. 'It's not safe.'

'Then you'd better come round in the morning,' she said.

And when he did she shouted at him, she shouted at him with anger that had accumulated over two years, a whooping fury that took a warped pleasure in being wronged. When the man turned his head as if to deflect the full blast of her, she saw that she was too much, in every way too much. And she did not care; she did not pull back, she did not soften, she did not forgive.

'I thought you were meant to be moving out,' she said. 'Not renovating.'

'I can't,' he said. 'I tried. You know I tried. I just can't. Not yet. Maybe in another year or two.'

'Another year or two,' she yelled. 'Do you think I'll still be here? What about your wife? How'll it be for her then? I don't suppose that matters. Look at you! You make us both promises, and you never come across. Not to her. Not to me. *You'll leave when you're ready!* And in the meantime this is information I'm meant to swallow and she isn't even allowed to know. You'd treat a dog better.'

'Come here,' he said, putting out the hands that had so recently caressed her and now, in that familiar gesture, could only wound.

'You must be joking,' she said, and opened the door.

In this ugly way he left, two years of love, two years of plans and promises, gone, just like that, into the smoky, polluted air above the city. Where once he had lingered on the doorstep, circling her mouth with his tongue, now he hurried past, scurried one might almost say; and with her arms crossed and her voice raised as loud as any fishwife's, the mistress watched as he set off down the street.

What did she, this mistress, feel as she stood in her empty hallway and watched the man she had been sure she loved, turn in o the traffic that was grinding its way towards the city? She felt a fool, to be so easily duped. She felt grief as the sharp possibility of the future evaporated into the loneliness she had thought to escape. She felt an unexpected shaft of compassion for a man caught in the mire of the present. She felt the fullness of the complexities that kept him from her. She felt love, and the gentle wash of memory. She felt hard and ungiving. All these feelings and sensations existed in her at once, not jumbled, not in sequence, but layered, like a scroll of possibilities that exist only in the con- figuration of the moment, though had she been asked to name them she would have said they passed too quickly for her to grasp.

'I still mourn her,' the man said to Louise over lunch that day, edging towards the question he wanted to ask, the question to which his story had been directed. 'How is she?' he asked, and although Louise understood his meaning to be *is she still mine, is there someone else*, she answered only that as far as she knew she, the mistress, was fine.

'I know I could be said to have made a mistake,' the man said. 'But what do you do when you have children, responsibilities. I couldn't put them through it.'

'You could have helped them through it,' Louise said.

'I couldn't jeopardise their schooling,' the man said.

'They say kids from broken homes can lose grades very quickly. It's a lot to let your children risk, their whole futures maybe.'

'Change,' Louise said, 'doesn't necessarily mean loss.'

'No,' the man said, 'I suppose it doesn't. But try telling that to your kids.'

'I did,' Louise said.

Mourning the Past

When Gerhard died, some people got it wrong and thought that Ettie didn't mourn for him. Compounding their mistake, they concluded that the marriage had therefore not been happy. Within days of the funeral, within hours, Ettie was back in the garden. That autumn she extended up the gully on the other side of the pool meeting native gorse with stands of azaleas. For the rest, her mourning was incorporated into the daily round she'd lived when living with him. But it wasn't this that confused those who saw little change in her behaviour so much as an attitude that spoke of him without the lowered voice that usually flattens out the dead and muffles their reality. He remained sharply imaged, as if he were simply away – on a trip, or in the studio, or up the garden. She didn't pass him over into the shadowy realm of reverence that she never accorded him in life.

Alec, who has his own reasons for not wanting that particular past to be too perfect, says the reason Ettie wasn't cast into the grief that is expected of a widow was not that the marriage was unhappy, but that it was fully itself. Not happy exactly, that easy word, although it was a source of contentment and pleasure to them both; but fully inhabited, so that the breaches, the moments of doubt, the pin-prick betrayals, were as felt as the moments of desire, the days of harmony, the coded jokes, the stories that blended and matched. The loss was as deep and as real as the love had been, and she lived it with customary courage. But she was spared the pain of mourning an absence: possibilities denied, hidden recriminations, insidious memories of distrust, passion cut off too soon. Every moment of that marriage had been lived in all its complexity. There was nothing missing to hurt her with its ghostly presence.

That's what's so awful about not being told of an affair, Louise says. Not only do you feel your humanity violated, as if you've been cast as infant or invalid who cannot be trusted with the truth, but you have not lived the truth, and therefore the experience, of that part of your life. You're left with the corrosive of regret, with the open wounds that come with the memory of things not said, with gestures reinterpreted, and with the realisation that you were not accorded an equal value with the one you loved.

As to the mistress, she is left mourning the unlived gap between the future that was promised and the story that seduced her. The bargain she struck – be for me what I want you to be – was reciprocated in his request that she play mistress to him.

A True Story

Louise, if you remember, had known the mistress before her affair with the man, and although the mistress now lives in a distant city, Louise would still count her as a friend. But during those two years of the affair, the bond between the women had creaked and strained until, just for that time, even each other's profiles became ugly to them. It was as if each faced the other across a battle line. While Louise knew that the wife's story could not match the one the man told her friend, the mistress wanted Louise's approval, her participation in the story, her blessing. They struggled over competing versions, competing identities. When the affair was over, the mistress apologised to Louise, and Louise replied that the apologies should be hers. If they were to be friends, Louise said, they should try to understand the reality of the other's life, and relinquish their competing fantasies.

This conversation took place some months after the affair had ended while the two women walked one afternoon on the promontory of South Head, that neck of land overlooking the swell on which the harbour meets the ocean. In making this doubled-over apology it was as if words came from deep down in them and they had to heave them out onto that headland where everything was clear and bright before they could know what they were saying. As they spoke they watched the surf pound against the rocks, and in the distance, crouched against the horizon, the low shape of passing freighters. They turned their heads and rested their eyes on the still waters of the harbour with its life of ferries and sail boats, islands decked out in green. Up there, above where Christina Stead had lived as a young woman and where in *For Love Alone* her lovelorn Teresa paced towards a destiny that had to do with more than love, Louise told the mistress a story that Ettie had told her during that long winter of Don's departure, and which had become an accompaniment to her present life.

'Is it a true story?' the mistress asked.

'Very true,' Louise said, and then laughed because the story she was about to tell was a legend, and not true at all.

In the story which I first tell you here in this short-ened form, a maiden had her hands chopped off by her father. This was not because he did not love his daugh-ter, but because he was caught in a bargain with the devil. The maiden, escaping both father and devil, took refuge in the forest with her bound-up stumps. There she wandered for many months until she stumbled into a king's orchard. The king, falling in love with her, manufactured a pair of fine silver hands which the maiden, now his wife and therefore a princess, wore with the greatest pleasure. But the devil had not fin-ished his work and the princess was cast once more into the forest, but this time, wandering for many years alone with her daughter, her hands grew slowly back: first as a baby's hands, then as a little girl's hands, and last as a woman's hands. It was only then, when the silver hands were discarded, that she was reunited with the king.

Akim says Louise was slightly flushed when she told him this story on their first date. He says he recognised it as a test. She says he recognised it as a parable for the shape of a woman's life.

The mistress, standing on the the headland, raised her hands to the shining sky and saw that the index finger of her right hand curved slightly towards the others, bent by the pressure of her pen, she supposed, or by the knife she used to cut her food.

'Tell me again,' she said to Louise her friend. 'Tell me it properly, with every detail.'

And What of Our Players

And what of the players in our meagre story? Where are they now that several years have elapsed? Having had time to reflect, what else would the man say? He'd say the days go slowly. He'd say he never meant any harm to either woman. He'd say that he doesn't know what made him so afraid. Afraid of what? Of that too, he isn't sure. The determination of the women perhaps? Their expectations? Their capacity for anger? When Louise asked him why he'd lied to his wife, he said he'd never meant to deceive her, only to spare her. Spare her what? Spare her her own life. That's what Louise would say. And sparing hers, I'd add, he could be said to have missed his own. So now he daydreams of the woman he took to bed for the year that spanned those two hot summers. Now, wherever he goes he looks out for her car, on the alert for a battered red Toyota. His night dreams haven't improved, but he thinks he is slowly moving to the point where one day when she stops at the traffic lights, he'll open the door and slip in beside her and she'll smile and say, *ah, it's you*. He doesn't know, because Louise didn't tell him, that she sold it long ago, and now drives a blue Honda in another city.

He and his wife sleep again in the same bed. He rarely works late at the office. It was because of his sadness, which went on and on, that she realised the affair really was over. She built up her strength little by little, as sharp misery resolved back into the comfortable mist of routine. Nowadays she is quite cheerful; with the children older she goes out more, and finds that she is learning how to laugh again; in restaurants, she tells her husband, she notices that it is at tables of women that there is the most laughter. The man, her husband, glimpses in her the girl he'd married, glimpses the woman another man might love. Where once her body was weighed down, now it seems springy. The children no longer wet their beds, they're too old for that, their grades are good. Well, good enough. If the girl has a tendency to lie on her bed and stare at the ceiling, it's probably only adolescence, nothing to worry about. A casual observer would say that everything had returned to normal, and notch it up as a success. Everything, except that over these years the woman, his wife, has begun to think of her name, her *maiden* name, which is really only the name of her father. She thinks also of her mother's maiden name and that too is the name of a father. She thinks of all the women in her family stretching back and back and she realises she doesn't know their names. To her it's as if, nameless, they are lost. How many generations will it take for her name to be lost? Her daughter's? Her granddaughter's? Wherever she goes she takes with her these queues of lost women, well not really queues as they're never in straight lines, milling around is how she thinks of them; and every now and again one breaks free, swinging out, her old-fashioned skirts, her cream petticoats flying out over the street. Behind all these women, or alongside and beneath, inside and beyond them, is an unnameable sense of herself. As the women mill and throng, all the women of generations past and generations to come, her marriage is like a short train track laid down in their midst. Where once it was the marriage that flowed all around her and there was no seeing in any direction but it, now when she looks that track seems quite small, quite straight, almost meek. If she turns round to face ahead she doesn't see it at all. When this happens she gets tearful. *The children*, she says. *The children*. And she reminds her husband of the days and the weeks and the months she spent hauling herself back to the light from the dark pit into which he had thrown her. There's bitterness there, she warns him as she begins to speak of a different future, bitterness they could feed on all their lives.

What will become of her no one can tell. Women can live on a pivot like that for years, but once they begin to question the names they've been given, it's usually only a matter of time before they know on which side they will come down: woman or wife.

And no one can tell you either what will become of the woman, once mistress, who now lives in a distant city. She didn't mourn for long. Or she thought she didn't. There are plenty of fish, as the saying goes, in a sea like hers. But her taste for affairs, brief encounters, short partnerships, seemed not as it was. She felt the absence of engagement, of depth, of understanding. When she found herself again entranced, it was not with a lover this time, but with a woman half her age. Well, not really, but almost, she likes the hyperbole: a girl, a mere girl, one, it seems to the woman (herself not yet forty-five), who is born of another mould. An artist, this girl, she smells of turpentine and paint, there's charcoal under her nails. Is this an evasion, a shallow

recovery? Or a sign of things to come? I wouldn't pre-
sume to know. See how she walks down the street. The
girl beside her is telling stories which the woman has
to lean forwards to catch, for it's cold in their city and
the wind picks up their words and tosses them round,
they entwine and tangle, the girl's story and hers, until
neither is sure what's real and what's not, what belongs
to one, or the other. And nor, at this stage, am I. Anything is possible with a pair like that. Look, they've just
turned into a bar, I can see them through the window
ordering vermouth and wine.

Telling the Truth

Was Clara right when she said all that was required of
the three was that they should tell the truth? And if
they had, would it have been different? The truth isn't
an eraser we can use to eliminate responsibilities, con-
flicting needs, other loyalties. What good would telling
the truth do when they saw themselves as they did?
When the wife saw herself as wife; when the mistress
was mistress; and the man depended on both for the
name he called himself.

No, something more than telling is required. And
what that something is each has to learn alone.

Clara

Up in the mountains I was writing this story at Ettie's
table. I was minding the house for a week. Or, more to
the point, the garden. The bloom of spring was in the
air, scenting the house, fragrant and demanding, enticing me out. My days were quiet, clearing out under the

azaleas, weeding the long border, tying back the espalier pear, the newly planted crab apple, watching the wisteria bud on the verandah.

Then Clara came walking down the track with her pack. The first I heard of her was the scrape of the gate, and her call hello.

'You should have rung from the station,' I said. 'I'd have picked you up.'

'Do you mind?' she said. 'I won't disturb you.'

'I could do with some disturbance,' I said.

I gave her the verandah. In the mornings I'd get up early and turn on the radiators so she'd be warm for her bath; wrapped in Ettie's old shawl, I'd sit at the table and watch the sun come in through the mist that rolls out of the valley at that time of year. The sun was shining down by the time Clara was up, and the dew evaporating as if the earth itself was steaming. She'd come into the kitchen with an old jumper over her pyjamas, pour strong black coffee into one of Ettie's large French breakfast cups and sit on the doorstep in the morning sun looking out into the garden.

She told me she'd become attracted to someone else. And what did the second one, this pawn in the game she played with Tom, think of this? Clara let him believe what he liked. She didn't lie, she said, and he didn't ask. Nothing, she said, had actually happened. I didn't comment. In any case this was not why Clara had come to the mountains. She didn't want my advice; and to her credit she didn't talk of it much, leaving the air calm around me for the strange exertions that gardens demand. She'd come, she said, to do some work. But she rarely opened her books. Instead she propped a mirror on the ledge in the bathroom and adjusted the skirt she was making. Or else she lay on the verandah as I have so often done, floating in a wordless reverie. Sometimes I heard her moving around, the soft pad of her step, the thump as she bumped against furniture, rearranging rooms to suit her mood. Sometimes I caught an acrid twang when she opened the tiny pots of ink she'd brought with her.

What Clara wanted to talk about was not the love affair that was drawing to its close. What she wanted to talk about was Ettie. And about Jock and Helena. She circled around the subject for days, and even then, when she homed in, she took me by surprise.

'You don't think Jock was any good as a painter, do you?' she said.

'No,' I said. 'I don't think he was. Not really.'

'Do you think I've inherited whatever it was that made him fail?'

'No,' I said. 'I don't. I think our talents are what we make of them.'

'That's a cop-out,' she said. 'What about Ettie?'

'What about her?'

'Why didn't she paint more?' she said, going into Ettie's bedroom and taking from the wall the only painting of hers that survives, the one she painted in the George Street studio at the end of 1938 during that southerly buster: the gouache of the eye straining against the threads that tether it to the ground, each held down by tiny plants and flowers. Clara leaned it against my typewriter.

'She had talent,' she said. 'Perhaps I inherited that.' She laughed. 'Don't worry,' she said. 'I'm joking.'

'You're not,' I said.

'I don't understand this painting,' she said. 'Do you? Why an eye trapped like that?'

'You should ask Ettie.'

'I'm asking you.'

She looked at Jock's portrait of Ettie that was on the wall above where we sat. 'Look at her eyes,' she said. 'They're mine.' I looked, and saw what I have strained to see and always missed, that Clara's right, the eyes are hers. The coil of the secret that awoke that night when Louise first told the story, and entered the house with her arrival, rose up like a great hooded snake. She said looking straight at me that now Helena's dead she could say that she never really believed in her. 'Don't get me wrong,' she said. 'She was kind to me, endlessly patient, and it can't have been easy landing me at her age. But I never believed she was my mother.'

'She wasn't,' I said. 'She was your grandmother.'

'When I was a kid I used to think Ettie was my mother.'

'You knew she wasn't. Dorothy was.'

'But who was her mother?'

'Oh Clara, Clara,' I said. 'Why are you asking this?'

'Because I want to know,' she said. 'Because I went through the paintings in the attic after Jock died and before Helena got back. Do you know how many there were of Ettie? Do you?'

'No.'

'Twenty-three,' she said. 'That's how many.'

'What's happened to them?'

'I don't know. I asked Helena and she said they'd never been there. I was furious. I stomped up to the attic and they weren't there. It was the only time I felt angry with her, really, truly angry. Do you think I dreamed them?'

'Do you?'

'No. And I'll tell you why not. Every one of them had my eyes.'

'Oh Clara.'

'Will you tell me the truth?' she said, but she didn't look at me. Instead she picked up the pages I'd already typed.

'Don't,' I said, but she jerked away from the hand I put up to restrain her.

'Look at this,' she said. 'The man. The woman. The wife. Who are these people for christsakes? I know about that affair you had with Jack. Everyone knows about it. You're the only ones who think it's a secret. Why don't you write about that? It's why Hal moved to the bush isn't it? Go on. Be honest. Or don't you dare?'

She sat down, and put the pages gently back where they'd been. 'Sorry,' she said.

'It's okay,' I said, and at that moment we heard a car spitting up gravel on the track, a voice calling out, car doors banging.

'It's a bit early for tourists, isn't it?' Clara said.

We go out together, walking slowly toward this well-timed interruption. We open the gate so the car can turn round and we explain that there is no way down to the valley. When the tourists drive off, much too fast up the track, kicking up dust, filling our throats with fumes, we walk along the line of the fence, through the orchard with the apples coming into blossom, across the lawn to the trees – oreades, blue gums, banksia – along the top of the escarpment. In one direction we can see Mount Solitary, like a huge maiden waiting to be scaled, in the other the folds of the range stretching into a distance where the buckled earth smoothes out along a road as thin as a string.

'This garden is like a launching pad,' Clara says. 'A transition. A place that lets you move between other places.'

'Or somewhere that allows all the parts to meet,' I say.

Walking back to the house, she puts her arm round my shoulder, as if she is the one with the strength, the authority, the knowledge. I feel my body small against hers.

'Will you tell me the truth?' she says.

....

[1] Virginia Woolf, 'Women and Fiction', *Collected Essays*, Vol. 2, London, Chatto and Windus, 1966, p. 145

[2] Stella Bowen, *Drawn From Life*, first published London, 1941. Virago edition, 1984, p. 63

[3] Stella Bowen, *Drawn From Life*, p. 64

[4] Stella Bowen, *Drawn From Life*, p. 168

[5] Stella Bowen, *Drawn From Life*, p. 162

[6] Stella Bowen, *Drawn From Life*, p. 160

[7] Marie-Louise von Franz, *Projection & Re-Collection in Jungian Psychology*, translated 1980, La Salle, Illinois, Open Court Publishing Co., p. 141

[8] Stella Bowen, *Drawn From Life*, p. 63

[9] Stella Bowen, *Drawn From Life*, p. 168

[10] The dance of domination is a phrase used by Jessica Benjamin in *The Bonds of Love*, London, Virago, 1990, an excellent and detailed analysis of the foundations and implications of this dance of domination.

[11] Jean Rhys, *Quartet*, first published as *Postures* by Chatto & Windus, 1928. Penguin edition, 1969, p. 97

[12] This 'dedicatory letter' is reprinted in the Penguin edition of *The Good Soldier*.

[13] Stella Bowen, *Drawn From Life*, p. 165

[14] Stella Bowen, *Drawn From Life*, p. 163

[15] Thomas Merton, *The Power and Meaning of Love*, London, Sheldon Press, 1986, p. 7

[16] Stella Bowen, *Drawn From Life*, p. 188

[17] Julia Kristeva, *Tales of Love*, New York, Columbia University Press, 1987, p. 109

[18] Julia Kristeva, *Tales of Love*, p. 215

[19] Thomas Merton, *The Power and Meaning of Love*, p. 7

[20] See Mary D. Garrard, *Artemisia Gentileschi*, Princeton University Press, 1989, Appendix B

[21] Mary D. Garrard, *Artemisia Gentileschi*, p. 416

Sight
and
Solitude

1 Far away and long ago, in the place where I grew up, there was a driveway through dark trees – yews, rhododendrons – that met overhead. So twined around each other were they that on a dull day it was as dark as dusk under there; no shade, no light, just a dim grey murk; not darkness, not light, a nether-region to be traversed as fast as possible. Ponies, bicycles, were urged on. On bright days the sun, during those few months of the year when it was high, pierced the dense leaves and dark branches in bright roses of light. Then was the time to dawdle, to watch the light-specks dance. Sometimes, suddenly, without warning, for under there you couldn't see the sky, a cloud would pass over the sun and it would darken as if the switch had been turned; all that remained was dim, uncertain, shadowy, a tunnel inhabited by all kinds of fears and mysteries. The question then was who dared stay there the longest before bursting out into light and a world that spread around us in the wide familiar arc we rode smoothly through.

I had forgotten about that place, after all it was a stretch of road no more than fifty yards in length, and, as I say, it was a long time ago; but it came back as much premonition as memory when for several months not so long ago my eyes dimmed, casting me into a region as murky as it was under those rhododendrons. But this time I couldn't hurry out into the light when the fears rustling in the undergrowth grew too loud. I had to remain, there was no choice, and while I knew I was not far from light, I couldn't be sure, not entirely sure, that I would ever burst back into it. Friends said I would, of course I would; in emergencies people rely on platitudes and assurances. But that first day Dr —— said I was on a precipice, an image that was as real to me as the tunnel and not in contradiction with it at all. As I staggered out of his darkened room into the winter light of Macquarie Street, shading my dilated, jumpy eyes against the low slant of the sun, it was indeed on the edge of a chasm that I felt myself. A chasm of darkness into which I might soundlessly drop. Plop, and I'd be gone.

Of all the disease-fears I've had, none have been focused on sight. Indeed all my life I have been complimented on my eyes; as a child they were considered my *best feature*, as a result of which I grew up knowing two things, both in their way quite useful. I learned that *real* eyes are not blue, but brown (in other words that the obvious is not so obvious); and I discovered the ease with which one can maintain illusion (the moral is much the same). My eyes might look dark and luminous, as if they miss nothing, a misapprehension I naturally encouraged, but it's merely the effect of the myopia that is carried in my genes. They look as my mother's eyes looked, and hers did miss very little; but they see as my father's faded eyes see - without the aid of lenses nothing much beyond the range of a closely held book. Tennis balls, parrots in the trees, people waving in the distance – these are rarely noticed until they're upon us. Gardens are appreciated for their colour and form, our taste running to paths that loop and weave, secret corners, unexpected nooks. Grand vistas hold little beyond an obvious magnificence for eyes like ours. Even when my eyes filled with black swirls and orange flashes, I didn't foresee that the guardian angel of visual certainty was about to desert me. Like falling in love, it was a sudden shock which changes how you see the past, a narrative of signs missed at the time but rewritten into the story you make of it once it has happened.

Nothing was as it had been two hours before when I'd walked into the building. Lights glittered and jumped, people loomed along the pavement, purposeful, busy, belonging to a world from which I had been abruptly excluded. The pharmacist said I was in good hands and wrapped the parcel with his own delicately pointed fingers. Though I caught the same train home everything about my life had changed. But while I confess to an excessive interest in health, and will doubtless be one of those old ladies who talk about their operations at the bus-stop, I will, on this occasion, spare you the medical details. I find myself reluctant to speak of them. Instead the journey I wish to describe is a journey undertaken – with such resistance, with toes dug in – less by the body than by the soul when it is forced into a darkness from which it must find its own rescue, and its own source of light.

At first it ʼeemed that everything had stopped. And in a sense it had. With sight threatened, everything had to stop: working, reading, writing, errands, walking, visiting. I was grounded and afraid. The first days passed in furious debate. On the one hand a list of rationalisations, often in the form of requests for reassurance, as I recounted the wonders of modern pharmacology. 'Surely,' I said. 'In this day and age.' Etc. On the other hand, there was blind terror, the terror of blindness. A darkness from which there would be no escape, trapped forever in a hot black box. Not just a dimmed world in which the centre of my field of vision blurred while the edges flickered, but a world of darkness: a world that is present to others, but you open your eyes and it's not there; nothing is there, only blackness, and wherever you put your foot, the blackness slips away taking you further into it.

On that first weekend, I was besieged with memories and fears. Every detail of my past, every occasion on which I had been cast into loneliness or danger, revisited me in a grotesque, magnified form. I was ten years old and Clarissa Larkin, a mean girl I never liked, shut me in the coal hole. Her brother upstairs, who was supposed to be looking after us, lay on his bed reading poetry and dirty magazines. I screamed, I remember screaming, and the realisation that I could scream until I was nothing but a voice, and forcing myself to sit quiet and still watching through the crack in the door for Clarissa's mother's thick stockinged legs, she'd have to come back sooner or later; and in the meantime breathing in, breathing out, as if I consisted of nothing but a heart and lung, contracted into these essentials, warding off the s irits and the rats that lived down in the dark where the coal used to be and now there was a rustling junk heap of old bed-springs and bicycle parts. And then I was dancing, and my first boyfriend left me on the sidelines and chose another, and there I was for all to see abandoned and alone. Self-pity is a heady drug; once it starts one's whole life can be composed of wretched incidents.

I rang Ettie. She came down on the train, bringing with her the angel that has flown over her bed for twenty years, an angel to guard over me. As neither of us had the reach to hang her from the ceiling she lay stranded on the table, a beautiful reminder. Ettie's old hands stroked my hair; she hushed me like a baby; she cooked food; she made up my bed with fresh sheets. 'The fear is enough,' she said, encouraging me to dwell there, to learn its shape, to feel its edges. 'Don't build on it with memories and slights.' She had spoken to the doctor, she knew the risk, and she knew that total darkness was the fear I conjured, and not the prospect that was offered. 'What is the fear?' she asked. 'What is its real nature?' It was not a question I could accept with grace, and I wept afresh when she said that if I shifted my way of seeing (she used that word), what this episode offered was an opportunity.

'For what?' I wept.

'For solitude,' she said. She was right: for years I had avoided that empty space we call solitude, filling up my life with work and lovers, distractions of every sort. 'Go into it,' she said, 'and you'll find it richer than you expect.'

When she left I closed the door behind her as if to a cell of which I was both inmate and gaoler. I turned the key in the lock and lay on my bed. Next door the old lady swept her yard with a straw broom. I knew, because I'd seen it many times, that she kept that yard as neat as a Japanese garden with the grain of the concrete's sandy residues streaming in one direction. I listened as she fed the parrot on its perch with seeds and tiny scraps of bread. 'Pretty Polly,' she said, delivering to its beak a single seed as it repeated her words, 'Pretty Polly,' hopping from perch to roof and back again. Every day the same routine: the only shape I could give to days that grew bare and repetitive. I could hear the scrape of her broom, the rattle of seeds in the jar as she shook them into her hand, the scratch of the parrot's claw, even the soft slink of the cat. I'd asked her once how they got on, the cat and the parrot, a disingenuous question as I had seen the cat stalk through the rubbish bins neatly lined along the far fence line, and past the geranium pots and the lemon tree that had somehow broken through the concrete, past the fish tank. She replied that she'd trained them both. 'I think,' she said curling her fingers over the fence, 'you could say they understand each other.' Inside I snapped down the blinds; but still I listened for the squawk and soft fall of feathers.

During those first weeks I rarely went out. People visited. Clara came with a pomegranate. I held it in my hand, a heavy golden orb at once irregular and balanced, glowing and curved. Louise rearranged my music, so that as one sense contracted another could open up: these are the things one remembers, the best of all gifts. During the long hours I was alone, as well as my neighbouring crone, I listened to the voices of Hildegarde of Bingen's nuns – a present I at first considered eccentric – as if to a dim trace of distant light. The quieter of my visitors, Clara perhaps, or one of the others, read to me of the abbess and her convent of women dressed in the most glorious of robes and wearing crowns on their head, 'diadems in niello enamel work in three colours, symbolic of the Trinity, with four roundels showing the Lamb of God, an angel, a cherub and a human being.' *This emblem*, Hildegarde wrote, *granted to me, will proclaim blessings to God, because he had clothed the first human creature in radiant brightness*.[1]

Here, three centuries before the *Malleus Maleficarum* and the torture of women for far less than their visions, we find a woman cloistered from the age of eight, who wrote scientific treatises on natural history and medicine, as well as commentaries on the gospels; who corresponded with popes and archbishops, an emperor and a king, as well as running her convent and maintaining an intimate intellectual contact with her sister convents. All this from a woman with a painful illness that left her *with periodic bouts of blindness*. It was at forty-three, during that difficult passage of mid-life, that she began, at the command of God, to record the visions full of the symbols of transcendence that came to her. I listened to *the symphony of the harmony of celestial revelations*, written for her crowned and cloistered nuns. At first these voices were strange to me, but strangely calming, far beyond the reach of the life in which I felt myself to be incarcerated. Outside on the street people walked past the window with collars turned up and scarves around their heads; and so strange were these passersby that I should have photographed them. Even the friends who bounded in from their lives of meetings, errands, shopping, working, reading, seemed less real to me than the gloriously appointed voices of Hildegarde's nuns.

Sometimes my living room filled as visitors coincided, and then all around me was the chatter of now, conversations studded with expressions like *I'll have to see*, and *if you look at it this way*, and *I'll look it up*, and *so you see*. Our daily language is full of visual references. But then sight is perhaps the dominant sense. It is the source of most of the information by which we regulate the most ordinary of dealings. And yet it seemed to me that no one knew what anything was like. No one could describe to me a daffodil. Not exactly. Not sufficiently. When I asked, Clara rushed out and bought me a bunch. I looked into their hooded hearts and couldn't see the stamens. Had anyone, ever, really looked? Other than Wordsworth, or botanists?

About halfway through, when the tunnel was all I knew, when the light at the end I'd entered from was no longer a bright beacon of incomprehension, and the other end was not yet in view, I became fractious and irritable. Where once I'd called people to me, now I shooed them away. The language I was familiar with, the metaphors and stories I'd based my life on, seemed to disintegrate. Nouns sank into a fixed and sticky mire so that the names of things weren't certain any more, or else were too certain to convince; adjectives floated around, slippery, changeable beasts; verbs I lost sight of altogether in the inertia of forced inactivity. Plots and histories didn't make sense; narratives veered along

strange pathways; the written word seemed empty and
inadequate, and anyway I wasn't able to read; there was
no salvation in novels. I knew at once that writing was
no cure, at best a substitute, and I couldn't even manage that. Where once I had stood aside and made order
of the life that swirled around me – a spy, Hal said, in
the lives of others – I was down there in the ruck of it
myself. Pushing through the gloom it was all I could
do to keep my balance against the snags and snares that
pulled at me. So low was my angle of vision that I saw
nothing further ahead than the ground on which my
nose was pressed, and even that was a blur.

I took the step of going out. It was Louise's birthday,
and other people, though not she, coaxed me as if it
would be an occasion on which I could step back, just
like that, into real life. It was a daytime party, in the
house with large windows opening over the ocean, in
the house where the glittery blue washes over you, as
seductive as sunlight, with the strange illusion that you
are part of the sky and there are no borders, no hori-
zons, only that encompassing light. But on the day of
the party the room was full of people, and there was no
such possibility of reverie. Party cheer blew the paper
blinds against the windows, flirtations eddied across the
room, guests loaded their plates with huge helpings of
food that is meant for delicate tasting. Funny stories
competed for attention, and not one of them made me
laugh. And in the midst of it all I could see how little I
could see. In a room full of people viewed against a
bright light, I could sense the ambitions and the sor-
rows that stuck to them, but I was unable to make out
the features on their faces. I found myself cast into a

shadowy land of silhouettes where voices roared and I was no longer part of that controlling order of seeing and being seen. Shapes and noises bore down on me; the space between sight and thought thickened into a roar.

It is only now when I recount this experience, that I can say people in dark phases of their lives should not be obliged to go to parties. The two realms do not connect and to be inadequately in the world acknowledged as normal only emphasises the sense of exclusion, the outcast nature of the other. The chronology of the heart does not sit easily with the time-span of parties. Surprisingly few people understand this, although in the event Louise did. For the rest, they will tell you that going out will *cheer you up*, take *you out of yourself*, or *your mind off things. A bit of good fun*, they say, *never did anyone any harm*.

That night, softened to my silence and even to the shuffle of my ancient neighbour, I dreamed I was a strange creature, half fish, half fowl; no, not that, and not half man, half woman either, but a creature indeterminate and made of many parts. In the dream, this strange amorphous being that was me squatted on the earth deep under the trees and gave birth to a fat white grub. I could see that it was born of me, this ugly creature, and before it wormed its way under the leaf mould, I could see that although pale and without a proper skin, it was fat and juicy. There was nothing about it I could recognise, except that it had been delivered of me; that I could tell by the way I crouched and by the ache in my belly. Who could have sired this creature, I had no idea. In the dream it was my task to watch over this graceless grub, though in reality I woke with a rush

of anxiety and snapped the light on until its image
melted into the quiet sounds of a building contracting
with the night.

When I looked at myself in the mirror the next
morning, I saw a face that was strange, and strangely
shocking to me. I saw, perhaps for the first time, or
maybe only since childhood, a face that was not poised
for the regard of another. I saw my face empty, so to
speak, naked seems hardly the word, unveiled is not it
either, though the sensation was as if something had
dropped. Not lifted, but dropped. I saw a face that at
that moment had ceased to live for, or in, the regard of
others. It was as if, in the dimming of my sight, I realised for the first time the exhaustive, exhausting moni-
toring that is made of us wherever we go. Eyes that
look, that see, that watch. As if our lives swim in a sea
of seeing, and being seen, our view of ourselves gliding
backwards and forwards, up and down, over the slippery surface of our bodies, and the gestures and mes-
sages they permit, conceal, attract, trap. I looked at
myself in the mirror that day and saw that the inability
to see how others saw me, which at the party had
frightened me so, was a dark blessing: for a moment I
had stepped, or been stepped, out of the onerousness
of that exchange; I had withdrawn, or been withdrawn,
into the image that lay between me and the mirror: the
raw solitude of a private reflection.

When you are threatened and afraid, unable to live by
the capacities and capabilities that have gone without
question all your life, a great deal about how you live
changes: your values, your sensory perceptions, even
your loves and friendships. This Ettie had told me, but

it was only by living it that I learned the lesson of her words. It seems to be, and I've heard it said by others similarly afflicted with illness, or grief, or losses of other kinds, that by being forced to live within a curtailment not of one's choosing, there can be a corresponding expansion in the heart's capacity. It is this I came to glimpse. I came to see that what I feared, though I called it blindness, and I would never underestimate that fear, or the courage of those who live without sight, was not of blindness in itself, but of solitude; the solitude that necessarily comes with the curtailment of a robust daily life and that, on first encountering it, brings with it the shadow of the solitude of child separated from mother, lover from lover, friend from friend. It is the emptiness that brings you slap up against that naked reflection in the mirror.

I wouldn't say that I came to like it, not at all; it remained dark down there in the tunnel, and damp. At best it was as if, with my body rather than with my eyes, I could sense its shape, lift my arms safely towards the leaves, push my fingers into the loamy soil to find they weren't immediately snapped off. Limited though it was, I began to stretch and grow into the space around me. I didn't yearn any less for that childhood capacity to run out into the light where flowers open and birds ride in the up-draughts, and the sky, shining down, houses all that you know. I began to find ways of existing there, that's all, each day made up of small repeated gestures, memories and sensations to which I became as attuned as I was to the symptoms I read with the precision I once gave to books. I came to see that what is required of us at such times is not performance – that endless dance of display – but the simple task of being. In a world in which movement is equated with achievement, and pain with failure, in which established creeds have emptied out into stale rhetorics, the question that was put to me was how to live with any bigness of spirit when the soil from which it must flourish had shrunk to a small handful of loam.

2 In early England being blinded – having your eyes cast out – was an alternative penalty to death; outcast bands of blind beggars roamed Europe, moving from village to village, region to region, evoking fear without pity. *Hark, hark, the dogs do bark / the beggars are coming to town.* It seems that there has long been a connection in our culture, or at least in our psyches, between the loss of sight and the loss of self. Consider the metaphors of darkness and light with which the Bible begins. With God came light. And with light came human life: self and selfhood born in God's light. *And God saw the light, that it was good; and God divided the light from the darkness.*

No wonder a threat to the eyes, even one that on the scale of things is not so severe, can be experienced as life threatening. As if loss of sight literally means loss of self. And yet it might be that the connection is in fact the other way round: that a dimming of sight, a changed condition of seeing, and therefore a change in our social relations, forces us not into loss of self but into confrontation with the self. The clatter of distraction is removed and there is nothing to keep us from the noise in our own heads. We live in a culture that overvalues relationship and undervalues solitude. Maturity, popularity, our success in life is marked by our ability to win and keep our lovers. Our sense of ourselves is bolstered by the capacity to look into another's eyes and see our gaze held and our eyes reflected there. But what is it we see? What do we really see? The fleck of iris. The dark contraction of a pupil. The play of light and shadow on reflective tissue. It is not ourselves we see. It is the illusion of a seen and therefore safely loved self. In this culture to be alone is to be pitied, or feared – the crone, the spinster, the table set for one – when it may be quite the reverse: that the capacity to be alone, alone with ourselves, is as great, indeed possibly a greater marker of maturity, of intimate human success. Then why do we fear it? For we do: look what we put up with to avoid it.

Could it be that our fear of solitude is that it will throw us into the outcast state of blindness?

John Hull, an Australian theologian living in England, went blind in his forties. Black, black blind from detached retinas. His book describing the profound disorientation of self in blindness was the first I took up on my return to reading. It took some time to finish so closely did it echo my fears: the fear of the loss of self, of being cast from God's light. The journey he recounts is as much of the passage of the soul through darkness as of the daily reality which came with a blindness so complete that he knew that he faced the sun only by the sensation of heat on his face. Even food, unseen, lost its appeal. He was no longer hungry. Life as well as sight dimmed within him.

While he struggled with the real limitations of a life without sight, treading his way with cautious steps to avoid the sudden slide when the ground slopes, or the path diverges, or obstacles block the way, he struggled also with the archetype of blindness within which he felt himself enclosed. At first the meanings he could give to the dark were as closed and as isolated as the world he inhabited even in the midst of a loving family. And indeed it is true that in many cultures, and certainly in ours, blindness has been crudely associated with a condition of unrelatedness: of being cast out, alone, ignorant and confused. Because blindness disrupts the distinction between the known and the not-known that is regulated for the rest of us by sight, *it represents*, he says, *dissolution, the borderline between being and not being.*[2] An alternative to death; as good as death.

Immersed in this archetype, unable to deny, or refuse it, yet not accepting it either, a glimmer of light flickered, a small beacon which took the form of a paradox, which as a theologian John Hull was quick to grasp, though as a blind man slow to understand. For of course there is a paradox. For God, that transcendent being, as the blind psalmist sings, *darkness and light are both alike to thee.*[3] It is for us with our dualistic either/or thinking that one is cast from the other, that one is held in opposition to the other. But a greater reality, and one we resist in our fearfulness and limitation, is that of light in darkness, and, more to the point, that of darkness in light. None of those who dwell so noisily in the realm of light wish to consider that light might contain its own darkness. And there is little in our culture to help those who inhabit the darkness grope their way to light.

On the darkest of my dark days, I lay in silence accompanied only by the squawk of a parrot as children came down the side laneway on a short cut to the bus-stop, calling out crudities to the parrot until the old lady opened her door on the upstairs balcony and shooed them away. 'Witch,' the children cried, as she stood looking down at them. 'Piss off,' they cried to the mad boy who lolloped along behind. 'Piss off, loop-head.' Their voices echoed, their footsteps pounded down the laneway and onto the street. The abandoned boy crashed his arm against the fence, waking the cat and sending the parrot in a flurry onto the roof and the old lady scrambling down the steep steps into her yard. 'There, there,' she said, her arms fluttering along the fence. 'There, there,' she said to the crazy boy, to the parrot, to the cat. Inside I lay still, listening to the quiet rhythm of my breath, the golden orb of the pomegranate on the table beside me catching the sun from the windows that face in the other direction.

When I visited Dr ——, attending my early morning appointments, the streets still rang with the rush of workers to their offices. But where once I regarded them mournfully, now it was they who seemed strange to me. Sometimes I'd meet Clara for a coffee before I left the city, and as the weather warmed we'd sit outside and, with a sort of astonished wonder, I'd watch the padded shoulders and Italian suits stream past. How can they bear the noise of lives without silence, I'd ask

Clara. When do they reflect? On what do they reflect? She said it was obvious, didn't I remember that doubt gets swallowed up in the rush. One knows who one is. She herself was running late, and left me for the library. In solitude, as I had discovered, it is not so much a knowing of ourselves that is forced on us as an unknowing.

One of the harsh truths about fear is that no one can accompanv you through it. Friends may be near, lovers may share your bed, children cling to your skirts, but it is you alone who must endure the darkness of that dank and chilly tunnel. When the fear is the result of illness, there is an additional harsh truth, for we live in a culture in which illness or disability (for all our liberal disclaimers) is considered a form of moral infirmity. Our fears trigger the fears of others; for the robust we are the spectre of what happens when activity is stripped down and silence revealed. Some turn away. Others flock around with too eager sympathy. Few can last the distance. Friendships, once solid and unquestionable, became fragile and chancy. I could hear the clocks tick, marking down the empty space that opened up between those I held away and those I called in.

To Louise who has been dearer to me than a sister, I held out my hands as if she alone could save me. 'Please come,' I said. 'I can't do this alone.' She came, although she had little to spare from the demands (and desires) of a new job and a new love; as the days stretched into weeks, the bond between us creaked and strained. I held out my hands and saw that I was too great a burden. To her alone I made the demand, *please save me*; not to lovers, not to doctors, only to Louise. Those of us who live outside family structures, choosing our intimates, our mentors, our loved ones, still make the demands the family spawns and permits. I found myself disappointed in one I loved, and stricken by my own failures, rushed impulses, terrible demands and weakness. But I don't regret the difficult days when my demands and her resistance hung in the air between us, and I think that she would say the same; for it was in those moments, with small steps taken this way and that, showing ourselves capable of fullness and limitation both, that we came to understand that all that was required of us, of each of the other, was that we be.

'Please,' I said.

'I can't,' she said, 'I'm going to a dinner with Akim,' but she came anyway and packed me some clothes, thick socks, a toothbrush, my own pillow, and took me down the hill to her house by the beach. I knew she was disappointed, her mouth was lined with tightness, it was her week without the boys, but still she cooked us dinner and sat beside me as I dozed on her sofa. When Akim came home he was courteous to me, no, more, he was welcoming. He lifted Louise's hand to his lips. For three nights I slept in the little downstairs room while Louise and Akim moved around upstairs. I could hear the floorboards creak under their feet and above my head. I could hear the low murmur of their voices on the phone, the click click of keyboards. When I joined them for meals, I saw the pleasure they took in each other, and late at night I could hear their voices murmuring in the darkness; and though I knew how little time they had to be alone, when I went down to my room it was not because they wished me there, but that I wished it myself. With the knowledge that Louise, gentle and irritable both, was nearby, I could stretch to be alone, and slept easily. In the morning I awoke to find I was still breathing, one breath in and one breath out, still in the same room with the door opening onto a tiny patch of garden: jasmine, rosemary and lavender in pots, parsley along the fence line. Upstairs I could hear Louise in the kitchen. I was sitting up, ready, when she came down with a tray of green tea and fruit, a bowl of spiced rice.

After three days, during which I lived as it were on the end of a thread that was held by Louise, I said it was all right, I could go home again, she didn't have to keep looking after me.

'Stay one more night,' she said. 'I'll take you home tomorrow.'

This time I packed my own bag. All she had to do was drive. Up the hill and round the corner, back to my place. It was then, after I'd unpacked, and opened the windows, and made us tea, that she stood on a chair with a cup hook cadged from the old lady next door, and hung the angel from the ceiling above where I lay: the wooden angel with green and gold wings, the gift from Ettie, my guardian angel. She has the face of a warrior; fierce, outstretched arms and fingers tipped with brilliant red. With her flying above me, though everything I saw remained blurry at the centre, indistinct against the light, nothing more was required than I listen to a silence broken only by the rattle of seeds in a jar. To have been brought a pomegranate: that was enough. Feeling the curved heaviness of the fruit in my hand, I settled to the stillness that stretched day into day. And during those days, as I lay quiet and still, I learned that I might be cast low but I had not ceased to exist; layers had been stripped from me, but I was still there, here, my breath rising and falling. The weak winter sunlight that caught in the prism set in the window, still crossed the room on a long angle, dancing on the wall beside me: a rose-coloured beam of light that was never still. Outside in the street, trees still grew, pedestrians still passed, and in the distance I could hear the rumble of traffic wending its way into the city. It was as if I had been let into a secret.

Hal drove in from the river to stay, a man who had for some years been my lover, and was at that time making his own retreat into a distant solitude. As presents he brought Glenn Gould's recording of *The Well Tempered Clavier* in which the distinction between the simple and the complex loses its meaning, and a copy of Thomas Merton's essay on the philosophy of solitude. I received these gifts with such grace as I could, for his presence disturbed me. Where once I had considered a lover essential as a bulwark against just such an emergency, I found myself resentful at his presence. Not because I did not love him, or had not, but because his presence evoked in me the remnants of the needs we'd once looked to each other to satisfy. I called out to him, more from habit than desire, and at the same time I warned him off. The demands I made (love me! rescue me!) exactly matched the refusals exacted (don't ask anything of me! expect nothing!). That courtesy and affection remained between us is a token of his good faith, and also of mine, as we manoeuvred ourselves through the transition from a love affair to friendship. Something in both our lives had sprung us from the grooves we'd steered along together. There was a lot we did not speak of, or spoke of only glancingly: the sudden shaft of brilliance, impossible and dangerous, that had burst around me in the months before I had been cast in the other direction, into dimness. It was by necessity a secret I kept from all but Hal, Louise and Ettie. Not that this affected Hal's retreat from me; he had moved to the river by then, and it occurs to me now that perhaps something like this had happened to him too, as if both of us needed others onto which to settle the desires that had once existed between us.

'Not everything needs to be said,' Hal said, as I braced myself for a full confession. His role was not one of handing out absolution; and he did not ask that of me. Whatever had occurred, fleeting and propitious, in the end we discovered that the move we each made was not to another, but to ourselves.

'*Too many people*,' he read from Thomas Merton, as I watched him from the other side of my angel, '*are ready to draw back at any price from what they conceive to be the edge of the abyss. True, it is an abyss: but they do not realise that he who is called to solitude is called to walk across the air of the abyss without danger, because, after all, the abyss is only himself.*'[4]

'Herself,' I said, not resisting the churlish impulse. 'The paths of the spirit aren't yours alone.'

'Okay,' he said. 'She,' he said, changing the pronoun as he turned the page. And while he read, this parting lover, I understood that no lover would save me from the abyss any more than Louise could, and suddenly, quite clearly, I no longer wished that he would. When Hal left, closing the door quietly behind him, I contemplated a life in which I might live beyond the gaze of a dearly loved man. As to the other, I had no desire to see him; but that's another story, and though I may tell it later, I won't tell it now.

To withdraw one's ego from the egos of men is a difficult move to make. I doubt that I would ever have made it had I not been forced by the threat to a capacity even more precious to me than the glories I'd known in love. I felt as if a part of myself had been hacked off. Like the princess in the story Ettie told Louise, my hands were useless stumps. Whatever had been there before had been forgeries, serviceable, even elegant; silver hands admired by the men who loved me, and loving me saw me, so that I, in that gaze, saw myself. Unseen by that confirming gaze, I felt myself to be out of sight, invisible, uncertain of identity or substance. The children's cries of *witch! witch!* applied as much to me as to the one who waved her broom at them. But with the blinds angled against them, those pounding, laughing boys were not able to taunt me.

The prurient Victorians with their vivid sexual guilts, attributed a host of visual disorders, including retinal haemorrhage and trachoma, to sexual licence and masturbation. In the Catholic church there are three minor saints, all of them virgins, who blinded themselves as a result of their own lustful thoughts, or the lustful approaches of others. Their stories are much the same, though they vary a little from version to version. Each plucked out her eyes in shame at her desires, and threw them at the feet of her lover or – in the case of St Triduana, a wild Scot – presented them on a skewer to the unfortunate man who'd admired them. In each case, the virgin's eyes were restored by the wisdom of God. Each went forth as a saint, with finer vision. Only in St

Odilia's case was there a hitch. Her new eyes were too large for the sockets left by their predecessors. For the rest of her life she carried them carefully in her arms *like a handbag*, I read. In *The Lives of the Saints*, Alban Butler assures his credulous readers that the story of St Lucy's restored sight is 'quite unhistorical' despite the fact that it occurs in the authoritative seventh-century account of her life made by St Aldhelm.

When, ecently, I first heard these saintly stories I took them to mean that God was telling us a virgin's passions should be proudly worn, but Catholic friends assured me I had it wrong. The virgins were being rewarded not for their passions, but because they were prepared to sacrifice even sight before virginity. St Lucy in particular is credited with extraordinary feats in protection of that frail membrane, including such immobility when ordered into a brothel that no man could make use of her. Her eyes she plucked out to deter a princely suitor. Nevertheless, here we do at least have legends of wisdom residing with the blind, a reversal of the archetype: blind and *single* women at that: spinsters all of them. Odilia was an abbess of great learning whose shrine and abbey, Butler reports, 'were favoured by the emperors from Charlemagne to Charles IV.'[5] And let us not forget Hildegarde, depicted in twelfth-century illuminations of her visions with heavenly flames leaping from her eyes and head.

The usual bearers of wisdom among the blind are old men, and therefore, one presumes, past the temptations of sexuality: the soothsayers and prophets who foretell history. *Blind Thamyris and blind Memides and Tiresia and Phineus, prophets old*, goes a line from blind Milton. But is the source of their wisdom, their power, to be attributed to their blindness, or to their solitude? To the solitude that blindness brings, or encourages? For it is in solitude, rather than in blindness itself that we are relieved of *the constant flood of language that pours meaninglessly over everybody, everywhere,*[6] and opened to other, more mysterious images, realms, and sources of knowledge.

Is it purely coincidental that in the arts, myopes and the visually impaired form an honourable roll call: Schopenhauer, Goethe, Schiller, most of the Medicis, Keats, Dr Johnson, Sir Joshua Reynolds, J.S. Bach, Yeats, Dante Gabriel Rossetti, Edward Lear, James Joyce, Monet, Cézanne, Pissarro ... The list goes on. Even in this age of contact lenses, consider how many spectacled faces turn up in photographs of writers. In one sense it is obvious: those who are short-sighted and as a consequence likely to be bad at things like sport, compensate by growing up as bookworms: a defence against all those balls flying around in the air, hurtling suddenly and dangerously into one's field of vision. The world of books, of pen and ink, or canvas and paint, is full and rich, and *in focus*; and through it (though I don't suppose this applied to the Medicis) one is likely to learn early a taste for solitude, and a confrontation with the self, for it is a world that relieves one of the unthinking rush of life as well as of the indignities of team work and the compulsions of sport. The ophthalmic theory of culture! And it does have to be said that there are landscapes of Cézanne, say, or Monet, which offer quite accurate representations of uncorrected myopic vision. When Cézanne was offered spectacles, he is said to have replied 'take those vulgar things away';

and Monet shuddered at the idea of corrective lenses which made him see with the conventional naturalism of Bouguereau. *Quelle horreur.*[7]

Tempting as it is, I won't try to push this theory far, though I would now never underestimate the impact of *blunted sight* on a person's creative work. It is only those who have never had to doubt the detail of the visual world delivered to them without effort who would contradict me. But there are few who would not take seriously the link between solitude and creativity. Read the biography of any artist or writer, even those who write of the passionate life, Tolstoy, say, or Proust, or Henry James, and you will find a taste or tendency for solitude, and periods of time lived alone. By solitude I do not mean isolation: torturers know how effectively solitary confinement can break someone. It is those who understand solitude who are often best at friendship: that capacity to be with others as ourselves, and allow others to be themselves with us. Women are often irritated by accounts of great men artists and writers who turn out, like V. S. Naipaul in *The Enigma of Arrival*, to have an unnamed wife tucked away in the background of their solitude; and it is indeed unequal, for it is less often, though not unknown, that a husband will play that role for his artist wife. When I speak of those who live with solitude, I mean a continuum that takes in the recluse, but can include those who give their attention more to the movements and images that come to them from within, from silence, and from long hours alone, than those who live their lives in devotion to the drama of the romantic dyad, seeking meaning in the eyes of the lover, in the drama of the marriage bed, in the sanctity of the family. The forms that solitude can take will differ for men and for women, but if they have the courage to enter those chthonian regions, neither gender will be denied its discoveries.

Two of the great recluses of twentieth-century Australian painting are Ian Fairweather and Grace Cossington Smith. Fairweather's reclusiveness was lived in cheap passages from one country to another, a rooming house here, an empty hut there; and finally the strange dwelling on Bribie Island where he painted his greatest work. Grace Cossington Smith's was lived from childhood to old age in the family house on the northern suburban fringe of Sydney. Their work could not be more different: her domestic interiors, his orientalised landscapes and numinous abstracts. Neither, I should say, had particular problems with their eyes, though both have changed the terms on which Australia sees and is seen. In the great work each did at the end of life, each discovered the paradox of the light that is to be found in darkness, and the intimacy that is permitted to the self in solitude.

3 The irony was not lost on me that my sight had become compromised just as I was beginning research on a group of artists. It happened in the very year that I was first spending my time in galleries, learning the tiny details of visual work, examining brush strokes, clots of impasto, the striations you can see under a side light, looking for the faint lines of pencil grid marks below watercolour, teaching myself to read a sketchbook as fluently as a diary. For months such detail was denied me, and now that I have the ability again and am no less fascinated with the details of composition, with the work that art is built of, that time in which sight was dependent not on detail but on other perceptions, has shifted my thinking about the nature of art itself. For months I felt myself to be peeping over a very high wall. Even as I strained and reached, I knew it could only exhaust me. What I needed to do, but how I did not know, was learn to see from another part of myself; explaining this to one of the few I could trust to understand, Louise, perhaps, or Ettie, I dropped my hands, which I'd held just below eye level in the position of the wall, to my heart. I held my hands level with my breasts and said: 'I must learn to see from here.' That is the insight John Hull has achieved in blindness. And I suspect it is the capacity to see from the breast, or the heart, that artists (whatever their refractive index) have, or struggle for.

In 1948 Grace Cossington Smith painted one of her few self-portraits. It is not a great painting: the colours are muddy and lack her characteristic clarity and sharp manipulation of light. Its composition is unexceptional. Nevertheless, in thinking about Grace Cossington Smith in particular, and women artists in general, it is a painting I return to, and not because it is the only one I know in which she is wearing spectacles. The spectacles slightly emphasise the size of her eyes, from which I infer they were reading glasses: I have no evidence that she was a myope. The painting has, however, everything to do with sight: with seeing, with being seen, wanting to be seen; and with not being seen. And there is nothing straightforward about any of that if you are a woman and an artist.

The portrait is striking for the uncompromising plainness with which Grace Cossington Smith presents herself. Photos of her as a young woman show a pretty, smiling girl. In middle age she paints herself stark and unadorned. A private face, a face without compromise: the face, it seems to me, of a woman who has renounced the vanity of being seen, and yet presents herself in her not-to-be-seen face. Simone de Beauvoir, at about the same time, in 1949, when *The Second Sex* was published though not yet translated into English, was arguing in ways that were then quite startling, and now hardly commonplace, that the function of woman in our culture as man's other is intimately connected with speech, and with sight. By being all that man is not, woman reflects him back in glory: transcendent to her immanent, subject to her object. He speaks; she listens. He sees; she is seen. Like a mirror, it is she who reflects: it is she who is seen, and in being seen, sees. The face Grace Cossington Smith paints is the face of a woman who is not available for this service, yet sees, and demands to be seen, in the seeing of the non-seen. It is an uneasy challenge she makes to herself, and to her viewer.

The self-portrait was painted just before the first of the interiors that were to dominate Grace Cossington Smith's late work. It shares the same technique: those small blocks of colour in broad brush strokes which require us to move backwards and forwards to find our own focal range. In those late interiors, in the last phase of her work, Grace Cossington Smith was painting out of a daily solitude, living alone in the family house where parents had died and from which siblings had departed. Do we see here the representation of a spinsterly existence: single beds, neat cupboards, empty hallways? Or the riches of solitude: empty rooms filled with possibilities? Doors opening onto hallways, windows opening onto verandahs and gardens, drawers and cupboards allowing us to glimpse their treasures? To my eye these interiors are by way of being self-portraits of a woman who has resolved the tension between her own ability to see and the seeing, or being seen, that is required of her: a woman who has fully withdrawn from the gaze of the world to discover not a defensive retreat, but the fullness of a solitude that society deems empty. They are the work of a woman with strong hands.

Take *Interior with Wardrobe Mirror* (1955) which is held by the Art Gallery of New South Wales. In it the mirror of a wardrobe door swings open in the centre of the painting, where it invites our own reflection – and in that invitation we see the absence of the painter whose image should face directly into that shiny surface. Instead it reflects a door which opens across a verandah, across a lawn, to trees and a distant sky. Where the artist should stand, stands instead an invitation to the world, to all that is beyond. That is the fullness her solitude has produced.

Whereas the colours in the self-portrait had been murky - dull greens, muddy browns, flushed pinks – in the interior they are clear and luminous: the yellows of sunlight and ochre, every shade of red, vermilion to the tenderest pink, touches of green, pure blue, a surprising mauve. In the self-portrait seeing and being seen are held in a painful tension, a dark and punishing solitude that contains as much refusal as release; in the interior we see the fullness of a feminine space once so ambivalently inhabited, and connected, in Grace Cossington Smith's words to *a golden thread running through time*, and to *the silent quality which is unconscious and belongs to all things created*.[8]

While I was rugged up against winter, and in full retreat, Hal, on a second, more harmonious visit, pointed out to me that Hildegarde was a healer, an expert on plants and animals, an advisor to popes. Was I romanticising her solitude? he asked. Did her retreat take her from the world, or bring her more fully into it? Solitude, he said, and he is one to know, is not in itself a virtue, and can take many forms. He doubted, he said, that the way of the hermit was for me. He asked if I was using it to step aside from the world of men, a sort of denial. Among the voices of Hildegarde's nuns, he said, are three tenors. Listen, he said. Perhaps there were things he still wanted from me; perhaps he spoke as a friend who had come to know me well; perhaps it was time for us to speak of the disappointments that had passed between us. In reply I said I wasn't well enough to argue, and instead I made us lunch. Afterwards I took the pomegranate from the windowsill and cut into it. I held the plate to Hal, but the fruit made disappointing eating. Outside, the rain poured down.

In those months of retreat I felt myself close to blindness, as if, no longer able to judge the distance from chair to door, I had to learn again the simplest of negotiations. When Hal suggested he stay another day, I said no, I wanted to be alone, and filled the thermos for his drive back to the river. But already the knowledge was moving in me that I couldn't live without work, or without friends, and probably not without lovers either; but nor could I return to them, or to the daily routines of life in the condition in which I had left them.

At the beginning of spring, on one of those days when it is unaccountably and miraculously warm, and the windows are open all along the street, I took Louise to lunch at Bondi. That is to say she drove and found the table I'd booked. The doors were open onto the brilliant colours (yellows, blues) that are represented everywhere as Australia, a language that even in the original at first seems overstated, but that day, as they swam back into focus, greeted me with the smack of memory. The lunch, my first out for many weeks, was a private celebration, and a gesture on my part to make up for the demands I'd made of her, which were referred to between us not as the time I had spent in her basement room, disturbing the first bloom of her life with Akim, but the night she got poor Dr —— out of the bath. It had been the Friday of a long weekend, and besieged with symptoms I didn't understand, streaks of light that disturbed the edges of everything as if the world itself was flickering, I turned to her. For what? For help? For rescue? What could she do but ring Dr ——, chasing him from number to number until she tracked down his wife at their holiday house and had her get him out of the bath. But weep as I might, and try as they might, neither of them were able to do anything to stop either the flashes in my eyes or the terrible constriction in my heart.

I felt then, and I still did as we went into lunch, the vulnerability of a child who must learn to step into the world alone. The last day of the holidays: a meal of my choice, and in the hall my school trunk already packed and waiting. In the hesitation of that moment when memory pressed into the present, I had to learn again, as if for the first time, the possibility of recognition that passes between two people, in which dependence is held in balance with our acknowledged separateness. Like a raw and skinless creature, something out of a butcher's shop, I faced Louise across the table; I faced the restaurant, and the world that glittered beyond it. In that bright paper-thin strip of life, I was overcome by a moment at once public and private, where all around us people spoke of who knows what, touched each other's hands, laughed with their mouths open, and allowed their eyes to fill with tears; and where people spoke with voices raised and opinions offered as much for the next table as for their own, shouting and gesturing amidst the clatter of dishes and the silent work of enzymes and digestive juices. If the problem then was to speak across a table, to clothe rawness in a voice that could express itself in a complex dance of retreat and advance, that could acknowledge both dependence and separateness, love and disappointment, if this was the problem with the dearest of friends, what shape would I ever give the silence that spread around me in wavelike gestures to the future. Even the first person pronoun, which once tumbled from my tongue, became lodged like a fish bone in my throat.

I've heard it said by writers who are men that to write in the first person is an inferior method, and that with few exceptions (Proust and Thomas Bernhard are often cited) it is the third person which makes literature. I have also heard it said by writers who are men that the writing of women is *sadly weakened* by the closeness of the personal. I would not be the first writer who is a woman, even when she is alone with her inkpot or powerbook, to know that lurking somewhere, in her throat, in her feet, I'm not sure where, but somewhere, are the opinions of men. The problem with the opinions of men is that they are as transparent as air. Because the masculine assumes the universal, men wear their certainties, their agency so lightly that very often no one notices: it is like the air we all breathe. Well may men scorn the first person. It is theirs by birthright, that particular subject of the sentence. All they spurn is the obvious, and every writer must do that. For a woman writer there is nothing obvious about writing that much despised pronoun at the beginning of a sentence, a paragraph, a book, and pronouncing it feminine. A man writes 'I' as he sees, and in writing it is therefore seen. The relationship is clear. When a woman writes 'I' she must reconcile se-ing with being seen, and negotiate the transposition of the first term to her own use. How is she, the object who is seen, to see herself, both seen and seeing? She cannot assume the same authority when she begins the sentence.

Artemisia Gentileschi's portrait of feminine agency in *Judith Slaying Holofernes* still has the power to shock. It is not only Judith's knee on the bed, the brow furrowed with concentration, the blood-spattered dresses; it's the sight of Holofernes' still-alive eyes, seeing what every man must dread, but surely never expects, pinned back against the bed as if he were the one to be penetrated: the powerful agency of the first person in the knife at his throat held by a woman's hands. No wonder the painting was relegated for centuries to back corridors and the basement of the Uffizi.

A decade after the second *Judith*, Artemisia painted her only known self-portrait. It is an equally striking, though more subtle composition, made in 1630. By then she had lived the better part of a decade as, in the terms of the 1624 census, the head of a household comprising herself, two servants and a daughter. After the rape trial she had married and moved to Florence. Her husband, one Pietro Antonio di Vincenzo Stiattesi, an artist, was probably related to a Stiattesi who testified at the trial. But while her career was immediately and (for a woman) spectacularly successful, not much is known of his. After her death scurrilous verses, no doubt motivated by envy, called her a temptress who cuckolded her husband.

It seems that Artemisia Gentileschi, whatever lovers she may or may not have taken, lived from the age of thirty as a woman alone with her household which soon comprised two daughters. Not that this meant she was beyond the control of men; she may not have had a husband to contend with, but she had a series of patrons, *Illustrious Lordships* to whom she wrote (or dictated) high-toned flourishes of admiration in her negotiations for money. She might have to declare her gratitude and service, but when it came to her work she was tough. *If I were a man*, she wrote after being chiselled down on the price of a painting, *I can't imagine it would have turned out this way, because when the concept has been realized and defined with lights and darks, and established by means of planes, the rest is a trifle.*[9] She had one great advantage which she used to good effect, certainly in her work (those recognisable, strong, engaged women), but also in her dealings with the Illustrious Lordships. This was her ease of access to the female model. Drawing from the nude was not yet the standard procedure it was to become, and the accuracy of figures was highly valued. Women, she informed her patrons, make expensive models and, on requesting fifty ducats, she explained that *out of the fifty women who undress themselves, there is scarcely one good one. And in this painting I cannot use just one model because there are eight figures and one must paint various kinds of beauty. Forgive my daring to ask this of you my patron. I kiss your hands with all reverence.*[10] She knew that seeing and being seen, controlling and being controlled were complex passages between people, particularly between those of unequal power. The Illustrious Lordships had one sort of power: an obvious, showy, potentially dangerous power. She had a subtler, rarer, more oblique power; and she made good use of it. It is her grasp of psychological intimacy and the power of the personal in its folded-over convolutions that infuses her work with the sting of life which reaches across to us nearly four centuries later.

In her *Self-Portrait as the Allegory of Painting* (1630), Artemisia makes a brilliant move. Where men in the tradition of self-portraiture with which she was familiar liked to adorn themselves with the trappings of their success, trussed up as gentlemen not artisans, she presents herself casually, without the masks either of grandeur, or of seduction. Her eyes are not on us seeing her, but concentrated on the canvas. Her silk dress and gold chain are worn without affectation, barely noticed, her hair is arranged only for the house; her face is full not from voluptuousness, though it is certainly a face that knows eroticism, but with a focus and knowledge that comes from deep within. Male artists, as the masculine subject of the portrait, could not also be the object that they painted, as art was thought to reside in the beauty of the feminine form; but Artemisia, as woman, could be at once subject and object, process and image, the creator and the art itself. She lifts a hand stained with paint to the blank canvas in order to make the first mark that will create the work of art which, as self-portrait (and we can see her lean to catch the mirror out of sight behind, or beside, the canvas), is also the image the artist will produce of herself. Her eyes, averted from us in their concentration on the canvas, on this complex process of bringing herself into being, focus not on the external world that would reflect her back, but on the inner contemplations that will produce herself. It is the image she is to create that will face us, not the artist who paints it.[11]

Writing four centuries after Artemisia's birth in 1593, and one century after Virginia Woolf's birth in 1882, there is still a problem of sight and language for women as writers and artists, and few have solved it as deftly as Artemisia did. It is a problem both of the eye and the feminine 'I'. Even Hildegarde would preface her far from modest revelations (reported in the first person) with a disclaimer such as *I am no man of learning* . . . but she had the advantage of writing in Latin and could use the word *homo*, the undifferentiated term that English translates inadequately, rather than the *vir* she surely was not. *I am no man of learning . . . but deep in my soul I am learned.*[12] And Artemisia Gentileschi informed one of the Illustrious Lordships that he would *find the spirit of Caesar in this soul of a woman.*[13] For all the confidence of our American sisters, how many women do we hear saying that today?

Artemisia wrote her lavish letters that read to us now as parody – *I pay my most humble reverence to Your Most Illustrious Lordship with the assurance that as long as I live I am prepared to carry out your every command* – and even then contained a recognised rhetorical flourish. Virginia Woolf did battle with the Angel in the House, that creature with shiny, silver hands she describes as *intensely sympathetic . . . immensely charming . . . utterly unselfish . . . ,*[14] whose shadow falls across the page as we write, warning us of the dangers of causing too great an offence, of putting oneself forward, of airs and graces; of inevitable humiliation, failure, poverty, neglect.

All these years later, killing the Angel in the House is still part of the work of a woman writer, time Virginia Woolf thought would have been better spent learning Greek grammar or travelling the world having adventures. As it happened, like many of my generation, I did learn Greek, but I was too young and feckless, or perhaps just too sad and girlish, to recognise its importance; and I have now quite forgotten it. I even travelled the world, but the truth of it is that I took the Angel of the House with me, and a difficult companion she proved. And as an indication of how inadequately I killed her off, though many was the time I thought I had, I found her waiting in that tunnel, still alive and doing quite nicely. How much harder, she whispered, you'll have to work now for the compliments that used to come just by looking into your eyes; how much harder to conceal *this terrible disability*, how charming you'll have to be if they're not to guess how little of them you can see. How hard. How very hard.

Forced into the silence of an incapacity which, while it proved to be temporary, at the time was extreme, I realised that for years I had been dancing a painful double dance, learning, I thought, to live – and to write – on my own terms, but at the same time caught in that endless little jig with its fancy footwork that said, although I might venture an opinion here, an idea there, I did so sweetly, do not be alarmed. I might not be utterly unselfish, but I am sympathetic and charming enough (though not, I fear, *intensely* and *immensely* so).

One of the many images that tumbles to mind when I consider my earlier self is a hall of mirrors in which I see myself reflected back in the reflections I offered; this way and that I turn to see myself from every angle receding into an endless repetition of my own diminishing image. The words I spoke, even the words I associated most closely as my own, were scrolled across the fancy footwork of this endless dance. It was as if I said to the whole world and not just to a lover, that though I turn from you in bed, and do not invite you into the room where my desk is, I still want you to watch me; I might withdraw a little into other preoccupations, but I still want you to desire me; I might write as I will, the first person personal, but I still want you to admire me: *how well she does!* Watch me spin. Watch me dance. *How well she does!*

If I am literal about it, in that tunnel, despite the whispering Angel, the jig stopped. Movement, I was told, was dangerous if bleeding was to be avoided. And so, just like that, I stopped. I cancelled appointments. For the first time in my life I had no compunction about saying no. No, I said. No. No. No. I was neither sympathetic nor charming. Frosty would be nearer the mark. Selfish and cantankerous. I refused invitations to coffee, to lunch, to dinner, to read, to write, to work. I opened the door only to those who could enter without expecting the jig, who could sit still, who could speak out of and into the darkness. No more of those conversations sat through remembering to look intelligent, keeping up the appearance of interest, keeping the plot going, keeping the mirror bright and clean. I did nothing, for there was nothing I could do. And doing that nothing, I saw at last how much I'd done, and hadn't done, and what the doing of it drained out of me as I danced and danced, and danced that jig.

The statue of St Odilia reveals a dumpy saint with the figure of a middle-aged woman. She carries her eyes in both hands, not like a handbag at all, but tenderly as she would an offering, perhaps, or a baby held across her body just below the heart. While St Lucy holds one pair of eyes on a plate, she, unlike Odilia, is depicted at the same time with her neatly restored eyes raised to heaven; but then she is a young and lovely virgin, fresh and tender, whose aspect would be spoiled by blank and empty eyes. It is she, St Lucy, who is claimed as the patron saint of opthalmology. With a slight rewriting of her story, I propose St Odilia as the patron saint of women writers and artists. Not rewriting perhaps, just a reinterpretation. She cast out her eyes not to reject her own lustfulness, not at all, that's the Catholic interpretation; not to reject desire in itself, but to reject the desire to be object to another; to reject her availability as the one seen, the reflector of the needs and agencies of others. It was by renouncing the vanity that comes with the display of sexuality, the courting of the ones to be mirrored, and in that mirroring to be seen always as a diminishing reflection, that she was blessed with eyes larger than life, to be forever carried with the greatest of care in that view from the heart.

The canvas, blank but prepared, waits. The wardrobe door swings open, and in its mirror we see not the woman, not the artist, but the world that opens beyond her.

4 When the gaps between my appointments with Dr —— stretched to two weeks, then to four, I packed a bag of clothes, stout walking shoes, and, out of habit or optimisim, I'm not sure which, a stack of books that looked as folorn as if they'd been left out in the sun too long. I rang Ettie and caught a train to the mountains. When I arrived at the house, the taxi backing up the laneway behind me, all the doors were open: I could see through from the front door, down the wide hallway to the verandah at the back, and beyond, to the sheer drop of the scarp. There was no answer to my call. I put my bags in the hall and went round the side, along the wall with the crab apple and pear, through the orchard of almonds and greengages not yet in bloom, apple trees with the first white buds appearing, and found Ettie in the gully brilliant with azaleas.

'Dear girl,' she said, stretching out her wrinkled hands, and levering herself up from the edge of the pool where she was clipping back ferns. 'Make yourself at home,' she said. 'I'll be up as soon as I've finished this.'

I went back towards the house, circling the other side of the garden, past the banksias and oriades that cling to the top of the cliff, round to the old cane couch on the verandah that in spring looks out through a screen of jasmine and wisteria opening bud by bud, to a mist of forget-me-nots and the honeysuckle that Ettie closely guards, a noxious weed under state regulations, an escapee she promises one day to root out. And then the drop of the cliff and a cleft in the earth that on misty days seems the edge of the universe, but on a day like the day I arrived is filled with a hazy, smoky blue that gives a name to the mountains.

For several weeks I lay on that verandah, some days rugged up against the mist that threatened to suck us down into the arms of the trees, or against the wind that whooped up the valley; on other days my wintry skin welcomed the sun. I watched parrots flash by in a pack, the print of the book beside me taking shape before my eyes. Ettie in her hat, or raincoat, came and went, tramping past with her trowel and rake, entering my dreams as if she were a part of their reverie. Every day she coaxed me a little further from the verandah. In the garden I helped her pull weeds and sweep the fallen leaves from the lawn. She led the way along the path that winds down the cliff-face, taking us into the valley. Every day we walked further, venturing in small steps. Along the side of the cliff we passed the rock-face close enough to touch; we saw cracks, and grooves, and springs seeping like tears. We saw the great trunks of the angophoras thrusting up through the rock towards the sky. No longer did I feel like a traveller passing through a place without the least affecting it. No longer did ideas appear more real than a physical world that for a moment had disappeared from view. Only the finest and most permeable of membranes seemed to exist between the terrain I traversed in my dreams, or in thought on that verandah, and the plants that grew in Ettie's garden, the wild tangle of bush beyond. Words began to regain solidity, though their meanings were not always as I expected. The verandah, once a place of transition and borderline, re-formed around me as harbour and essence. Day and night, light and dark, no longer seemed such easy opposites as I watched, morning and evening, the dawning of one and the coming of the other. Though each remained distinct, I could never say, never see, the moment at which light transformed the world and all it held from darkness, and the darkness reclaimed it from the light.

In the evenings when the house drew in around us, Ettie and I sat at the table and ate the soup, the thick stews, I made from the vegetables in her garden, and the order that was brought down from the town twice a week. We spoke quietly, at first of nothing much, as if Ettie saw my need for rest and gave me wide steerage. But as the weeks passed, and each day I walked a little further, and she caught me now and then humming a tune, or lying quite still, barely thinking at all, floating as if towards the future, she began to speak of my return to the city. I knew it was not to tip me out; on this occasion, this occasion only, I knew I could stay as long as was required. But still she rubbed her weathered hand on my arm, poured me a tiny glass of brandy and said there were times when it was necessary to return. She said I had work to do. She said there were the people I lived among, should I not return to them? There was Hal, was it really settled with him? And as to the other, was I not going to contact him? It occurred to her, even if it did not to me, that he would be worried, that he might feel the constraints that kept him from me as bitterly as I had felt them.

'Good,' I said. 'The worse he feels the better.' The anger I felt towards the man who'd encouraged in me the love he knew he could not honour, had simmered, unacknowledged and put to one side, throughout my retreat. Disregarding anything he might feel, I felt duped, and a fool. Any avenue of returning the hurt, I took; if it meant withholding myself, withholding information about myself, then withhold I would. I responded with scorn to the gestures he made. I did not listen when he spoke to me: it's all excuses, I said, I'm not interested in the machinations of selfish masculine power, go conquer someone else, or better still look to the one you can't love and can't leave. I returned his letters unopened. When he rang through to Ettie, I refused to walk the distance from my chair to the phone.

'It's a curse to hate too long,' Ettie said, 'for it'll surely come flapping back.'

'Ha!' I said. 'Why should we accept the things they do.'

'We do them too,' she said. 'I was cruel to Helena, I was cruel to the child, and look how that ended up.'

For a second time she told me the story of Jock and Helena and the baby. But this time she spoke of the war, the ambulance she drove in the blitz, the silence of Shropshire where she lived afterwards, up under the scree two miles from the village with only the canvas and a palette she didn't use for company; and the temptation to pitch it all in, to stay in England, to leave the baby, Jock, Helena, on the other side of the world, to recreate herself as artist, as a woman without a past. But she didn't. She knew, she said, that resent it as she may, it was necessary to return.

When Ettie arrived back in Sydney, coming through the heads at dawn, Jock met the boat and drove her out to Wollstonecraft where he and Helena had moved, and where the child they'd named Dorothy was growing up. As they parked in the driveway and Jock carried her bags into the house, holding the door for her to enter, Ettie felt as if she was witness to the life that had been denied her, a sanctuary from which she was excluded. So there'd been a submarine in the harbour, a few nights of panic. She was told the details as if it were she, who'd been picking limbs out of the rubble, lifting children crushed beyond recognition from their mothers' arms, who was the one to have escaped the danger. Jock, who was teaching art at the Teachers' College, took her into his studio to show her the gaudy work of his students, twisted images of a war few of them knew. She felt, she said, the impulse to kill. Nothing less. She had returned – and for what? For her there was no work, no child, no home with a red tile roof perched above the harbour. Not for her. Nothing. Not even a shared and understood past. Just entanglements and a legacy of secrets. She spent one night under that roof, and in the morning Jock gave in and drove her to a boarding house in Kings Cross. She volunteered to work with the refugees, and accepted the pounds her old mother, who still had the garden in Pymble, had saved for her. She put the money on a flat in a wide street shaded by trees, a place where there was no garden and no room to paint: she had closed her heart against both, and would not re-open it until Gerhard arrived with his own refugees and both their lives found a new shape. In the meantime she attended to the children, not her own, who poured off the boats with stories it was her task to bring from their eyes.

On visits to the house at Wollstonecraft, the sight of the child filled her with rage. She could hardly look at the eager little face that turned expectantly to Helena. That first afternoon she had seen in the child all she had despised in Helena. That she despised Helena had been hidden from her until that moment, under the mantle of a friendship that had existed before the affair with Jock. Where once she saw Helena's care of her in late pregnancy as generosity, two women stranded together in London, now she saw it as the greed of a woman who was determined on a child. The war suited Helena very well. In the child Ettie saw Helena's capacity to dissemble, the coy way in which she got what she wanted by flattery, a feigned helplessness, and a turned-in sweetness that made it impossible to deny her. All this she saw that first afternoon as Jock stood beside her on the verandah looking out towards the child who played on a strip of mowed grass. *Look at me,* the little girl said. *Auntie Ettie, look at me.* But Ettie turned her head as well as her heart against the child. She preferred to see Jock in town, but that was rare, and when she did she felt a hard contempt for his amiable acceptance of a house governed by the falseness of Helena and her simpering child.

'I'll tell you this,' Ettie said. 'I enjoyed the capacity for cruelty that I felt grow in me. I enjoyed the tears that sprang to the child's eyes when I brushed her hair. I enjoyed her polite disappointment when the gifts I gave failed. I told Helena that I'd seen Jock in a cafe with a woman he'd once taught and was in the papers after a successful first exhibition. I told Helena I doubted there was anything in it. I told the truth. I did doubt that there was anything in it, I knew Jock's tastes; but I also knew that precisely because I wasn't filled with doubt, Helena would be. So much for the truth,' she laughed, 'that nasty little weapon. I'm warning you, that's all, that giving in to the desire for cruelty will come back on you.'

'When did it end?' I asked.

'It didn't,' she said. 'Not until Clara was lifted out of the wreckage of that car. I mourned Dorothy in death as I never loved her in life.'

This is a story Ettie hadn't told before. At least not to me, and not, as far as I know, to Louise.

'How do you live with something so hard?' I asked.

'The correct attitude to painful events,' she said, 'is not blame and denunciation, but grief and mourning.' This, she said, is something as a culture, as a nation, we do not understand. People think blame is easier than grief, she says. But grief is passed through and brings understanding. Blame remains.

On the wall above where Ettie sits at the table with her cup of coffee and the one cigarette she allows herself each day, is the portait of her on Jock's couch in the

George Street studio. Despite the eyes her younger self shared with Clara, it is not a good likeness, for Jock was flirting with cubism at the time, and he was never the painter for that. You won't find him in any of our galleries: an amateur, a muddler, a trier. He was flirting with cubism and at the same time painting a monument, or so he thought, to a pure love. It is not a combination made for success.

As Ettie told her story and I watched her, blurry from the candlelight not from my eyes, the question formed in my mind: why did she keep that painting there, above where she sits in the kitchen, when in the hallway, in the sitting room, in her bedroom were Gerhard's paintings, many of them of her, and all of them better, that the insurance worried about and the gallery angled for.

'It was my last act of revenge,' Ettie said. 'Marrying Gerhard made its mark. Every time Jock came here he winced when he saw the portrait.'

'So why keep it there now?' I said. 'All these years later.'

'As a monument to my shame,' she said.

In the hallway is a portrait Gerhard painted of Ettie in the fifties during one of Dorothy's visits when she had grown into a lumpish, awkward girl. He did what he could for the child, pampered her with treats, let her ride in the front seat of the car; he deflected Ettie's gaze from her. It is a portrait I have looked at many times over many years, coming and going, entering and leaving; but I had not seen it until that visit when sight was compromised. I walked in from the garden one morning and it was as if the painting reached down and pulled me towards the cruelty of that much loved face. There in Gerhard's portrait, positioned so that it can be

seen on entering or leaving the house, is the capacity
for darkness and for light that had warred in Ettie for
so many years. The tendons of that splendid neck are
taut and ungiving. Over the chair where she sits is Jock's
pastel of empty romanticised youth. In Gerhard's oil is
a face that was known in all its moods, a face loved but
not spared. In the muscle and skin of Ettie's aged face
that I watch across the table, are the complex lines of
her knowing and being.

Every day of those weeks that I was with her, Ettie
coaxed me a little further down the cliff-face, until we
reached the base of the waterfall that tumbles from the
eroded creek at the top to the deep pool where it is too
cold to swim on all but the hottest days when the air
itself is thick and steamy. Every day that we descended,
I felt myself to be travelling further into the gaping
emptiness that had stared back at me from the bathroom mirror. When we reached the bottom, Ettie led
me along the path that skirts the flat rock onto which
the spray falls, and tucks itself in behind the waterfall.
The mist that blew from the water touched our faces.
We stood safe in a cool silent cave, viewing the world
through a curtain of fine water which caught shafts of
light and shone like crystal. Back in the gully, Ettie
hacked with her bush knife at a stand of blackberries
that had taken root in the only spot the sun reaches.
Above us the cliff shone iron-pink in the afternoon
light, and high in the sky even I could see the vapour
of a plane flying overhead on its way across the conti-
nent. I had no desire to be on it. Nowhere tempted me:
not Paris, not New York. Certainly not London, though
I was due there in a matter of months.

'I'm getting a taste for solitude,' I said as Ettie removed the stubborn bramble roots.

'I've had you up here in love,' she said, 'and now it's as if you're the first to discover solitude.'

'That must be an improvement,' I said.

'Do you think your life goes in a straight line?' she said.

'You live in solitude,' I said. 'Look at you, day after day up here on your own.'

'I'm an old woman,' she said.

'Not that old.'

'Old enough,' she said, 'to have made the necessary returns.'

We walked back up the track in silence, that is to say without speaking, for all around us were the sounds of bush creatures and snakes that rustled and slithered at our aproach. Overhead was the constant traffic of birds. When we reached the house, the phone was ringing. It was Louise. Hers was one of three calls that came within the space of a week like outriders heralding my return.

The first had been from a neighbour to tell me that my neighbouring crone was under threat of being put in a home. The crazy boy, my neighbour said, had put his hand through the glass of the phone box one night, and when the old lady went out in her dressing gown, the boy had flicked his pouring wrist at her and she'd become distressed when she couldn't calm him. The police rang her son, a red-faced man from Brisbane, my neighbour said, who wants the house packed up and sees this as a good opportunity for a sale. We've been onto the welfare, my neighbour said, but you're the one who saw her most.

The second call was from Jack, my secret love, and

this time I walked the distance to the hall and picked up the phone. All right, I said. Come on Friday. Just for the afternoon. Yes, I said, I'll listen, I'll even try to talk.

The third was from Louise. She had seen an advertisment for a house in a valley across the river from the town where Hal lives. Hal had been to look at it and had reported that yes, there'd be room for us all: a shack for him, a garden for me, a house and a river for Louise.

'It's cheap,' she said. 'Should we look at it?'

'Are you sure there's room for a garden?' I asked.

'Heaps,' she said, reading from the advertisement. '*Old orchard, outhouses, fruit cage.* Come down at the weekend and we'll look. Hal'll meet us at the ferry.'

On my last morning on the verandah between the soft interior of the house and the steep descent of the cliff, I woke early to the sound of Ettie's feet on the bare boards as she walked to the kitchen. I heard the hiss of steam and the chink of china as she made her morning tea, the gurgle of steam radiators as she switched the heating on. I heard the spring of the back door screen, and her voice whispering to the birds, and to the day unfolding around her. Lying there, contemplating my return to the filaments of a life I'd abruptly left, it came to me that the folded-over intricacies of language and sight in which I had felt myself to be immobilised, were both impediment and blessing: a complicated birthright. The task I faced was not to surmount the impediments as if they were a mountain range to be scaled, nor to refuse them, retreating into a sanctuary that could as well be a prison, so much as seeing them through,

and seeing through them. Facing the necessary return
to the noise of the city as one who would never again
see as she had seen before, I understood that the capacity to love foolishly, and to love well, to retreat and to
withdraw, were not a shame to be concealed by a proud
ego, but practice for a heart that sets its own limits. All
of this I had tried to explain to Jack. He'd arrived in the
afternoon while I was napping in the orchard, so warm
had the weather become. I awoke to see him loping
along the far side of the border, coming round the long
way from the gate. his thatch of hair catching the light,
his face a crease of smiles; his step was as familiar as a
heartbeat. As he stood looking down at me, I reached
up a hand to him. He turned my palm towards the sun,
and smoothed its crease of lines with his thumb. 'For
you,' he said, dropping a tiny silk pouch onto my open
hand. Inside was a silver and lapis bracelet which he
clipped around my wrist. In reply I told him that I
could never again live the way we had. And nor, to his
credit, could he. What can change in his life, what will
change, remains to be seen; and although Ettie is right
when she says love comes in inconvenient ways and we
turn our backs on it at our peril, right now it is not for
me to stand on the sidelines and wait.

'Are you still going to England?' he asked.

'As soon as Dr —— says I'm well enough,' I said.

'Are you going there to get away from me?' he asked.

'I'm going,' I said, 'because I have work to do,' and
in part I told the truth.

That evening, after Jack had left, Ettie lined three paintings along the dresser in the kitchen. The first was Jock's

failed pastel; the second was Gerhard's oil of her capacity to harm; and the third was the gouache she had painted at the end of 1938 in the George Street studio during a southerly buster that dried the paint too fast. The one of the eye tethered by many strings, each of them reaching down to a flower, or a plant that was clinging to its hold in the earth, as the eye strains to make its escape from the net that held it as if it were a hot air balloon.

While we drank the wine Jack had given Ettie (Cloudy Bay, her favourite), I said that at least two of the three should be in a gallery. But Ettie said, no, she'd decided to give them all to Clara.

'When?' I said.

'Now,' she said. 'Before she leaves for Europe.'

'Good,' I said. 'In time for her to understand their significance.'

'While I'm still alive you mean,' Ettie said. 'Well, maybe.'

'What will you hang in their place?'

She lifted from its position unhung against the wall, Clara's pen-and-ink drawing of two silver hands, delicate and beautiful, but as macabre as hooks.

'That story is like a seed,' I said. 'You never know when it will flower.'

[1] Marina Warner, *Monuments and Maidens: The Allegory of the Female Form,* London, Picador, 1985, p. 190

[2] John M. Hull, *Touching The Rock, An Experience of Blindness,* Melbourne, David Lovell Publishing, 1990, p. 48

[3] Psalm 139.1, quoted in John M. Hull, *Touching The Rock,* p. 49

[4] Thomas Merton, *The Power and Meaning of Love,* London, Sheldon Press, 1986, p. 56

[5] Alban Butler, *The Lives of The Saints,* Vol. XII, London, Burns, Oats & Washbourne Ltd, 1938, p. 157

[6] Thomas Merton, *The Power and Meaning of Love,* p. 60

[7] Patrick Trevor Roper, *The World Through Blunted Sight,* first published by Thames and Hudson, 1970. Penguin edition, 1990, pp. 37, 38. Thanks to Marion Halligan, an honourable myope, for drawing this book to my attention.

[8] Quoted by Daniel Thomas in his catalogue to the 1973 Retrospective of her work: *Grace Cossington Smith,* Art Gallery of New South Wales, 1973

[9] Artemisia Gentileschi to Don Antonio Ruffo, November, 1649; Mary D. Garrard, *Artemisia Gentileschi,* Princeton University Press, 1989, Appendix A, p. 398

[10] Artemisia Gentileschi to Don Antonio Ruffo, June 1649; Mary D. Garrard, *Artemisia Gentileschi,* Appendix A, p. 393

[11] For a full discussion of this painting, see Mary D. Garrard, *Artemisia Gentileschi,* chapter 6, to which I am indebted.

[12] Quoted in Marina Warner, *Monuments and Maidens,* p. 192

[13] Artemisia Gentileschi to Don Antonio Ruffo, November, 1649; Mary D. Garrard, *Artemisia Gentileschi,* p. 397

[14] Virginia Woolf, 'Professions For Women', in Leonard Woolf (ed.), *Collected Essays,* Vol. 2, London, Chatto & Windus, 1967, p. 285

The
Winterbourne

PART ONE

The Photo

It was Clara's idea to visit Carn. If I'd been alone that day, I may well have let the moment pass, put down the photo and shaken off the fumes of memory. But as soon as Clara said *come on, let's go*, I knew it was, if not what I'd come to England to do, then at least an explanation for subjecting myself to a prolonged return to the country of my birth. But where for me a visit to Carn would be a return to the terrain of a past that, all these years later, still has its bite, for Clara the prospect was purely exotic. Too young to know either England's glory or her own colonial status, Clara had discovered in London a playground, sometimes bedraggled, sometimes inspired, that was filled with young people of every hue, a floating population who lived among the Dickensian architecture, decking it out in music and their own colour. To her the England of boarding schools and Wessex hills had no more reality than the

BBC dramas Helena watched on television in the country of her birth.

Clara and I were in a coffee shop in Soho on a dark, drizzly October afternoon, when I told her the story of Carn and Frances Petersen. And though I do not entirely believe in chance, I told her, for the shape of the story, that it was entirely by chance that I saw Frances Petersen's name, entirely by chance that I was waiting in that room, and that of all the magazines on the table, that was the one I chose. Out of date and tatty, it was tucked at the bottom of the pile beneath glossier possibilities. But there she was: Frances Petersen, professor of archaeology at a Canadian university, in a team that had recently returned from Mexico. I took the magazine to the window, lifted the lace curtain and peered at the grainy photograph. I could make her out at once, third from the left, unmistakably Frances Petersen. Thirty years had passed since we were at Carn together, and it showed in her figure which had, like mine, thickened around the middle; but nothing had tamed the hair that the Asp had called a mop and ordered her to cut.

But while I made a story of it to Clara, at the time, standing at the window with the photo, looking out onto a crescent of Georgian houses hunched against an iron sky, it was as if all that had passed between then and now were as naught, and we were at Carn again, girls at the mercy of a woman who, according to the perversities of British wisdom, was said to be a brilliant teacher, a figure to whom legends are attached, an archetype of those responsible for a generation of educated girls. The sort of woman Virginia Woolf might have been proud of: a woman who set store by Greek as a discipline for the mind, and on intellectual training that would sweep women into the professions. Dancing classes, art appreciation, the cultivation of feminine wiles and good contacts were not the terms of her girls' education. We were to rival the boys. And we did, leaving Carn boys embarrassed and confused in the race for scholarships, exhibitions, bursaries. Merely to be at Carn was a privilege, and we were not to forget it. Our fathers footed the bill, our mothers put us on the school train when we were still too young to part from them, and the Asp, Miss Astrid Stuart Parker, waited by her window overlooking the cold slopes of learning. There she would take over our training, and ensure that the substance of our character would win through, moulded and adorned for the future she upheld, and that Britain, fearing to contradict, was said to need.

Sometimes, I told Clara, making a point of it, things did not go according to plan, and a girl would prove herself *without substance*, that's how the Asp put it, slipping the mould of the Carn design. Frances Petersen was one such girl. She had springy hair that in itself the Asp regarded as a sign of bad faith in a Carn girl. It was a dark reddy-brown, her hair, the colour of a fox. It spilled out from under her beret in winter; and the spring of it made a straw hat impossible in summer. Her eyes were the colour of stormy seas. They were balanced by a wide, well-shaped mouth in a pale, freckled face. The daughter of a botanist, she had read *The Origin of Species* by the time she was thirteen and already in the lower fifth and I, at twelve, arrived in the upper fourth.

This precocity did not endear her to the Asp. Nor did her capacity for stillness. When Frances Petersen walked, the air parted for her so that she moved through classrooms or along corridors without a ripple. The uniform, composed of drab greens and browns, hung from her as if it were *meant for an orphan*, the Asp said. While everyone else fussed and bothered at skirt lengths and coat sizes, Frances wore these ugly garments as if they were of no consequence, no consequence at all. A silent child; that's what was said of her, and that, I think, was what the Asp resented in her, that ability to keep her own counsel. She wasn't like the good girls, the girls the Asp liked, the girls that crowded around to hear the prefects: the team girls, the girls who sang rounds and madrigals, the girls who acted in the house play, organised matches and picnics, and kept the score. The good girls, the chattering girls who controlled the house morality, saw only that Frances was silent. 'It's not right,' they said. 'It's unsporting and rude,' they said. 'Did you see her?' they asked each other in loud tutting voices as Frances stood in the hall learning the Latin for that day's punishment.

But Frances Petersen, who could keep her silence for days on end, was the only girl I knew who could talk to the kids at Holme Farm. When Leah worked in the kitchen, she'd put her head round the door.

'Leah,' she'd say. 'Did that calf get born?'

'Yeah,' Leah would say. 'My dad's got her in the barn. She's that small. You should look in. I'll show you.'

The good girls huffed and puffed in the corridor outside. 'I don't think she ought,' they said. 'It's embarrassing,' they said.

It was Frances Petersen who showed me the winterbourne. Although I was a year younger, and friendships outside the years were frowned upon, I was the one she chose as a walking companion. Perhaps she recognised something of herself in me when, in my first week at Carn the Asp stopped me on the stairs and said, *what kind of a girl are you, dressed like that?* and I was startled, even frightened, for the only deviation I had made from the uniform that every girl wore was the addition of a little knitted hat that in Australia would be called a beanie. My mother had made this hat for me in the house colours, a parting gift to keep me warm in that windy part of the country. I wore it less for my ears, than as a part of her. The hat was confiscated; gone, just like that, into the box in the prefects' room where it would stay until the end of term by which time moths had chewed small insidious holes in it. Thea Linton, head of house and adored of the Asp, was on hand to carry it off. She walked down the stairs holding it out from her by two elegantly raised fingers.

'Imagine it's still there,' Frances Petersen said as tears gushed into my eyes. She put her hand on my head. 'See,' she said. Her hand was warm like the hat; but when I put my own hand to my head, all I could feel were shocked follicles where the hair grew.

Imagining was no use at all against the wind we pushed against along the edge of Holme Farm.

'Is the winterbourne running?' Frances asked the boy in tight trousers leaning on the gate.

'No,' he said, raising his eyes to a dull, dry sky. 'Not in this weather. Wait till the rain comes.' He swung off the gate. 'Come back then,' he said with a half-smile at Frances as he disappeared into the barn where we could hear the sounds of milking.

We walked through the woods to the fields on the

other side of the farm, to the dry stream bed of the winterbourne: a grassy indentation, maybe three feet deep, meandering down the slope until it joined the running stream at the bottom. As we followed this dry trough-like groove across the fields, Frances Petersen described to me how it would be when the water rose up through the chalky soil and bubbled out in the spring that fed the winterbourne where we walked – a runnel that was hard to distinguish from the surrounding fields – transforming it into a river flowing over grass. When that happened, she said, the seeds that had collected in the bottom of the trough during the dry burst into life, and in spring, when the water has gone again, the winterbourne becomes a river of flowers.

Anyone who sees the winterbourne flow, she said, is blessed. Her father told her so.

Frances Petersen's mother had died when she was small. Her father, a botanist, had not remarried. He'd brought her up, *father and mother both*, he said, and he sent her to Carn because, like my father, he believed in education for girls, and careers for women. When her aunts put her on the school train, Frances had tucked in her bag the thesaurus her father had given her, a rhyming dictionary, and leather-bound diary. A year later, I'd join her on the top shelf of the linen cupboard, and while she read proper books, or her secret passion, the *National Geographic*, I'd recite until she hushed me, wondrous lists of rhymes from her dictionary: arsenic, chivalric, choleric, limerick, turmeric, whitterick, maverick, rhetoric, bishopric, heretic, politic, lunatic. Her aunts gave her books like *A Room of One's Own* and *A Vindication of the Rights of Woman*. What she made of them I don't know; the books we discussed were the novels I preferred: *Jane Eyre*, *Tess of the D'Urbervilles*; or prisoner of war escape stories; *A Tale of Two Cities*, or Georgette Heyer, or Mary Stewart.

The good girls didn't approve of her reading. 'She thinks she's superior,' they said. 'She's anti-social,' they said. They'd rush to the prefects, to Thea Linton with complaints about the things they had to do – like moving chairs for play rehearsals or putting away the sports equipment – while Frances Petersen just kept reading. Thea Linton didn't like girls who were lazy, or dreamy. Or girls with noses in their books.

Or girls like Hannah Morgan, always scraping away at a violin.

Among the good girls, those patrollers of teams and the rights and wrongs of joining in, those arbiters of taste and standing, there were the devious and nasty, girls who, under a show of pursed lips and tutting noises, had a predilection for tales of cruelty: secret accounts of Nazi torture, the Spanish Inquisition, the witch hunts. They left these books in places where Frances read, hoping that Thea Linton would find them first and catch Frances in their trap. But Frances Petersen was not so easily caught. When she found these nasty books she'd return them to the common room without a word, leaving them for anyone to see on the table inside the door. When prefects held them up, asking in shrill cross voices 'whose are these?' Frances kept her customary silence.

'Why don't you report them?' Hannah Morgan asked, coming into the linen cupboard with Henrietta, my friend from home.

'There's no point,' Frances said. 'It'd only make them worse.'

'It's not fair,' Henrietta said, 'you getting into trouble all the time.'

'It wouldn't change that either,' Frances said.

'Do you mind if I practise in here?' Hannah asked.

'Not at all,' Frances said.

'I'll listen,' Henrietta said, climbing onto the shelf next to me.

The linen cupboard, despite its name, was larger than a cupboard, more like a small windowless room, where blankets and eiderdowns were kept in summer, and laundry was sorted and returned. The shelves, padded with blankets and pillows, were large enough to lie on; the air was warm and moist from the hot water tanks. Hannah Morgan, a wispy insubstantial girl, unpacked her violin. Thea Linton had chased her out of the common room where her practising disturbed the girls, and out of the dining room where it disturbed the kitchen staff.

Hannah Morgan was a scholarship girl. The good girls exchanged knowing looks as they passed this information from one to another, and before the school train bringing her to Carn for the first time had pulled in at the station, the news had spread that she came from a housing estate near Woking. Even I heard the news, and I was preoccupied with the seedlings I was nursing on my lap, and with Henrietta, new like Hannah, sitting beside me, her face pressed against the window, watching familiar landmarks disappear.

'It won't be so bad,' I said. 'I'll look after you.'

'I want to be at home,' Henrietta said, pale and trembly.

'There's my garden,' I said. 'And someone will be down to take us out soon.'

'But I don't want to be there at all,' she said. 'I'm not big enough yet.'

And she wasn't. The bones in the hand she held out to me were as fine as a bird's, with pearly nails as small as the crescents of tiny cowrie shells, the sort you find in the Scilly ·Isles, not the Pacific. That first term I tucked her in with me wherever I went.

When Frances Petersen's father arrived at the school in his battered Citroen, he'd swoop Henrietta and me into the back seat with his lenses and collecting cases. Sometimes Hannah too. Frances sat beside him as we dashed round corners and through villages, listening to his blustering tales about laboratories and experiments, the shape of seed pods, the length of pond weed, the properties of ragwort. We'd stop in one of the larger towns outside a hotel with white colonnades, and eat Dover Sole for lunch *to sustain us*, he said, for *the rigours ahead* – which I took to be the weeks of term that stretched before us, but by which he meant the exertions of the afternoon.

'Finished?' he'd say, and pay the bill as we trooped off to the Ladies.

'Ready?' he'd say, as we piled back into the car.

'Where to?' he'd say, though the itinerary was always his. He'd drive us to the coast and chip fossils from the mud-coloured rock; or take us on hikes across the uplands to see the rowans and the spindleberries; and of course to the winterbourne. He'd walk through Holme Farm with a cheerful wave at the children, offering the little ones a bob if they'd show us where the badgers were.

'I've been mother and father both to this child,' Frances Petersen's father said as we walked in the bright sprays of light that came dancing through the branches of beech trees, elms, chestnuts. 'And I praise her imagination. She inherited it from her mother as well as from me,' he'd say. 'When she's learned the discipline of schooling, she'll be an intellect to reckon with, mark my words.'

The Asp said she despaired to think what would become of Frances Petersen, *a sullen wretched girl like that, just look at that hair, and when did she last iron her skirt, surely she wasn't intending to go out like that. A Carn girl: what was she thinking of? That was the trouble,* the Asp said, *she didn't think, always with her nose in a book.* On this the Asp was wrong. Frances Petersen thought. She thought a great deal. And if I learned anything about thought at a school that prided itself on its academic standing while mistaking obedience for schooling and propriety for learning, it was through Frances Petersen that I did. It was from her that I first glimpsed what it might mean to learn by heart, not from the rote requirements of the classroom. For the rest there was, during those years, a dumb unknowing quality about my life. It was only in the garden or in the linen cupboard that, looking back, I'd say there was hope or understanding, any continuity between my life then, and my life now.

'Do you see the way the grass grows?' Frances' father would say, parting its strands at the bottom of the winterbourne. 'Do you see the way the blades already bend in the direction that the water will flow? See! They are flattened to withstand the water. And look!' His fingers scratched among the roots where seeds and egg cases collect, blown into the dry winterbourne by the wind.

He'd take out one of his lenses and we'd stare at the tiny specs of dirt in his palm. 'These grains that we can't make out even with a magnifying glass contain the germ of life,' he'd say. 'And when the water flows, beetles will hatch and water buttercups flower. You are very lucky to be so close to a winterbourne. I was nearly twice your age before I saw one. That's how you should think of school,' he'd say, and later when he dropped us back at the house, he'd give me tiny envelopes of seeds for my garden, each marked in elaborate copperplate. 'The grains of learning that collect in you will burst into life years later,' he'd say.

'Oh Father, really,' Frances said. 'All they're interested in are exams.'

'Other things,' he said, dusting off his hands and scattering seeds back into the grass. 'Things you can't see yet.'

He romanticised it, that school, Carn with its tradition of fine women, and he left his daughter to its far from romantic consequences. While other girls wept and prostrated themselves for less, Frances took whatever punishment the Asp handed out – always public, always humiliating – and in her doing of it, even with the good girls eddying around in gleeful disapproval, it seemed not a punishment. Frances reading Shakespeare aloud during lunch; Frances learning Chaucer in the hall; Frances scrubbing out the prefects' room.

Standing at that London window, looking at Frances Petersen's photo, all this passed through my head less as thought than as sensation, a sudden rush in which the strongest emotion that came to me was a dogged sort of loathing – for the Asp, for Carn, for the place itself. Not the hatred that flares up in the shadow of love, but a dumb smouldering refusal. It was by telling all this to Clara in the noise and clatter of a coffee shop that memory shifted into story – and immense curiosity. For there was Frances, Professor Petersen, hardly the failure that the Asp predicted; and failure is not a word I'd use of myself, or ever have, though for many years my intellectual life was lived as if I were travelling on forged papers, a disassociation I put down to the slur that was cast on me at Carn. Of Hannah Morgan's progress I know nothing.

So when Clara said *let's go, let's visit Carn*, I said *of course*, as if it had been my intention all along, and that very evening I wrote to the headmistress. I made no bones of my intention to investigate Carn as an example of the education Virginia Woolf was promoting when she published *A Room of One's Own* in 1928: an education she thought would assure women access to the great world of intellect and learning. Revenge was not a word I used. But it was what I meant when I spoke of the price that was paid for this education and its privilege, the enforcing of a conformity that regarded itself as individual, yet had no place for the idiosyncratic, the quirky, the reclusive, the dissident or wayward feminine. It's what I meant when I spoke of the differentials of privilege in Thatcher's England. I was staying near Clara in North London, on the edge of the borough of Hackney, less than two blocks from a school where the kids had more chance of being knifed than of matriculating.

As I told Clara this story and as I wrote to the school,

I knew exactly what I was looking for. As a result it didn't turn out quite as I expected. For a start I hadn't anticipated that the reply from the headmistress would come over the signature of Miss Dorothea Linton.

PART TWO

The Town

Carn is one of those towns that the postcard industry thrives on. Quaint, tucked in the Wessex hills, with its abbey, winding streets and narrow bridge over the river – tourists think they have found the quintessential England.

To get there you take the train west from London, or you turn off the A30 at the corner where Hannah Morgan stood the night she climbed out of the cloak-room window after the prefects had gone to bed, and cocked her thumb in the direction of London. The trucks didn't stop, but the police did. Hannah Morgan, clutching her violin case, was returned to the house at midnight in a blaze of light. The Asp and Thea Linton were waiting in the hall in their dressing gowns. Hannah Morgan had to eat lunch at a separate table for a week. That's the sort of town it was. Not so pretty for the girls incarcerated there.

'*Honey coloured*,' Clara said, reading from the guide book. 'It doesn't look honey coloured to me.' So I knew it wasn't just memory and its dysfunctions that rendered the town grey to me, for that's how it seemed to us both, crouched there under the hills. A dull flat grey. This is Hardy country, where the hills are austere, where stone walls run in vertical lines down the hills, where the tracks leading from one farm to the next collect water in deep ruts of mud; and where Tess of the D'Urbervilles was created and seduced as if she were real, in a hymn to feminine masochism which as girls we read with the eyes of self-punishing desire. What we learned was not, as the Asp would have said, that our passions were dangerous, but that this place was, with its sudden mists and weepy skies. On the train Clara had the novel open on the seat beside her as she looked out onto a sodden landscape.

At Carn the London train still arrives on platform two, the other side, so that you still have to cross the footbridge with its rusting stairs and wind-trap of a roof, down onto platform number one, through a shrunken entry passage – hall would be too grand a term – and out into the forecourt. Even the taxis hadn't changed, their drivers still reading the *Mirror* as they waited for trade. The park across the road with its curved laurel and box hedge smelled exactly as it had: damp earth, spiders' webs, dead leaves, Mars Bars wrappers. All that had changed as we walked up the main street was that the Spindleberry cafe, which had served waffles with Canadian maple syrup, had gone. In its place was a Wimpy Bar.

Clara and I were expected for lunch at Perceval, the Asp's old house. Carn, as I had explained to her on the train, is a school dominated by a system of houses in which the girls eat and live. A housemistress, as in the case of the Asp, could become a figure as powerful as any Head for she was the point of reckoning for her girls. The current housemistress, Mrs Sheila Glassop was expecting us at 12.45. Our appointment with Miss Dorothea Linton, once Thea the prefect, was at 2.30, 'between parents'. After that we were free, her secretary wrote, 'to walk around the school as we pleased.'

As we had an hour to spare we spent it in the abbey, which was at least out of the rain, where the Sunday ritual of prayer had been enforced but not understood; and where at concerts shared with Carn boys, the good girls would arrive in a self-satisfied knot, cooing and pointing while the pretty girls, the sexy ones with names like Georgia, Lisa, Caroline, pushed their hats to the backs of their heads and turned innocent eyes and fluttering handkerchiefs to the boys being led under supervision to their seats on the other side of the nave. The pews were hard and there was no heating, but should a girl dare complain of chilblains, a sore throat, tired back, or bruised knees, she would be reminded that privilege attached to mere association with a monument as ancient as Carn abbey.

Carn takes pride in its history; tourists come to see the traces of the Saxon stonework in an abbey that had once been a centre of religious learning before the bishops moved to the cathedral town, and the abbey became a monastery and extended into the buildings which are now the often-filmed hub of Carn boys' school. All this

we knew and were taught time and again, and somehow we were led to believe that when we sat cold and
hunched on those hard pews, the abbey was just as it
had been all those centuries before, and our complaints
and miseries were attributed if not to ingratitude, then
to a shallow sense of history.

It wasn't until I visited Carn with Clara, who had
entered this expedition in the spirit of research, that I
could see the significance of the history we were not
taught. 'Listen to this,' Clara said, reading from the guide
book of a century-long rebellion against the monks.
She understood at once that Carn, as a place, was redo-
lent not of an uncontaminated English picturesque, but
of the defeat of proud, independent Wessex. As children of a United Kingdom we were taught nothing of
Jack Cade's rebellion in the fifteenth century during
which a bishop was killed in the cathedral town, man-
ors were fired, and the abbey placed under town guard.
The parishioners took up *swords and cudgels*, Clara read,
against the monks, and won. But though the names of
Saxon bishops were handed down to us girls as the
names of the houses we lived in, the name of Jack Cade
was never uttered; the conflicts and histories we studied
– regal, parliamentary, imperial – did not touch our
lives. And those that did, the struggles that had occurred
right here where we lived, were never mentioned. Yet
we felt them in shame and hostility every time we passed
Holme Farm with its population of surly, unwelcoming
children. They were the depressed inheritors of old
Wessex, we the children of their defeat, which arrived,
finally and conclusively, with the trains, the agricultural
technology, the telegraph: those heralds of modernity
against which swords and cudgels had no edge.

Our school was founded in the same decade as *Tess of the D'Urbervilles* was published, the money put up by the same family – old squires married to the new money of the Percevals – that had funded the clearing out of the abbey, a victory over the townspeople that was named restoration. Out went the town's fire-fighting equipment, the box pews, the galleries spanning the aisles, the coaches, the weapons, the gun powder. No longer in the service of the town and its villages, the abbey was claimed by the squires and their new allies, whose power spread down the railway line to Wessex. The confidence of their right to order the world declared that this was how God had always intended churches to be.

If I had read *Tess* through a lens other than the clouded masochism of girlish youth, I might have seen that what Hardy lays out in her ruined body is the destruction of his beloved Wessex, broken, as surely as Tess herself, by the coming of new money and new ideas that were as insidious as the threshing machine was dangerous. It was Clara who pointed out that while the skirmishes and defeats that Hardy wrote of happened here, within a day's reach of London, the same imperial passion for taming was being enacted on grand colonial scale on the other side of the world in the Maori wars and the massacre of Aborigines.

In the abbey, Clara and I inspected the brass plaques recording the county regiment's colonial conquests: the North West Frontier, Cyprus, South Africa. We read the names of the officers killed in Flanders, Dunkirk, Burma. The townspeople killed in war, and those co-opted from farm and village, are listed in small letters

on the hexagonal base of the grey stone memorial outside in the close, where tourist buses stop for photographs. More than two hundred men from one parish
killed between 1914 and 1918.

Walking round the abbey with Clara that day, I saw not
the temple of permanence I had knelt in as a child, but
a decoy of class and authority posing as tradition. There
in the stone rafters, like faultlines, are the red stains of
Jack Cade's fire, and if you look carefully you can see
where the galleries were once affixed to the walls. There
laid out before us in the stone of the abbey was the
evidence of the taming of rural Wessex, the dying of
that tough and independent breed that Hardy chroni-
cles so bitterly. The monks could be fought with sword
and cudgel, and even into the first half of the nine-
teenth century the coastguards could be evaded and a
supplementary economy maintained; but there was no
defence against the power of the new classes, new ways,
new money, new ethics that were backed by the railway, the internal combustion engine, telegraphic com-
munication, sweeping aside the old forms of agriculture
and tenancy, precipitating rural poverty and depression
from which there was no escape. The descendants of
the smugglers and arsonists and dairymen of Hardy's
novels worked in the kitchens and grounds of our
school, their grandfathers listed in small print on the
war memorial in a close of clipped grass which we girls,
lined up in pairs, considered our own, and where once
animals and children had roamed while the townspeople and villagers made their own arrangements with
the deity.

The House

From the windowseat I saw at once that the garden had disappeared under a car park.

'Oh, no,' Clara said as I pointed towards the tarmac on the other side of the hedge. 'Seeing the garden was part of the point.'

'We were short of space,' Mrs Glassop explained. 'It was a luxury really, a garden for the girls, and there weren't that many interested. After all there's still the rest of the grounds.'

We were standing at the first floor window of the drawing room that had once been the Asp's, and it was true that with a slight adjustment of neck and eye, we had a long view across lawns, paths, tennis courts, the chestnut walk and playing fields to the chalk hills in the distance.

'It's a lovely view,' Mrs Glassop said. 'I never tire of it. And now, a sherry?'

Mrs Glassop was not as I expected, and not as I'd led Clara to believe, bringing her to Carn with a view of housemistresses based solely on stories of the Asp. Young, with a wide face, well-cut short hair and a stylish suit, the tone Mrs Glassop took with her girls was relaxed, slightly teasing. At lunch she encouraged me to tell the stories which made them shudder in relief that they were hers and not the Asp's. For although the girls sitting at the table that day would barely have been born when the Asp retired, her reputation lives on, magnified into some kind of mythology, a counterpoint to the privilege of progress and the smooth workings of the present. So I told the story of how it had fallen to my lot to sit next to the Asp on the day Princess Margaret had her first baby, and how I'd ventured sympathy for this grand natal event, only to receive the full force of the Asp's scorn for girls like me, the newspapers and the BBC, indeed anyone who paid maudlin attention to such a minor, and private, event. Birth was not something to be spoken of at lunch. 'After all,' the Asp said, closing the subject, 'gypsy women have their babies behind hedges without the slightest fuss, and are back at their tasks the same day.'

Another of the Asp's maxims was that British women think nothing of tearing up their petticoats on an ox cart to Simla.

The girls roared in their chairs.

'What did they tear them up for?' Clara asked.

'That's a good question,' Mrs Glassop said. 'What did they tear them up for?'

'Bandages, I suppose,' I said. Bandages for wounds inflicted by bandits, mutineers, or bears perhaps.

'Perhaps they tore them up in the agony of labour,' suggested the toothy prefect serving out at the end of the table. Plates of a pale chicken dish were being passed along the table.

'Oh, I doubt it,' Mrs Glassop said.

'They were behind the hedge, you mean,' the prefect said.

'Now, now,' Mrs Glassop said.

'We don't even wear petticoats,' a small girl from the lower fifth said.

'I'd like to, though,' another girl said. 'You know, for parties and things.'

'Not on an ox cart,' Mrs Glassop said. And everyone laughed.

'We'd be safer in leggings,' a tiny girl, surely not yet at the menarche, ventured.

'Quite so,' Mrs Glassop said. 'I wouldn't want you on an ox cart in anything less.'

I liked Mrs Glassop. I had noticed of course that her title denoted that she was, or had been, married. I'd assumed she was a widow, or possibly divorced, though that seemed less likely as a model of suitability for the girls. So I was surprised by her youth, and more than that, by her vigour, which was quite different from anything displayed by the women who taught us – with the exception of a gym mistress who arrived to a flurry of excitement one summer term, and left at the end of it. She played tennis with young men on the front courts at weekends, while rows of mesmerised girls sat on the bank and watched. She was the first person I ever saw in jeans. From America, Frances Petersen said.

As soon as I saw Mrs Glassop I wondered what strange twist had brought her to Perceval; but none of the possible scenarios that had whizzed through my head – early death, a temperament unsuited to marriage – prepared me for the truth which she dropped into the lunchtime chatter, that her husband lived in the house with her. Nothing could have surprised me more; no terrible accident involving lions, no papal annulment.

'What?' I said. 'Here? In the house?'

'Yes, here,' she said, and her wide face widened with her smile.

'In the Asp's bedroom!'

'It's our bedroom now,' she said, just like that, with a table of girls around her. 'It's good for the girls to have a man in the house,' she said. 'Much more normal than all those stitched-up spinsters.'

I'm not sure that she used the expression *stitched-up*, and nor was Clara, but if she didn't it's what she meant, and she easily could have; she spoke that way, in a vernacular that overlapped sufficiently with the girls', and indeed with mine. Her husband was a scientist at a nearby research establishment. At weekends he helped the senior girls with their prep, Mrs Glassop said, and rehearsed the sixth-form band.

After lunch, as the stairs and landing pounded with the feet of girls, and the bannisters swayed as they swung round the corners, Mrs Glassop, doing nothing to check the noise, led Clara and me back to her drawing room for coffee, she said, with the prefects. The room, with its large bay windows facing south and west, which no Perceval girl of the Asp's era will ever forget, had subtly changed its shape. As Mrs Glassop held the door for us to enter, I saw it was not far off the square. In memory it remains as long and thin as a hockey field, and the walk into the light of those windows where the Asp waited was deep and treacherous.

'It's changed shape,' I said.

'That's what all the Asp's girls say,' Mrs Glassop laughed. 'The drama of walking towards her.'

'What happens to your girls when you want to speak to them?'

'I don't make them do that,' she said. 'I go to meet them. But then I don't have arthritis.'

'True,' I said. 'She must have been in pain a lot of the time.'

'Severely so, I believe,' Mrs Glassop said.

The girls who jostled in behind the tray were hard to take seriously as prefects, those creatures that work their way into the psyche of even the most wayward girl and remain there for life, working their authority. Some were plain and stocky, others looking out from long curling fringes; some had bands on their teeth, others had red knees. Yet these were the ones who, in the absolute hierachy of Carn, no doubt still mete out power in grand gestures of mercy, and petty moments, deliberate and calculated, of daily control. These wholesome, jolly girls asked Clara questions like *are you up at university?* and *what do you read?* Daunted by the prospect of a university as distant and as unlikely as Sydney, about which they had nothing to say, they informed her of their prospects. 'Oxford,' one said. 'Mummy was there.' And although they mentioned the Foreign Office, medicine, the bar, as future destinations that were theirs as if by right, this startling confidence was contradicted by the predictably adolescent anxieties that filled the room like an odour, stale, slightly sweaty. There was that afternoon's match against Holme, Perceval's traditional rival. And, rather more interesting, the Perceval dinner party which was to be held at the end of term and for which the prefects were drawing up the invitation list. Boys from Carn were to be invited. But which particular boys? The problem, it seemed, was deliciously immense.

'How brave,' Clara said. 'Do you invite one each?'

'Oh, we don't invite them ourselves,' the head of house said. 'We make a list and send invitations which say *Perceval invites*. Not us. Gosh no.'

'And we ask a few extras,' Mrs Glassop said, 'in case any of them turn out to be duds. We pair them off with single members of staff.'

What makes a dud? I asked. You know, they said, the

ones that don't talk, or boast all the time. 'Or aren't sexy,' said the one who's expecting Oxford. It was my turn to say *gosh!* All this scheming in the room where the Asp burned the valentine cards. February 14th was the one day of the year on which every girl hoped to be called in to see the Asp after lunch. Every year the rich and pretty girls were summoned, girls with names like Georgia, Lisa, Caroline, of whom it seemed life required only that they shine. The junior school hung over the bannisters to watch as they waited their turn, went in, closed the door, and emerged five minutes later with a little lace hanky held to their rose-bud lips. It was winter. The Asp, sitting not on the windowseat, but beside the fire, fed the cards to the flames. Slowly, one by one. *A vulgar habit, not befitting a Carn girl.* All they had, those pretty, sexy girls with names like Georgia, Caroline, Lisa, was a glimpse as love, still in its envelope, curled in the flames.

These days Mrs Glassop's girls make their plans with the dexterity of a society wife. The point of the dinner party, it seemed was to get an early picking before the boys' end of summer dance.

We never saw boys. They didn't come to the house. We didn't go to theirs. Except for the same few girls, those rich and pretty ones, who were invited to the same end of summer dance at the boys' school. For everyone else romance was the domain of gossip columns, radio plays, and notes passed across the prep room. Until the dance that is. Invitations arrived early in June, and the same girls lined up outside the Asp's drawing room; girls with tiny waists and neat feet, girls with names like Georgia, Caroline, Lisa. Every detail had to be approved by the Asp; and every preparation was made under the gaze of fifty girls hanging over the bannisters to watch. Dresses arrived in flat boxes from London: organdie over-skirts with yards and yards of rainbow net petticoats, taffeta and satin bodices, bunches of tiny silk roses. Little pointy white and silver shoes were inspected from every angle, sequin bags, gossamer shawls, even lipsticks and nail polish of the discreetest shades.

When at last the great night arrived, girls going to the dance were excused supper. While the rest of us toyed with our food in the dining room, they lounged in baths sweetened just this once with oils and salts. After supper, senior girls not going to the dance retired to the prefects' room and closed the door without a care in the world, while the rest of the house rushed to the aid of the chosen, grateful for the humblest of tasks: folding a hanky, holding a mirror, opening a door. At last, dressed and adorned, the favoured and the beautiful were escorted to the Asp's drawing room. Outside on the landing, girls swooned in each other's arms. Thea Linton shooed them away. It was her task, as the senior girl not going to the dance, to meet the boys at the door and show them up to the Asp. Introductions were made, orange juice provided, conversation held, and glances cast. Then, with the exhortation to be back by eleven o'clock, not a minute later, the couples set off down the stairs, in those days painted a gloomy blue, to the accompaniment of fifty girls fluttering in cotton nighties between upper balcony and windows. Excitement swished through the dormitories, making sleep impossible, while at the other school the girls in their net and taffeta dresses were more aware of the effect they were having in the house they'd left than in the arms of the ones with whom they danced.

All this I told Mrs Glassop's girls, with embellishments that have become practised over the years. But where an Australian audience always laughs, these girls leaned forward attentively, and did not laugh.

At eleven o'clock, I said, every window was open and studded with tiny moons as the faces of fifty girls kept watch on the front door. The Asp sat in the hall, her gaze fixed on the panel of frosted glass. Thea Linton was instructed when to open the door. The heads of the couples making their farewell had only to incline towards each other under the porch light for the door to spring open. Fifty voices of fifty girls hanging from the windows could be heard drawing in their breath in a long disappointed *ooooh*. All this is true. Having done her duty downstairs, Thea Linton climbed the stairs to lock the windows against the murderers and rapists conjured up by the excitement, and chase girls in their white nighties back to their beds.

'It's not like that now,' Mrs Glassop's girls said, with regret in their voices. 'The juniors don't take the slightest notice.'

'That's not quite true,' Mrs Glassop said.

'They don't admire us,' they said. 'Not like that.'

For the last days of those distant summer terms, romance was the topic that prepared us for home and the disturbing possibilities that holidays presented. Names were tried out on every tongue; the postman was met at the door. But when boys were spoken of, it was the boys of Carn school we meant, that undifferentiated mass who were nonetheless boys of our class, boys of our world. That has remained the same. Town boys are not invited to the Perceval dinner party; town boys are not of interest; town boys are embarrassing. Or worse. The year Frances Petersen got a valentine card, the hand on the envelope and the postmark from the town down the railway line where the state school was, gave her away. The flames were too good for this card. It lay on the table between her and the Asp. *Who sent this?* the Asp demanded. Frances could not say. She said she did not know. Beyond that her power was her customary silence. She sat very still. It was not that her attention was elsewhere, rather that some other life moved in her even as she attended to the words that turned the Asp plum purple, brows hooded over her beak of a nose, as if it were she, not Frances, who confronted the worst part of her nature. *You sullen girl. Sullen wretched girl. Has the cat got your tongue? Sullen sulky girl. What possible hope can there be for a girl like you? Look at you, sitting there like that, sullen, wretched girl. Lazy beast of a girl. Look at you. Your hair cut like a mangy cur.* The Asp's fury filled the air. On the other side of the door the house simmered not with excitement, but with shock. 'Who can it possibly be from?' The good girls composed their faces. 'She should be ashamed,' they said. In the linen cupboard, Frances lay flat and silent on the top shelf. Hannah didn't take her violin out of its case.

This is not a story I told. I waited until the train and told it to Clara as we jolted through the dark, back towards London.

'I can imagine it'd be much the same,' Clara said. 'The place reeks of class, and being civilised about it doesn't make it any better.'

When the prefects had gone to prepare for the match,
Mrs Glassop showed Clara and me around the house.
As she explained to Clara the arcane routines of a school
that still has evening lessons and ritual pashes which
require younger girls to prepare the beds and run
errands for the senior girls, it was as if I was on a film
set for which someone had unexpectedly changed the
script. The dormitories had the same names and the
same dimensions, but now there were power points for
hair dryers and posters on the walls. The girls lying on
their beds reading, or changing, were the wrong girls.
The only girl of my era who had a hair dryer was, I
think, Georgia and she had to plug it into matron's
power point. The good girls jostled to hold the mirror,
there, just there, to admire, to compliment, to praise. We
passed the dormitory where Henrietta and I had slept
that first term she was at Carn and it was cold and she
crept into my bed, tired out from the tasks Georgia had
exacted from her, running to and fro, polishing shoes
she'd only polished the day before, turning down her
bed, fetching her book, waiting while she asked matron
for a special face cream.

'We don't let pashes go too far these days,' Mrs
Glassop said.

'How far is too far?' Clara asked.

'You know,' she said, 'just one or two tasks a day.
None of the humiliation that used to go on, with girls
having to scrub out the prefects' room while they all
watched. That sort of thing.'

On the top floor a telephone had been fitted in the
linen cupboard, and beside it a battered chair in recognition of the enclosed comfort where Frances read, and
Hannah Morgan took her violin as if the rest of the

house and its rules and prohibitions ceased to be, and she, unnoticed and unheard, could safely let her heart play into that warm moist air.

From the attic window, one floor above, you can still see across to the hills on the other side of Holme Farm, but as the town has spread it was hard to see the route we took, or recognise any landmarks.

'Does the winterbourne still run?' I asked Mrs Glassop.

'Oh yes, I imagine so,' she said. 'I should take the girls in the summer, now that you've reminded me.'

Downstairs the common room was still lined with the lockers Thea Linton used to inspect on Thursdays; there were the same bookcases with the same editions of the same classics. But the radio had been replaced by a stereo; postcards, photos, magazines were strewn about in a clutter the Asp would never have allowed; and the portrait photographs of the first two housemistresses in black dresses with white lace collars, had been replaced by posters of Michael Jackson and a print of Picasso's doves.

In the cloakroom the lacrosse captain was exhorting her team to alarming feats. 'What is this game?' Clara said, watching as girls with over-developed shoulder and neck muscles raised their sticks and trembled. Lacrosse is a game that in England is considered suitable for girls. A hard ball is thrown through the air as girls fight to catch it in the stiff scoop attached to their sticks. For girls in glasses it can be alarming, and also dangerous. That afternoon Perceval was playing Holme, the house where the myopic Letty Browne had served in the ungraded team that was produced to play ours. We played wing opposite each other, positions chosen for their distance from the centre of action, and in matches that were usually unsupervised, so low-grade were they, we'd spent the afternoon deep in the life of Tess Durbeyfield, whose reincarnated spirit we allocated to Leah, the girl from Holme Farm who worked in Perceval's kitchen. Knowing nothing of her life except what we saw as she heaved the trays of baked beans and rice onto the table, we dressed her flushed and handsome face in tragedy. She was well equipped for the part, with long golden hair spilling out of the knot that was required in the kitchen, sad eyes – *as brown as a deer's and as deep as pools* - and a generous mouth that pouted with dissatisfaction. The mistake we made was to interpret as tragedy a stance in her we could not, from the inaccurate viewpoint of an uncertain privilege, understand as pride or determination.

When we left the house, shaking Mrs Glassop's hand, and leaving the team to its awesome preparations, I took Clara round the hedge to the car park where my garden had once been. It had been a wide bed concealed from the lower windows by a hedge, and backing in the other direction onto the quiet parade of vegetables which has now vanished beneath new buildings. In my day junior girls could choose a strip of this bed and plant it with flowers brought from home. Few were interested; one or two poked at it with their forks and planted the odd limp seedling. The effect was untidy and uncared for. I chose the strip that ran along the southern edge of the bed where in summer there was full sun. The northern edge where the bed was in shade was a more popular choice for reasons that had nothing to do with gardening and everything to do with proximity to the back door and the common room. Nothing that was planted

there flourished; as a consequence the girls became dis-
heartened and I encroached until the whole bed was
mine. Sid, the head groundsman, helped me dig it
through, and showed me how to take cuttings. I'd walk
round the grounds with him and snip from anything
that would fit my plan. He brought me seedlings from
his own garden across the road, and sometimes cuttings, or even plants from his sister's garden on the
other side of town. When Frances' father gave me seeds
to germinate, Sid would find a spot for the seedling tray
in the school's congested greenhouse. When the first
tips of the white delphiniums appeared, he was waiting
on the path for me after morning school and shook me
by the hand as if something of myself was pushing up
through the earth. 'Well done, Miss,' he said. 'Very well
done.' The seeds, which had come all the way from the
Crimea, had been given to me by Frances Petersen's
father. Known for their difficulty in germinating, they
were given as much as a challenge as a compliment.
When they grew and were transplanted, they formed
the centrepiece not only of the garden but of the under-
life I managed at that regulated and controlled school.

The School

Such was the gloom in Miss Dorothea Linton's office,
that it seemed the light was blotted from the window
by the ghosts of unhappy girls who had been handed
punishments and reprimands from the unsmiling headmistress behind that dark, laquered desk. The walls were
painted dark green. The glass cabinet along the wall
beside the door, which our headmistress the Dame had
used for books, was filled, shelf upon shelf, with dolls.

Dozens of frozen-faced dolls dressed in the traditional costumes that in real life nobody wears.

'From my girls,' Miss Linton said in response to Clara's enquiry. 'Aren't they lovely.' She took a tiny doll with a peaked white cap and wooden clogs from the shelf. 'This one,' she said, 'has just arrived. From my last head of school. She found it in an antique shop in Bruges. So thoughtful of her.' She put the doll back, making sure its balance was secure, and turned her attention to Clara and to me.

'Now what can I do for you?' she said, and for the first time in my life I began to stutter. The questions I'd devised fell out of my head, words tangled in my mouth, consonants rearranged themselves, verbs became as hefty as nouns, refusing to move the sentence along.

It was left to Clara to explain our task, part personal, part research on the education of girls. Miss Linton produced a sheet of paper with the last five years' university entrance results. They were indeed impressive. Those Perceval prefects may well find themselves at the Foreign Office or the bar.

'When did you come back to the school as a mistress?' Clara asked.

'In 1968,' Miss Linton replied.

'So soon,' Clara said. 'You could only just have left.'

'I was out for four years,' she said.

'Why did you return?' I asked, rallying slightly.

'It was my earliest ambition,' Miss Linton said.

'Even when you were a girl?'

'Absolutely,' she said. 'I knew from the beginning, from the day I arrived, that it was what I wanted.'

'I suppose,' I said, 'that by the time you came back

there was a younger, newer breed of mistress here, and things were beginning to change.'

'Not at all,' she said. 'When I came back my friends in the staff room were the women who'd taught us. The Miss Roses, old Miss Birkoff, and of course *dear Astrid*.'

I could imagine Big Miss Rose with her many chins being kind to any new teacher. In her day the scholarships, the glory, all were hers. When we reached the middle fifth Letty Browne and I joined Frances Petersen and girls from the upper fifth at the Miss Roses' Sunday teas. Thin Miss Rose, the Latin mistress, handed round cup cakes decorated with chocolate icing and tiny silver balls. 'Well, girls,' Big Miss Rose would say, 'what are you reading?' And Letty would lean back slightly and say, 'Proust, actually, Miss Rose.' Miss Rose would sigh. 'Ah,' she'd say, looking into her teacup, 'the paper flowers of memory,' and we would be embarrassed and not know what to say next. On the wall of the sitting room she shared with her sister in their small house on the outskirts of Carn, not far from the road that led down to Holme Farm, was a rather disturbing modern nude. We'd jostle to sit with our backs to it. There was a third sister, we understood, who lived in Australia. She alone of the three was married.

'Was that nude at the Miss Roses' a Stella Bowen?' I asked Miss Linton.

'I really wouldn't know,' Miss Linton said, showing little interest in Clara's enthusiasm for the possibility that flashed across the years. 'What's Big Rose got that on her wall for?' Letty would say as we walked back to school, dawdling along the edge of the boys' cricket flats, past the bookshop by the abbey, looking at the cakes in the Spindleberry cafe and the senior girls at the tables inside. There was more of interest to be seen through those windows, than on the walls of the Miss Roses' sitting room.

'In 1968,' Clara said to Miss Linton, 'there must have been changes coming.'

'I can see you live abroad,' Miss Linton said. 'The great thing about Carn is tradition.'

The interview was not a success. I wanted to know what manner of woman becomes a headmistress. Miss Linton wanted to assure me of the school's continuing tradition. She was proud, she said, to have held the line against the trend to co-education. When Clara suggested that movement between the schools might establish a more normal environment for adolescent children, Miss Linton simply said, with only the hint of a laugh, that most girls will always be more interested in house matches than boys. As if to prove her point, we could hear the distant chant of house mottos through the closed windows, and the roar of girls following their teams onto the pitch.

I reminded her of the great swirl of fuss that had surrounded St Valentine's Day and the summer dance.

'Some girls will always be silly,' Miss Linton said.

'The whole house was silly,' I said.

'What nonsense,' she said, a charming smile stripping the remark of rebuke, and thereby shafting it home. 'You always did have a vivid imagination. I can see it hasn't improved.'

'You must remember,' I said. 'You used to have to open the door for the girls who'd been to the dance, and then try to settle the rest of us down for the night.

You had half the junior house on detention for weeks.'

'I think you've been abroad too long,' she said with that glittery, reflective laugh. 'Most of us got on with our prep.'

The view of the school that she offered, based on good standing and tradition, was, by any other standard, as empty of meaning as our conversation. But that, I suppose, is the role of the headmistress: to patrol the split between body and mind that our culture avows; to deny the messy and difficult terrain of the body and its wild desires. Are we left believing, somewhere, secretly, that we need to tame ourselves in order to harness our capabilities of mind? Is this her legacy? Clara and I asked ourselves these questions on the train back to London.

'When did Big Miss Rose retire?' I asked.

'When Julia Rose married,' Miss Linton said.

'Thin Miss Rose?' I said. 'I didn't know that. Who did she marry?'

'A master at the boys' school,' Miss Linton said. 'It was a shock to us all. Poor darling, she died soon afterwards.'

'What happened to Big Miss Rose?' I asked.

'She went to her other sister,' Miss Linton said.

'The one in Australia?' I asked.

'I believe so,' Miss Linton said.

'Do you know where?' I asked.

'Somewhere in Melbourne,' she said. 'We didn't correspond.'

What had happened? Why didn't she correspond with a woman who only a moment before she'd described as a friend? These are not questions one can ask of a headmistress. Besides we had touched on the uncomfortable subject of Australia. The mere fact that Miss Linton told us that Big Miss Rose went there implied a failure of some quite serious sort, for Australia is still regarded among the less imaginative sectors of the British middle class as the place girls went when they got pregnant. Now that is no longer possible, persistent images of antipodean vulgarity are used to reflect back Britain's tarnished view of itself as civilised and urbane. The irony is of course that as Britain comes to realise it's no longer anything more glorious than a small island off the coast of Europe, it contrives to see in Australia exactly the values by which it hoped to save itself during the Thatcherite eighties, as if by this complex fiction of projection and exchange, it could absolve its own faltering crudities.

'I gather Frances Petersen lives in Canada,' I said.

'Really,' Miss Linton said. 'I can't say I'm surprised. She was rather a tiresome girl.'

'I liked her,' I said. 'Why was the Asp so against her?'

'I wouldn't say that,' Miss Linton said. 'Astrid treated all her girls most fairly. She was an excellent teacher.'

'Not if she didn't like you,' I said.

'Come now,' Miss Linton said. 'You mustn't let your imagination run away with you. Adolescents can be very unforgiving.' She laughed. I laughed. Only Clara did not laugh.

'Do you ever hear of Hannah Morgan,' I asked, 'the girl with the violin?'

'Yes, yes,' Miss Linton said. 'I know who you mean. But no, I can't answer your question. Some girls just disappear.' She was turning the pages of the diary on her desk as if to signal that our allotted time was up.

'One feared that you had too,' she said. 'Disappeared, I mean.'

Miss Linton stood up and looked out towards the match that we could hear in the distance, beyond the tennis courts, on the far side of the grounds. Girls on the sidelines obscured our view.

'Perceval's playing Holme,' she said. 'I can't make out the score. Can you?'

'No,' I said.

Clara was looking at the dolls. Afterwards she told me there was one, tucked towards the back, which was in a nappy.

'Well,' Miss Linton said, putting out a firm hand, 'is there anything else?'

'The winterbourne,' I said. 'The girls don't seem to go there any more.'

'I see you are a sentimentalist,' she said, with just a hint of that laugh. 'They're putting the bypass through on that side of the town, where Holme Farm used to be. The geography master at Carn is upset. He wants a joint petition.'

'What happened to Holme Farm?' I asked.

'It was only ever a tenancy farm,' she said. 'Terrible state of disrepair. It was bought up years ago. They farm it from over near Exeter. Most of the buildings have come down. The ones they don't use.'

'That's awful,' I said.

'One's got to move with the times,' Miss Dorothea Linton laughed. 'That's what I tell the petitioners. High time we had a bypass. Much better for the school.' She opened the door. 'Lovely to see you,' she said, and the door closed behind us just a fraction too quickly.

'Imagine sending your daughter here,' Clara said. She

looked pale, and I have to say that despite the heating ducts in the floor, it was no less draughty than it ever was in the corridor outside the headmistress's room. That public place of waiting and punishment.

'Are you regretting coming?' I asked.

'No,' she said. 'It's fascinating. I can suddenly see what you mean about being English being a bit like being a man. That awesome certainty that your view of the world is *the* view of the world.'

'But it's girls they have here,' I said.

'Taming them,' Clara said. 'The message is that if they knuckle under they stand to gain.'

'And they do,' I said.

'Depends what you mean by gain,' Clara said as we let ourselves out through the staff cloakroom into the raw bite of the wind.

'What kind of a life would it be, a headmistress like that?' I said.

'What kind of a woman?' Clara said.

Later that evening we stopped in the town for a meal before catching the train back to London. At the hotel where we ate (Carn doesn't run to restaurants as such) Clara asked the woman who was the only other person in the lounge, and the hotelier who was bustling around us, what they knew of the Carn headmistress. *A splendid woman*, they said. *Absolutely splendid. Though mind you*, drawing close, after another gin, *things are said, you know. Not that one would believe them, or pass them on, not at all, a splendid woman like that. But well, they say there was a scandal at the school with one of the senior girls taken away after she'd been to London with a group from the school. To see an exhibition, or something, all perfectly above board, one wouldn't* doubt it, but the parents did take the girl away and one can't help but wonder. *One sees them sometimes, girls weeping,* the hotelier said, *I've had them in here when their parents are down for the weekend, begging to be taken away. The things they say. There's no doubt Miss Linton's strict. Well, you'd have to be, a school like that and all those girls, they can be very wild, and the boys no better than you'd expect. Not that one believes the things one hears, not for a minute. Happy looking girls they are when you see them outside the abbey of a Sunday morning.*

The taxi driver was blunt. *They're never what they seem, those women,* he said. *That headmistress,* he said. *I wouldn't let her near my daughter. They say she has wild parties during the holidays. A sight for sore eyes if you'll pardon the expression. I don't suppose there's anything in it, but you can't help but wonder, those righter than right types.*

Common gossip, and I repeat it only as gossip, for gossip it is, as well as to illustrate the universal truth that no one believes that such stern surfaces are as they seem. The more righteous a person appears, the more the regarding imagination dwells on the possibilities of a scurrilous under-life, and the greater is the desire to pull down the one who sets the standards none of us wish to live by.

The dreary reality is probably that Miss Dorothea Linton is much as she appears: a competent headmistress with a competent, sensible life lived out in the smooth runnels laid down by tradition and Carn. The telltale sign of this is the fact that Dorothea Linton looks not in the least like the Thea Linton I remember, but exactly like our headmistress, Dame Elizabeth Mainwaring Burton.

Like the Dame, Miss Linton is tall and willowy, with

the same white hair, the same straight back. The only difference is that her teeth are not good. Even her suit that day was like the Dame's, with a little squared-off jacket that could have been in the cupboard since the fifties. But where the Dame had been a woman who toured foreign countries as a representative of British education, who awed parents and debated with bishops, Dorothea Linton seemed somehow transparent. While it may once have been that schools like Carn offered an intellectual environment for women who might otherwise have had lonely lives as single professional women, Thea Linton went back to Carn as a young woman in 1968, to a town and an institution whose rigidity she had made her own. Where earlier headmistresses were forging a brave new world, she is defending a conservatism that depends for its identity on a discredited moral authority. Her girls with their bright futures were in danger of becoming a parody of all that Virginia Woolf had hoped. Rather than assuming full citizenship of a world of intellectuality and feeling that would reveal them to history in the fullness of their femininity, they were being cast as the silver-handed bearers of an embattled regime. In post-Thatcher England where ruling-class masculinity can barely conceal its uncertainty – the very week that I visited Carn *The Times* ran a full page spread on whether John Major was having a nervous breakdown – it seems that there is no crisis of confidence in ruling-class femininity. But at what cost? Walk round the back of Miss Dorothea Linton and you can see the struts. I don't believe for a minute that she has a secret life. I'd rather like to, wild parties and all. But I don't.

Perceval won the house match.

'Thirteen three,' Mrs Glassop said when we joined her on the path back to the house. 'Marvellous.'

The team captain came jogging past with her team behind her, chanting the victory chant.

'Well done, girls!' Mrs Glassop said. 'Very well done!'

'Brilliant!' the team captain said.

'Extra tea,' her offsider said, smartening up the pace.

Tea. Tea had not changed. The only unsupervised meal of the day. The only meal at which there was enough. Loaves of white bread, barrels of margarine, tubs of jam: strawberry, blackberry, apricot. Doughnuts, pink finger buns, rock cakes. Girls could help themselves; girls piled slices onto plates, balanced finger buns on their arm, retreated down the back stairs, sat at the window of the common room, or, in the summer, on the back doorstep and *scoffed*. The one comforting moment of the day. Down it all went into adolescent stomachs growing and expanding, fat slothful girls, spotty, smelly girls with smells and fluids spilling around, filling the air of the house, creeping into dormitories, under the door into the Asp's drawing room, into her dried-up starchy nostrils, settling on Thea Linton's shiny prefect's badge. It numbed our emptiness, kept us warm for the long haul of evening classes with nothing to look forward to but a miserly supper eaten at our places. When Henrietta crept round the end of the partition and through the curtain, I lifted my blankets for her to come into my bed. For years we'd slept together, since we were tiny children, top to bottom, side by side; a familiar warmth. I lifted the blankets and in she came. Her feet were cold. She put them on my calves. *Don't*, I said, but she did, and I wrapped my arms around her. *Don't cry*, I said, *Henny-penny. Don't cry.* Night after night. *Hennypenny.* That way she bore the shock of it. *Tell me your day. Tell me what happened.* We slept curved together, neither of us yet past the shapes of children; to sleep like that was as deep in us as the childhood we'd shared, and far from the realms of blood and desire that had yet to claim us. None of this mattered, none of it mattered at all, when Thea Linton drew back the curtain and turned on the lights. The bare bulb of the inquisitor.

'Get up at once,' she said, stripping back the blankets. 'Best dresses and straight downstairs.'

Down we went to the Asp, dressed in our Sunday best, blinded by the lights on those gloomy stairs. The Asp was beside the fire with a book on the table beside her, a biography of Disraeli, and a tea tray with two cups, biscuits shared with her head of house.

What was said? I don't recall. Our parents. Our parents were mentioned. Their disappointment. The Asp's surprise. Thea's shock. But what was it that we'd done? Nothing was articulated. It was years before I heard the word lesbian and when I did I thought *of course, of course*, that's what they thought. In so far as I'd felt the swell of a passion that had never been named, it was not for this shrimp of a girl whom I'd loved since we'd first crawled around the same rug; it was for Frances Petersen with those storm-grey eyes that still had the power to shock even in a magazine photo thirty years later.

What did Henrietta think, feel, that night? I don't know. The next day, supervised by matron, she changed dormitories with her sister.

'Really,' Stella said, coming round the end of the

partition between us. 'You should know better. We're not at home now.'

Stella was one of the good girls, and as the rest gathered around, tutting and sighing and casting sorrowful looks, I could see that we'd embarrassed her. It was never spoken of again. Not at school. Not by our parents. I don't even know if they were told. Henrietta and I never spoke of it. It wasn't that we avoided each other exactly, but with a year between us, and carefully separated arrangements for our daily routines, there were limited occasions on which we could be together. Weekend walks; not much else. We never spoke of it at school; and afterwards we never had the chance. A year after Henrietta left Carn, by which time I had already crossed the world, she was killed, *bang*, just like that, when her car went under a bus. I still weep for her, for Henrietta, for the companion of my infancy, for those nights we slept together against the cold. For this I weep. Not for the rest. For Henrietta, that's all. And at the heart of my long and dogged hatred for the Asp has been the charge that it was her fault. If not her fault that Henrietta died, then her fault that she died unrestored to me. Hers, and Dorothea Linton's.

The Asp

It was said that the winterbourne never flowed for the Asp. When she came to the school as a young mistress before the war, she'd take groups of girls there on hikes, explaining as they went the workings of the water table, the nature of chalk and the mystery of springs; but already her arthritis had begun and when the weather was wet enough for the water to rise up through the

chalk and flood down the winterbourne, the Asp was
in too much pain to make the journey, her hands and
feet bent in on themselves like hooks. But the tradition
lived on and the first girls to see the winterbourne when
it flowed wrote their names in the *excellent book* that the
Asp kept on her desk for the signatures of the clever
and the favoured.

The track to the winterbourne skirted the edge of
Holme Farm. There were gates to open and close, deep
ruts in mud that dried to a white dust in summer, dogs
yowling on their chains, and from the shadowy depths
of barn and house came small squawking children, and
girls our own age, older boys in dungarees or drain
pipes. The boys leaned on the railings as we passed.
Unless Frances was there, one would give a long slow
whistle, another would spit; their contempt and ridi-
cule scorched our coats, and made impossible the
democratic smile we had been trained to bestow. It
was their land on which we trod. It was a sensation
of trespass – worse, of deep and humiliating inappro-
priateness – that I felt with a stab of recognition years
later when I was living in a black country. The farm
girls would giggle and pout as we walked stiffly past;
they'd bunch up their hair which, unlike ours, grew
wild and long. Unless Frances was there, Leah stayed
out of sight and no one spoke. But Frances went over
to the rails while Hannah and I hung back. The children would smile up at her, Leah would appear at the
back door, and there was laughter and chatter we didn't
know how to enjoy. Leah's brother Ken, the one in the
drain pipes, would open the gate for her, and she'd turn
and beckon, and we'd follow her into the yards with
clumsy limbs and awkward hearts.

'Do you think we should?' Hannah would ask as we continued on our walk.

'Why not?' Frances said. 'When we leave we'll be able to talk to anyone we like. They won't be able to stop us. I'm going to come straight over here and invite Leah and Ken out.'

'You wouldn't, would you?' Hannah said.

'I would,' she said. 'You wait.'

By cutting across the fields before the farm, through the woods with their leaf-mould smells and sinister rustlings, and by fording the stream at the bottom of the slope, the winterbourne could be reached without venturing through the yards. Frances showed me the way, and it's only now that it occurs to me to ask how she knew. That was the way I went on the only occasion I saw the winterbourne run.

On that day, almost my last at Carn, the winterbourne bubbled and roared across the fields, through stark winter hedgerows, stroking the grass that seemed to flow in a snakelike movement all the way to the stream flooding its bank at the bottom of the hill. Climbing back to its source I watched the gurgle of water through the grass. There was no opening, no tap, no faucet, nothing to indicate where such a body of water could come from, but there it was, rising through the chalk with the grace of tears.

As I had gone alone in breach of rules that forbade any form of unsupervised absence, I couldn't tell the Asp; and as I couldn't tell the Asp, I never signed the excellent book, a failing that was pointed out to me at my final interview with the Asp. She hoped I would show more substance at my next school, and reminded me that no matter where I was or what I did I would

forever bear the responsibility of being a Carn girl.
Despite Big Miss Rose's recommendations, she was not,
she said, hopeful for my future.

When I'd written to the headmistress asking if I could
visit Carn, and declaring my intention to write about it,
I had hoped the Asp would still be alive. In so far as I
formulated a plan, I had imagined confronting her and
though I knew it wasn't possible that she could still be
in the house, I saw myself flinging open the door of
her drawing room and marching into the room, a presence to be reckoned with, my achievements shining in
the air around me. But such dreams and grandiosities
were dashed by the letter from the headmistress' secretary. Miss Stuart Parker, I read, had died two summers before after a bad fall. 'It was a mercy,' Mrs
Glassop said, for the arthritis that had crippled her for
fifty years had finally knotted her into a gnarled carica-
ture of her early stature. 'She was brave to the end,'
Thea Linton said, 'and always good humoured.' And
then, in a strange moment of confession, Thea, Miss
Linton, told me that on the day the Asp was moved to
a home, she was 'rather miserable'. Thea could only
call in briefly, though the Asp was querulous and asked
her to stay. 'She pleaded,' Thea said, 'but what could I
do. I was expected in London.' Telling this story, Miss
Linton did not laugh.

   'She had a marvellous funeral,' Mrs Glassop said. 'The
service was in the abbey and she'd left money for a
party so all the girls who'd come could see each other.'

   'Did many come?' I asked, seeing pew upon pew
empty of anything but shades; girls, mourners, I could
not imagine at all.

'Oh yes,' she said. 'The abbey was full. She was greatly loved. Many girls kept up with her all her life. I suppose you wouldn't have known, having spent so long abroad. They asked advice, stayed with her when they visited, sent books for Christmas, that kind of thing. She was immensely generous when it came to her girls.'

'She could also be cruel,' I said.

'Yes,' Mrs Glassop said. 'I believe she could.'

Later that afternoon, as Clara and I were leaving for our train back to London, Mrs Glassop gave me a copy of the memoir the Asp had written during her retirement. 'You might find this helpful,' she said. Not interesting. Helpful was the word she used.

Clara read this slim, locally printed and stapled book on the train whisking us through the night to London, while I lay back in the seat to rest my eyes. Through the drift of sleep and the rhythmic thud of the wheels, I listened as she read bits of it aloud.

'These aren't her memoirs,' Clara said. 'They're her father's.'

The Asp's memoir was a paean to an Edwardian age when maids attended family prayers, mothers read aloud after dinner and – most of all – fathers ruled. Her childhood had tipped the very end of this twilight world, yet she wrote of it as the brightest moment in her life, an ideal grieved for in old age.

'She'd only have been ten years older than Ettie,' Clara said. 'Less. And she still calls her father Daddy. Listen to this. *Since Daddy's day, sadly, there have been lesser standards in judging behaviour.*'

When I read the memoir myself, back in the London flat, I could see it was the writing of a colonised mind: exactly the intellect Virginia Woolf complained of in women: cautious, conventional, looking over its shoulder: that deadly style of avoiding opinion and when forced into it, backing everything with authoritative quotation. A nice style for a quintessentially English rendition of the perfect family. Everything covered up. *Nice*. That innocuous word the English use to conceal their real thoughts and fears and feelings. Not a whisper of conflict, dissent, ambivalence, thwarted hopes. Instead there are plenty of jolly good times: Christmas plays, happy holidays, evening reading. Even the 'loss' of a brother, blasted to smithereens in the war, is dealt with nicely. The only hint of emotion is kept for her father, a once eminent psychiatrist who was tipped out of a prestigious London clinic for his anti-Freudianism.* The Asp's scorn for Freud, her belief in substance rather than the unconscious, self-control rather than sexuality, is presented as a matter of family loyalty held across the full span of the twentieth century. It is not a

----

* By an extraordinary coincidence, while correcting the galleys of this book, I saw a letter from Stella Bowen to Ford Madox Ford in which she tells Ford she had taken their daughter Julie to see a doctor. The doctor was the Asp's father. When Stella and Julie arrived in London from France in the mid-thirties, Julie found it difficult to settle to English language, routine and, in particular, to an English school. Ford, who hadn't lived with them since 1926, was complaining that Stella was not bringing her up properly. Stella's letter to Ford, taking him up on this point, includes the information that she had taken Julie to this eminent doctor, the Asp's father, for a thorough physical and psychological examination. Even a man as conservative as he could see that the girl was suffering nothing more serious than adjustment to a new language and a new school. That of course could be serious enough.

voice that belongs to a modern world. Reading it, it was as if, bewildered and nostalgic, she understood life no more in retirement than she had as a child during one war, or as a young woman who served in the next which was to claim the life of her beloved brother.

'I don't believe a word of it,' Clara said. 'All that niceness. And do you know why not? Look! I'll show you.'

She passed me the book open at a fuzzy photograph of a handsome, rather androgynous looking young woman in full climbing gear standing astride a mountain peak.

'That's her,' Clara said. 'In 1932. On the Rimfischhorn. She was a climber. A real serious climber. She and her brother, they climbed the Grépon, the Matterhorn, the Aiguille. They *picnicked* on the Mer de Glace. All through the thirties she was climbing. And then by the time the war starts she's down here at this dump of a place with arthritis so bad she can't get to the winterbourne.'

'What happened?' I said. 'What could have happened?'

'You'll never find out now,' Clara said. 'She's well and truly dead.'

'I wonder what her father made of it,' I said. 'A daughter with arthritis.'

'He'd have been the cause of it,' Clara said, 'hooking her in like that.'

'But there must have been something in her that was rebelling. She must have been striving for something, that kind of climbing's not easy. And it's certainly not safe.'

'She might have been competing with him,' Clara said. 'Proving herself against her brother.'

'Look at her,' I said. 'What a strong, handsome girl she was.'

'Something happened,' Clara said. 'She'd lost that strength within a few years of that photo. Think of it. Not much older than me. Ettie goes on about calling ourselves wife or mistress. But imagine at thirty calling yourself a schoolmistress.'

'Especially one of that sort,' I said.

'The question that puzzles me,' Clara said, 'is why did she hate Frances Petersen and Hannah Morgan? And you? Why not the girls who played sports, did all the things she couldn't do?'

'She loved them,' I said. 'She used to laugh at their jokes. I suppose Frances and Hannah must have reminded her of some wounded possibility in herself. What else?'

'That,' Clara said. 'Or that she couldn't control you, and resented your capacity to withdraw into yourselves.'

Or was it our loathing of her she reacted to? Adolescents can, and do, bring violent antagonisms to bear on the adult world; they try to escape its grasp even as they reach out to take what it offers. None of us, not even the good girls and the sporty girls had the least interest in the Asp and her life and how she might feel. Which of us knew she'd climbed the great peaks of Europe or cared that her joints ached? We looked at the photo in pride of place on the mantelpiece above the fire that ate the valentine cards and imagined in that soft-focus uniformed young man a fiance lost in the first world war. Now I realise that she was much too young for a lover from that war, and the photo has to have been of her brother killed in the next. None of us, except perhaps Thea Linton with her evening cups of tea with the Asp, had any idea about her life and her being. And none of us cared. To us she might as well have been a hundred years old, or five hundred; even now it takes an effort of mind to realise that when I was first in her charge she wasn't much over fifty. Through the lens of our youth she was ancient, sexless, a cypher to our needs, there to serve or obstruct us. Even the good girls were responding to the prestige of the one who makes the rules; even they concealed, dissembled, mocked. Those of us who fell into disfavour were sullen, hostile, ungiving.

With Hannah the Asp's anger was directed against the violin to which she gave her first allegiance. The muffled sound of chords, filled with grief and perplexed self-pity, could be heard from beneath the door of the linen cupboard. But it didn't save her. The linen cupboard door flew open. 'Downstairs,' Thea Linton would bark, and Hannah, red-eyed already (she didn't have the stamina of Frances), was marched down, first to the Asp, and then to stand in disgrace and on display in the hall.

Upstairs, Frances lay low on the top shelf behind her barricades of blankets. Her crime was no greater than that she preferred to read. She did not join the games, she did not watch the matches, she did not dance the reels. Wherever she went she took a book. She was unobtrusive about it, but insistent. In her talks after Sunday lunch, the Asp would point to Frances Petersen as an example of the pride that should be understood as shame. Even this Frances bore, standing as the Asp spoke, a warning to us all. I only ever saw her cry once, and it was not in the house.

Had it not been for the garden, my own passage through school may well have been uneventful, marked by nothing more than the quietly dismal misery shared by many English children separated too soon from their mothers, and lacking a predilection for team sports. The Asp was not particularly kind to me, but until that last summer when the garden flowered in its full glory, she did not mark me out.

By my second summer at Carn I had taken over the whole of the garden bed that was set aside for the girls, and tending it gave reason to the day when I woke each morning. I designed it not in strips but in tiers that let light in to the plants that grew in the shade of the hedge. I planted in bands of colour, picking up the blues and yellows at the southern edge, carrying them into the creams, pinks and reds that blended into the dark greens and maroons which flourished in the shade by the kitchen door. My taste ran in the blue range to cat mint, lavender, lupins, Michaelmas daisies, and of course delphiniums, offset by the yellow of daisies, chrysanthemums, and the white of lillies. For the reds I chose phlox, columbine, roses, pinks and one magnificent peony. The centrepiece, slightly more than a third of the way back from the sunny southern edge, mediating blue to creamy yellow, was the white delphiniums. They grew tall and generous, a glistening white that caught the sun and reflected it back to the foxgloves which thrived in their company.

Sometimes the good girls came out to look. I'd see their legs through the hedge and round they'd come, flapping like dark birds, boasting and joking. Or they'd stand and watch without comment, and then, as they turned to go, they'd ask if I wanted to revise with them, or practise tennis, or reels, or reading aloud. I'd say *no, thanks, I'll just finish digging these delphiniums in*, and they'd run off, raising their arms like fluttering wings, their brown shoes spitting up gravel on the path, their voices twittering along the top of the hedge, and it was only later when I went into the house myself that I remembered their human origin. They too must have had inner lives, secret desires, longings for solitude and expression, painful reticences; but at the time I disregarded them, for life held more for me in the drops of water that gathered in the flowers than anything that occurred inside the walls of that house.

By the third summer there was shape to the garden, and by the fourth it had sloughed off the traces of its organised beginnings. The tiers were no longer tiers, but moved as a single entity; the colours blended with the assurance of a complex palette. Visitors vied in their praise for their favoured plants. Sid would insist on the delphiniums. Big Miss Rose preferred the peony. The prefects cut roses for the bowl on their windowsill.

At speech day that fourth summer, while mothers and aunts ate strawberries on the front lawn and talked to the teachers in their best hats, Frances and I took our fathers with their glasses of wine to see the garden. By a quirk of good luck Sid, who'd been on the gate in his best suit, was there with his sister who lived in the town and sometimes sent cuttings from her garden.

Sid shook my father's hand, and said he was real proud.

'It's beautiful, Miss,' he said.

'It really is,' my father said. 'Gertrude Jekyll couldn't have done better herself.'

'It's not often that those seeds germinate,' Frances'

father said, enquiring of Sid the temperature of the green house and the type of loam we used. 'You're clever girls,' he said, raising his glass to Frances and me. 'Your lives are a joy to witness.'

The tears that lay like a great lake in me did not spill over. Perhaps like the chalky earth beneath our feet, they had dried with a summer that had brought such profusion of growth and colour.

That summer, as it turned out my last at Carn, when the garden reached its peak and I was to sit my 'O' levels, the days dawned one after another dry and clear. Each morning, day after day, the sky stretched above us taut as a dome that had faded by evening to a pale gaseous blue. The sun touched everything that lay beneath it with a golden light. Sid helped me rig up a hose from the back of the house, and when the bans began, Frances and I carried buckets of washing-up water that Leah kept for us after lunch. The chalk under the soil was friable, and in the fields the grass turned brown; the little trough of the winterbourne was visible only as a dusty indentation where seeds and insect shells gathered, blown there by the puffs of wind that were all that disturbed the hills of Wessex that hot June term.

Letty would come over from Holme and sit on the grass and talk, or read aloud from the books we were to be examined on. Sometimes she'd lie back and, as if the air itself was affected by the garden, she'd breathe deeply and say not that it was beautiful, but that it was peaceful. The upper windows of the house caught the evening sun, and as we were unable to see through them against that shining light, we felt ourselves to be safe, out of sight, out of reach. On the other side of the hedge a window-sash moved, a door opened, a piano ran through its scales, a voice called out; but we remained in a pearly peace, never suspecting that there were eyes that could see us as clearly as through the sights of a gun.

Flushed out of the linen cupboard by the hot afternoon sun, Frances would sit on the grass with Letty whose comforting chatter needed no reply. With Frances she had a knack of asking the questions no Perceval girl would dare to broach: she'd ask about her father, and how her mother had died, and was it true she had to stand in disgrace while everyone else ate? And as if Letty's great rolling talking thoughts were catching, like tunes played on the harmonica, Frances spilled over with words: tales of her fairy mother, who'd carried her through forests and across rivers on expeditions with her father before she died of a fever in the middle of the night; the teas that her aunts made for her birthdays with cakes on china pedestal plates, and the paintings in their studio that smelt of turps and oil pushed back against the wall so that children could play pass the parcel and blind man's bluff; her father working late at night while she slept in the lamplight. And sometimes she spoke with such furies you could scarcely believe your ears, and the Asp's, if the saying was true, would have felt hers scorch. Still fuming with furious adjectives, she'd spread out her cardigan, lie down and deliver herself up to the sky. Letty would wait quietly, and I'd keep on in the garden, and Henrietta and Hannah would come and go, and after what seemed the distance of sleep, Frances would be amongst us again, quiet and still.

At the end of that summer, not long before the exams, Letty made a daisy chain. I remember she tried to put it over Frances' head, but it was too short. Then she tried it on mine where it rested like a crown.

'She won't let you keep it,' Frances said, and at first I thought she meant Letty and the daisy chain; but of course she meant the Asp.

'Why not?' I said, standing back to admire the garden that had brought me from child to the brink of woman.

'Why not?' I said. 'She can't undo it now. Everything's growing.'

'You should be prepared,' Frances said.

Although the pitch of her voice should have warned me, it did nothing to ward off the shock I felt like a knife, when, a few days later the Asp asked to see me after lunch.

'Well now,' the Asp said when I had crossed the vast wastes of her room and was perched beside her on the seat beneath the open window. Outside I could hear Sid's mower, humming gently along the lawn in its rhythmic turn and turn around. 'What have you to say about your garden?'

I had nothing to say. It was she, with her gruff cavernous voice, who wished to speak. My selfishness, she said, had been overlooked until now, but did I not think about the girls coming next year, should they wish to garden. No girl, she said, had ever assumed she could take over the whole bed. I was drawing attention to myself. Had I considered that? Should I not spend more time with my friends, with my classmates in house activities. Was I preparing to audition for a part in next year's school play? Did I not think of others left to man the teams without my support? Was I not ashamed at my discourtesy to girls whom I did not join in reels, madrigals, hikes? Did I think of no one but myself?

What preparations was I making for the exams? Did I not think of my father and the results he would expect? And how would I be of any help to my mother if this was my attitude? Had I not considered that she would need my help during the holidays?

There was nothing the Asp did not know. There were no depths of self-reproach she could not plumb for me. Must I be taught to take my place? she asked. It would seem that I must. I was not to return to the garden until the exams were finished. Meanwhile she had instructed Sid to dig up the garden and have it prepared for the junior girls next year.

Forcing myself to speak, I asked if I could keep one strip, just one strip for the delphiniums?

'You've had quite enough garden for one girl,' she said.

In the extremity of that moment I saw her with a kind of photographic intensity: the open pores on her great beak of a nose, the deep furrows down to her mouth, hands twisted with her disease, her tension, her disappointment, her incarceration. The sun coming though the window glistened on her mottled skin and caught the fine hairs that had escaped the net that clamped the sculpted roll of curls in place. All this I saw as if she were carved in wood, and I was the one with age and understanding. I never looked at her again. Thereafter I spoke to her sleeve, the hem of her dress. She had put a powerful curse on me.

The exams started the next week. And so did the rain. It smashed its way through the trees, knocking the candles off the chestnuts and flattening the lettuces in the kitchen garden. It hissed and spat on the paths as we ran between the school buildings and the house. I used it as a way of avoiding Sid, dashing past him with a mac held over my head. It wasn't until after the last weekend of term when the exams were over and the weather had cleared as suddenly as it had broken, that we spoke. Frances and I met him as we were making our way back to school from one last illicit walk.

We had been to the winterbourne. Although it was only days before the rescue of the school train, our mood was sombre as we crossed the ford and walked up the hill. There was no sign of life at Holme Farm. A small boy eating an apple; sounds of a radio from an open window; doors shutting; nothing else. There were flowers, germinated by the rain, growing thick along the course of the winterbourne. We traced its glorious path up from the bottom of the slope where it met the flowing river in a burst of water buttercups, all the way to its source. At the top, a damp indentation where tiny orchids grew among the anemones, we lay on the grass and watched the pale wisps of cloud that floated above us.

'I wonder if anyone will love me?' Frances said.

'I love you,' I said turning sideways to look at her. Tears were trickling into her hair.

'Don't be daft,' she said, still turned to the sky. 'You don't count.'

'You got a valentine card,' I said.

'He shouldn't have sent it,' she said. 'It's ruined everything.'

'Is that why you didn't want to stop at Holme Farm?'

'Don't,' she said, propping herself up on her elbow. 'I'll be a prefect next year. It'll be different. We won't be able to come out like this.'

Our eyes were level with each other. For a moment I thought she was going to lean forward and kiss me.

'Let's go on up the ridge,' she said, brushing down her dress, but the day was hazy and even from the top we couldn't see far. There was nothing to the west but empty hills. Behind us the town was hidden in the milky vapour rising up from the woods, the hedges, the streams. We were bolted to the ground as surely as if the Asp had put chains around our ankles, and were we not, we would surely have lifted up into the afternoon air and drifted over those hills where Tess had been seduced and abandoned, and made our escape.

As we came back into school, we met Sid in the lane outside the garden gate. He was pushing his wheelbarrow up the path to his cottage. The white delphiniums, carefully dug out, were lying limp against its boards.

'I'm real sorry,' Sid said. 'Real sorry.' Though we walked right up to him and he put the barrow down, it was as if I heard him from the bottom of a very deep sea. 'I'll find good homes for everything,' he said, 'and keep the plants together. I'll put some of them in the bed beside the gym, they won't attract attention there but you and me'll know they look good. I'm taking the best ones home with me,' he said indicating the wheelbarrow. 'And my sister Delia, the one who gave you them lupins, she says . . .'

I ran, abandoning Frances who was so soon to abandon me, crossing the line that would give her a place in the prefects' room. And abandoning Sid. Anything rather than hear the offer he was surely making, that I could visit his garden, and his sister Delia would be there for propriety's sake. I didn't want to hear what I knew I could never accept, and his kindness was more painful to me than the frank brutalities the Asp handed out from her eyrie on the windowseat.

PART THREE

The Dream

In the month after I had visited Carn, I dreamed a series of dreams. Some were fleeting; I'd wake with the edge of an image, a skirt disappearing up some stairs, a window opening, mist rolling in from the west. Others stayed with me as full and detailed narratives.

I dreamed that Miss Dorothea Linton had died. I was in the house, in Perceval. Perhaps I was Mrs Glassop, certainly I was an adult and in some relationship of responsiblity to the girls. I was not a girl, though girlness was close to me and I understood it. Perhaps this can be explained by the fact that Clara had drawn for me a long line of girls in white nightdresses, some holding their eyes in little saucers on the desks that were lined before them. I had this drawing pinned beside my bed. In the dream there was a lot of running around, agitation amongst the adults, details about how Miss Linton's arms had tingled, and the numbness had stretched into them before she collapsed. She had, the dream said, already had a small attack before I arrived, and this one occurred after I had seen her in her study. *Dear Thea*, the spinsters said and held her hand, their plaid skirts stiff and awkward as they bent towards her, their bony fingers stretched with the strain of lifting her, their faces pale and powdery, flaking as they wiped each other's brows. *Dear Thea*, the spinsters said, *Dear Miss Linton*, as she lay on the ground, her empty veins hardening, well beyond their reach. Amongst the girls of this dream there was lightness and quick movement; they moved as if a choreographer had arranged them, though I do not think the choreographer was me; they were not playing their brutal games, but floating, dancing, rising as if on the tide or swell of a sea.

In another dream I was walking up a steep bank, holding onto the railing so as not to lose my footing. But instead of reaching Sid's cottage, the path climbed and climbed as if to a volcano. Ash was on the path, sulphur in the air and deep rumblings could be heard from the earth below. As I climbed I met groups of girls coming back down the hill with mistresses hurrying back. *Turn back*, they said. *Turn back, it is not safe. Listen*, they said, cocking their ears and covering their faces as the volcano roared and spewed around us. But there was no volcano, only a battered cauldron in which a liquid substance, a metallic yellowy substance was bubbling. It had no odour at all.

In another the Asp sat up in bed dressed as a wolf with a pretty white bonnet on her head. In another the grounds were covered in white delphiniums and the girls laid down their arms: shiny swords, silver-tipped arrows, and suits of armour were piled on the seats under the chestnut trees. In another Sid wheeled school books away in a barrow. In another Henrietta and Hannah floated in the winterbourne, like twin Ophelias with chalk dust for blossom in their hair.

During my working hours I sat at my desk in the ugly London flat two blocks from the school where police cars were known to park outside during recess. At the top of the page I wrote *Carn* as title and intention. Underneath, not a word.

The Lunch

A week before I was to leave London, with still not a word written of Carn, a friend called Jane Carey rang. She was looking for Louise who was in London briefly for a conference. She suggested we all have lunch in Hampstead. Jane is not Australian, though it is through Louise, and through Australia where she worked for a while, that I know her; and against all the evidence – that I see her more often in London where she lives and I visit, than in Sydney where I live and she sometimes visits – she belongs in the antipodean compartment of my life. It wouldn't have occurred to me to mention the problems I was having with Carn, had it not been that after lunch the three of us set off to visit the Freud Museum. We had eaten in a light and airy restaurant of the sort you would expect in Sydney rather than in London. It was a crisp mid-winter afternoon, dry and not unpleasant, so we decided to walk.

'Come this way,' Jane said, cutting through to Fitzjohn Avenue. 'I'll take you past my old school.'

'I always forget you grew up here,' I said.

'Exactly here,' she said. 'I walked up this road every day of school until I was twelve.'

'I didn't know you were Catholic,' Louise said, looking at the school's heavy brickwork and plaster statuary.

'I wasn't,' she said. 'But it was a good school, and close. I was only there until twelve, and then I was sent off to a C of E school out in the country.'

'I went to one of those,' I said. 'Ghastly.'

'Mine wasn't,' Jane said. 'I loved it.'

'It can't have been Carn,' I said, as a joke, though of course it was no joke and what would you expect, given what was on my mind.

'Carn!' Jane Carey said.

'Carn!' Louise said, for Clara and I had both told her the story.

'Carn!' I said. All of us said, standing there in the street where we were to turn off for Maresfield Gardens.

'Carn!' we said, our heads turning to each other from the bleak gardens we passed, and bare trees. 'Carn!' we said, all the way to the Freud Museum. Jane Carey had gone to Carn! Not only that, but she had been one of the Asp's most golden girls.

'Are you sure it was the same school?' Louise said, looking from one to the other of us.

Jane Carey had been head girl of Carn the year before I arrived. She left as I came. The reason I had not remembered her name was that she was not a Perceval girl. Her association with the Asp came through the school. As well as Perceval's housemistress, the Asp was also history mistress; and Jane Carey, her star pupil, won a scholarship to read history at the Asp's old college. She was her shining success, the inheritor of the flame, a hand into the future. Her years at Carn, Jane said, still standing in the street outside the house where the exiled Freud had come to die, *were bathed in a golden light. Nothing has ever quite measured up to it since.*

'My memories are all of summer,' she said. 'The chestnuts in flower, the slow ping and thud of tennis balls, the smell of cut grass, those winter walks into the hills.'

'The winterbourne?' I asked.

'The winterbourne was a Perceval craze,' she said. 'I never saw it run.'

'Did you see it flower?' I asked.

'No,' she said. 'I don't think I did. In the summer I stayed around the school; it was always so pleasant lying about in the grounds, playing tennis, reading.'

Jane Carey: a good girl, a gooder than good girl she must have been to be chosen as head girl. Nothing about her conformed to my assumptions about the fate of good Carn girls. I imagined them all married to solicitors if they hadn't managed diplomats, part of the great unknowing complacency of the British middle class: crimped and pinched and putting on a good show. And there was Jane Carey, a woman who sails along the street on long legs, who would in her youth have spurned the vanity of watching herself in the reflection of shop windows, but might now catch a glimpse and not be displeased. There is nothing about Jane Carey that is crimped. On the contrary, she is a woman of expansive intellect and compassionate humour. So extreme was the unlikelihood of this connection, this sudden coincidence, that it might never have been discovered had it not been for the weather, and the proximity of the restaurant to our destination: the Freud Museum, into which we went.

In the large room on the right-hand side of the hall, running the length of the house from front to back, is Freud's study and consulting room, recreated as he left it. Apart from the couch, which has an obvious luminosity, and the desk with its sepulchral chair and tell-tale spectacles left resting on the page, the most striking aspect of the room is the clutter of antiques: busts, heads, vases, fragments of fresco, tiny statues crammed onto every surface. Over and over again feminine images of the siren, the sphinx: source of mystery and riddle of the unconscious.

'A powerful image,' I said as we looked at a sphinx, 'not one we grew up with.'

'But limiting as well,' Jane said. 'It projects the feminine as mysterious and wise, but cuts her off from the political world of the here and now, from the historical, the economic.'

'Our Carn inheritance,' I said.

'Yes,' she said. 'There's something there of value. In amongst all the rest. The trouble begins when thinking gets divorced from feeling. And it certainly did, and not only for girls like you.'

'The Asp's father was a psychiatrist,' I said. 'A dedicated anti-Freudian.'

'I know,' Jane said. 'I read that little book she wrote. There were copies at the funeral.'

'You went?' I said. 'What was it like?'

'It was one of those perfect Carn days,' she said. 'Early summer. You know, the abbey glowing in sunlight, the gardens a mass of blossom. England at its best.'

'Its BBC best,' I said.

'Quite,' she said, and laughed. 'Anyway, we walked

up to the school after the service. There was a party at Perceval. Everyone was there.'

'I wasn't,' I said.

Jane Carey put her hand on my shoulder.

'I didn't mean that,' she said. 'What I mean is all the ones I remember. Lots of Perceval girls. Stella was there. You'd remember her. Henrietta must have been your age. And Georgia. Do you remember Georgia?'

'Is she still beautiful?' I asked.

'She seemed old to me, with too much make-up,' Jane said. 'But glamorous in a flamboyant sort of way. Her daughter's there now and she's as pleased as anything Thea's in charge. She doesn't approve of this business with the boys' school and watches the poor girl like a hawk. She remembers what she got up to when we weren't allowed near. I said maybe it's less exciting, less enticing, now it's allowed. *Now what's allowed?* she said, looking at me sharply. She told Stella she was having an affair with someone in the government. *In the ministry*, she said in one of her stage whispers.'

'Maybe Thea's right after all,' I said. 'And some girls will always be silly.'

We laughed. An open-throated sort of laugh.

Louise said that to hear us talk it was as if Carn was a novel. Full of characters and landscapes and mad divergent narrators. The place, the buildings, the hills, the winterbourne: all this she could see, but for the rest it was as strange as a film spliced together from the reels of different directors. The stories we inhabited, and that inhabited us, did not match in the slightest regard; and yet because our association in the present is one of compatibility, even affinity, the bizarre extremity of our

Carn experience led not to positions that needed
defending but to a sudden expansion that was as much
of the heart as it was of the mind. The shock threw
into doubt the thinking I'd done during the weeks since
the visit. Doubt entered emotion that had been fixed
for years. It sat alongside it, rocking it, unsettling it,
freeing it. Like water flushing out the stagnant pools
when a river runs again after drought.

Because I had scores to settle, I had cast everything
about that school, and therefore my growing up,
through the lens of failure. Stories that Clara pressed
me to elaborate, told in the service of a subsequent
exile. But in Jane Carey I was face to face with the
benign aspect of a complex inheritance that has formed
me as surely as have the wounds it dealt. The connection she and I made as adults in Sydney, on the other
side of the world and light years from Carn, yet owing
to Carn, was based on intellectual recognition, the
capacity each of us has to think from more than one
angle.

'Don't give Carn all the credit,' Jane Carey said. 'It's
not a clearcut inheritance. There have been times when
I've felt it like a chain and collar.'

'But you loved it,' I said.

'The education of girls,' Louise said, 'seems to produce equivocal results.'

Were we the beneficiaries of the education Virginia
Woolf had pleaded for? We had learned Greek; there
was nothing in our brothers' classrooms that was not
in ours. Were we the ones on whom generations of
women had pinned their hopes? Were we the ones who

would step fearlessly into the world of ideas and decisions and power?

Virginia Woolf proclaimed herself undereducated, and though she grew up counting on her fingers, it was hardly true. She learned Greek with Janet Case, literature and history with her father. What rankled with her was that she was denied the schools and colleges that were granted to her brothers. But we should not underestimate her education, far less her capabilities, and the inheritance she has left. Precisely because her education was outside the great institutions, one could say, she became the writer she was, with a mind not untrained but untrammelled. Her fiction, her essays, everything she wrote, break with the expected, get rid of the consecutive, refuse division and exclusion, and present us with moments of shock, pleasure, understanding. She was an elitist through and through, and she was a snob. This she dressed up in her plea for the education of girls and there was indeed gross inequity on which to base it. That debate has been won, more or less, but do not let us forget that schools like Carn are precisely what she was arguing for in a polemic against the inheritance her brothers had stepped unthinkingly into. But was it what she wanted? Did she want women in the Whitehall through which she walked so resentfully, clicking in and clicking out, as she put it, at once part of the culture, and outside it. She wanted women to have access to the great world of being and thinking. That's what she wanted, and while it might mean women in the Foreign Office and at the bar, and almost certainly does, the flexibility of mind she admired and herself possessed, was, as she very well knew, a matter of a great deal more than that sort of education.

Standing in the Freud Museum talking to Jane Carey and Louise about the terms of a fully lived and fully feminine intellectual life, I was grateful suddenly for those generations of women stretching back a hundred years, and their fight for our education. Looking at Freud's antiquities I was grateful that we were taught Greek. But all of us agreed that we don't just learn Greek and step into shoes kindly vacated by our brothers, or little extra shoes laid alongside. If we do it's at our peril, and the price is a loss we do not recognise. The gain is a discipline of mind that should not be undervalued. The loss, it seemed to us that afternoon, was represented by the figures of the sirens and sphinxes that filled Freud's room: the repressed feminine that our culture denies. Our un-English, feminine waywardness.

'If you don't recognise the loss,' Louise said, 'you're spared the pain. But you're also spared the mess and toil of life.'

'It lives on,' Jane said, 'that loss. I see it in the faces of my patients. A sort of ghostly presence.'

When I left Carn, I left and that was that. Or so I thought. I met Frances Petersen in London shortly before I left the country. We had lunch near the LSE, and very little to say to each other. Letty wrote a few times but nothing came of the correspondence. Henrietta was killed. As for the Asp, I never saw her again. I never heard from her, or of her. Carn was baggage I left gratefully behind. I used the skills that it had taught me, but so successfully did I detach them from the environment in which they were acquired, that I acted as if they were mine alone.

Jane Carey, on the other hand, was still getting letters from the Asp at fifty; which wouldn't have been so bad had they not been so critical. The Asp never approved Jane's defection, as she saw it, from the pure discipline of history to the *pseudo-science* of psychoanalysis. And although Jane's writing always includes the historical, a hallmark of her work and reputation, for the Asp it was sullied; she could not forget Jane's early promise which had – this is my surmise - become invested with her own forgotten promise. Every time Jane Carey wrote, or spoke on the radio, the Asp would invariably read, or hear her, and the very next day she was at her desk. *My dear Janey,* she would write, *I was surprised to see . . .* She would criticise Jane's choice of subject, Jane's choice of words; she would lament the waste of Jane's talents. The letter would end, just as invariably, with an invitation – no, a command – to lunch at the University Women's Club on her next visit to London. And Jane would go; and the Asp would order sherry, and chuckle in delight at the prospect of having Jane *all to herself,* and a bottle of wine over lunch. She, the Asp, though retired on a schoolteacher's pension, would insist on paying. Her arthritic old hands reached out to embrace her still golden pupil as they parted. 'Dear girl,' she said, watching from the steps until Jane had disappeared across the square.

'The last straw,' Jane Carey said, 'was a few years ago, just after my fiftieth birthday when she wrote a scorcher about a discussion she'd heard on the radio: you know the sort of thing, feminism twenty-five years on, sex and personal morality. I was taking a fairly considered line, I thought, a post-AIDS commitment-if-you-can sort of line, none of the seventies nonsense we used to get on with. Positively proper. Carn-ish, in fact. The Asp's letter began, *My dear Janey, I was shocked to see you've reduced yourself to trading personal information over the air waves.* And so on for a page. *Mere lucre,* that sort of thing. I was furious and fired back a letter the same day saying it had to stop. And no, I couldn't go to lunch at the University Women's Club because I'd be in Berlin on the date she suggested at a symposium on the orgasm. It was naughty of me. But really!'

Louise bellowed with pleasure and mirth. 'This school,' she said. 'One trembles! What a relief to be a colonial.'

'They exported the prototype,' we said.

'Not to country high schools, they didn't,' she said. 'We did our lessons and that was that. We all went home at half past three even if it was a long bus-ride.'

'I felt awful, of course,' Jane Carey said, 'because she had that fall shortly afterwards and couldn't have come up to London anyway. I felt mean. And I heard from Thea, she wrote me a note, saying the Asp was distressed and kept asking *do you think Janey will forgive me?* So of course I wrote. I even said I'd go down and see her. But she died before I could. Poor old girl.'

With this story, told as we were leaving the Freud Museum, I felt my loathing of the Asp, that dogged ancient hatred I'd lumbered round the world with me, loosen, if not like a skin shucked off and gone entirely, then at least soften so that it was less scratchy to wear. There was no longer any animus. There never was a curse. Just an empty sort of sorrow as if at last by seeing the nature of her stringy old heart, a hard core of resistance in me loosened, not just my skin, but a loosening and a lifting of the spirit. But it may only have been the effect of the wind for it was late afternoon by the time we parted, and chill, that wind coming up the steps from the Finchley Road.

'If you look at the two of us,' Jane Carey said as we turned to leave, 'you could say that you've come off best.' And then, over her shoulder, as an afterthought. 'You should write to Frances Petersen.'

My time in London was not composed entirely of Carn. The last week rushed by in a round that had no thought to that particular past. Clara had gone on to New York leaving me with boxes to add to my own shipping back to Australia. Louise was trying to do too much in too little time. I had family and friends to take my leave of. I filed Carn away for consideration from the safer distance of Australia. Then, the morning before I left, Jane Carey rang to say goodbye, and to tell me one last story. *A cautionary tale,* she said.

In the early seventies she had written to the Dame asking if she could come down for a visit as she wanted to write a piece for a series the *New Statesman* was running by people on the left revisiting their old schools.

'I was perfectly frank,' Jane said. 'I didn't conceal my intention in the slightest. I was young and full of bluster, and wrote saying I was coming down to expose the iniquity of such privilege and the damage it does to individual expression. So on and so forth. The Dame wrote back at once saying *Dear Janey, Of course you must come. Do stay at the Lodge. We'll ask Miss Stuart Parker to dinner. Who else would you like to see? Let me know the time of your train and I'll meet you.*'

'Gosh,' I said, trying to imagine the Dame in a situation as mundane, as ordinary, as human, as meeting a train.

'I got on the train full of myself,' Jane said, 'with the article half written in my head and a pile of scandalous books to drive home my point. Shulamith Firestone I seem to remember. Anyway, it was a warm drizzly day in the middle of the summer term, everything was pale except the dog roses in flower all along the railway line. As we came into Carn I could see the Dame on the platform. She hurried down the platform towards me, took my bag and insisted on carrying it.'

'She carried your bag?' I said. 'Over the footbridge?'

'She insisted,' Jane said. 'Opened the boot and put it in next to her shopping.'

'Shopping?' I said, reduced to the exclamation mark of repetition. 'What had she bought?'

'I can't remember,' Jane said. 'Ordinary things. You know, shopping like anyone else. Washing-up liquid. Onions. That sort of thing.'

'And what happened?'

'I had a pleasant day, mostly sitting in the Dame's drawing room reading.'

'Shulamith Firestone?' I said.

'No, something off her shelves,' she said. 'Hardy, I think. I had a bit of a prowl round the school. Spoke to some of the staff, some girls. And that night we had dinner. The Dame cooked. It was all very delicious and civilised, and I remembered why I had liked growing up in the company of these women with their strong intellectual identities and resolute lives. We talked about the school, and what other old girls were doing, a bit about my work at the Institute and why I'd moved from history which the Dame at any rate seemed to understand, a bit about biography which was the Asp's great love. We even hedged around feminism. The Asp was surprisingly on side. Said it was time *girls took the reins*, but she didn't like all this emphasis on sex, she thought it diverting apart from anything else. *One would rather see a woman at Number 10,* she said. But there was no mention of my article for the *New Statesman*. Not a word. Not so much as a raised eyebrow. It'd have felt indecent for me to mention it, and I didn't.'

'Did you write it?' I asked.

'Not a word,' she said. 'I never wrote a word. I went back to London and sat at my desk. How could I write about them after that? I couldn't bridge the distance between Carn and how I was with them, and all those expectations and silences, and what I knew them to be, good women – and the London where I lived and worked and practised. The London that made everything about Carn seem obscene, grotesque, a last bastion of privilege, women in the service of a culture that wanted its ruling-class women either complicit or silenced. All that. I was stymied by the gap.'

'I'm not surprised,' I said. 'I can't even manage a letter to Frances Petersen.'

'Why ever not?' Jane asked.

'I don't know her address,' I said.

'You know which university she's at,' Jane said.

'It was an old magazine,' I said.

'It can be forwarded on,' she said.

'I think I'm afraid,' I said.

'What of?' Jane said.

'Of disturbing her. Of opening up the past,' I said. 'After all she doesn't even live here.'

'Now you sound like them,' Jane said. 'Afraid to disturb the settled surface. It may be that because you went away you're best able to tell the story. I was thinking that last night. The clarity of distance.'

'Of exile,' I said.

'Of freedom,' she said. 'A sort of freedom. You and Frances Petersen. Come on,' she said. 'You're making me sound like head girl again.'

She hung up after plans had been made for her next visit south of the earth's bulge, leaving me to contemplate the chortling nature of her laugh, my wayward packing and the still blank page. I put on my coat and walked up to the post office for an airmail envelope and stamp.

The Letter

'How extraordinary!' Frances wrote. 'I was in Sydney a few years ago, and I'd heard you were living there, or at any rate in Australia. I looked you up in the phone book but I couldn't be sure what name you'd use. There was no one listed with the right initial and anyway I wasn't even sure if you'd welcome a call. I'm glad you took the risk. How strange it is to know so little of someone one once knew so much. The linen cupboard. Of course I remember. You used to make yourself completely invisible under an eiderdown. I don't think Thea ever had any idea. She probably thought you were in the garden. When I didn't ring you in Sydney, I thought well anyway she's probably living out in the country amid lilac and wattle. I could imagine how Australia's spiky plants would add to your repertoire. Do you suppose the delphiniums still flower at Sid's cottage? Would anyone have collected their seeds? I like to think they have. You see, I'm quite the sentimentalist. My father brought me up to be a scientist, to observe things as they are, not dream about how they might be. Maybe that's what made Carn easier for me. I like to think I shrugged it off.

'So the Asp is dead. Well. No sentimentality there, though I confess myself moved (a little) by the image of her asking if Janey had forgiven her. But then I thought, the manipulative old crone, still at it from beyond the grave. You're right, it must have been a wretched life watching generation after generation of golden girls leave and slip from her grasp; but don't give her too much credit. The damage that was done to her doesn't cancel out the assaults she made on us, even if they did come from her own cramped nature. I won't forgive easily. And I won't go back, there'd be no point. For you there seems to have been some ambivalence. For me there was nothing.

'By the way, I agree with you, Carn was grey, grey, grey. But Janey Carey: now there's a different matter. *She* was bathed in a golden glow. She was head girl when I arrived. I remember my first prayers in that ghastly ornate assembly hall, and she was up on the podium. It must have been a trick of the light or something, but I remember her blazing and luminous, drawing in the whole school, as if she wore a halo. She did have very fair hair which caught the light. I was a new girl; I'd probably have seen halos anywhere. Though I can't say I ever spotted one anywhere near Thea Linton. Yes, I know she's headmistress. I bumped into Stella once in Harrods, where I'd taken my aged aunts as a treat, and she told me. 'Can you imagine,' she said. 'Well that's scotched any idea of putting my girls down for Carn.' She told me you were in Australia, and no longer married. That's how I knew.

'I know about Holme Farm too. But not from Stella. From Ken. Remember him? The valentine card? I used to see him in London when I was at the LSE. He was in one of those very right-on left groups. We went out a few times, even to bed once or twice; but somehow that awful history hung between us and he'd be aggressive as if he could make it all up by possessing me, but he could never believe I wasn't ashamed, just being in the street with him. It was hopeless. But we remained friends of sorts. He runs a youth centre in Brixton and is married to rather a nice black girl. He writes strange elliptical letters. He says Carn's a good place to get out of and why have another generation of kids grow up at the farm to be looked at by the toffs and taught their station. So the sentimentality about Holme Farm is yours, I'm afraid. Leah is married. She lives in the north and has six kids. Her husband is a rich man, Ken says, a farmer, richer than I'll ever be, Ken says. She wanted to send the girls – there are four of them – to Carn. A sort of equalising. I think she wanted to swan into Thea Linton's study and say, *Well now headmistress, this really will not do.* And give the girls a chance. But Ken says she didn't. When it came down to it, she couldn't be so cruel. He says it's only the upper classes who think it's all right to send their kids away. For other people it happens out of desperation and failure. So Leah's girls go to a day school in York and the boys to an agricultural college. All this I know from Ken. But nothing else. I haven't kept up with anyone, and let's face it, why would I? But sometimes I see things. Or hear things. Just before I went to Canada I read a news article in one of the evening papers saying that a member of one of the Philharmonic orchestras, a Miss H.T. Morgan, had fallen from a train while on tour in the Soviet Union. I assumed it was Hannah, though I don't remember her other initial, do you? This would have been 1981. The implication was that it was suicide. But those rags are so unreliable, it's hard to know. Even if the report was true at all. It's odd that Thea would say she hadn't any news of Hannah if something like that had happened. She could have been covering up, of course. I wouldn't put it past Thea. She was very good at appearances and is probably capable of persuading herself that black is white if white is required. And then there's the overriding virtue of school. That'd explain it. A suicide is not a good recommendation. Not that it would imply a causative connection to anyone else. Or not necessarily. Carn girls don't throw themselves off trains. Or end up in the evening papers. Poor Hannah. A clever girl who should never have been there. She didn't have the resilience, and why should she. Why should she? There was probably something wrong with those of us who did.

'Reading of her death, of that death, whoever's it was, and whatever it was that caused it, whatever Carn had to do with it, or not, was a factor in swinging me round to accepting the Canada job. I had been dithering. My father was old and as you know I'm all he has, and I didn't want to abandon him. But it was a position and a univeristy which would give me more scope than I'd ever had in England. It was a good move. It wasn't until I was there that I realised how cramped I'd found England, even in post-Carn London, as if what really counted was the form of the thing, even the thought, the style. Never the feeling. No sharp edges, ragged margins, blots, about-turns. It was an immense relief to be in a country where one could blunder, change one's mind, take off in flights of fancy and still come back. Someone told me once that in Russia instead of saying what's it all *for*, what do we live *for*, they say what should we live *by*. It wasn't until I left England that I could begin to see what it was I was struggling to live by: a much harder messier question than what to live for. Carn girls live *by* the Carn code you might say, but that code is a *for* code par excellence.

'And as to my father, well it was only a question of money. I was earning well, and what's money *for* if not to enable you to live *by*? So I lived by my debt to him and made sure I got back to England as often as he needed me. And I brought him over on extended stays, which he loved. He was down in the botany depart-ment in a trice, and the year before he died he joined an expedition collecting specimens in the north. He found a lichen that hadn't been classified. So that's a good story. His death was a great loss, and another free-dom of a kind I hadn't anticipated. It was after his death that I lived by my love, never acknowledged before, of women. I also gave up the university. It had given me a great deal, but there was too much back-stabbing and getting ahead, and sometimes it seemed that thought was reduced to fashion. It was too easy to get tangled up in it. I'd spent years flying in and out of Mexico and central America, always on research raids, it seemed at last time to live by a commitment that was real but until then was only paper thin. So here I am working at the INAH, an institute of anthropology and history.

I'm researching and teaching, that's the same I suppose, but the context is profoundly different. Where once I was interested only in an ancient past, as if that way I could bypass the perils of the present, now I make my enquiries, everything I do, to understand better the present – and the future – of the people I live among. I don't know how long we'll be here, nothing is secure, but for the present it's enough. I live with a woman by the name, as the strange twists of fate would have it, of Astrid. She has three children and it is not always plain sailing, but she is a person with a much clearer understanding than I will ever have, of what it is she lives by.

'So that in summary is my life. And yours? You tell me tantalisingly little. If you do ever write of Carn, will you let me see what you have to say? Perhaps that way I'll discover who you are, the grown-up version of the child who planted the finest garden in southern England. It wouldn't be too much to say. And germinated the white delphiniums. Where did they come from? The Balkans, did he say? Some war zone.

'Well. What a long letter. The ease of the word processor. Do you always use ink? It's not easy to read, written that way, but I enjoy the signature of the pen. Your hand still bears the traces of Carn; but it is the hand of someone I would hope to meet.'

That's what she wrote. The letter came packaged in a neatly typed airmail envelope, so neat that with its Mexican stamps I didn't realise who it was from. As a result I opened it without expectation or preparation, and perhaps that's the best way to do these things: suddenly, as I had written to the headmistress of Carn that afternoon in London when I first saw the photo. As I sat at my open window in Sydney's autumn sun with Frances Petersen's letter in my lap, I knew that, though not a word was written, the score was settled. When I took up my pen it was in reply to Frances. 'It was entirely by chance that I saw your name,' I wrote, explaining to her as I haven't to you, that I was visiting the opthalmologist that afternoon when I picked up the magazine and saw her photo; a routine visit, one of the many I will have to make, to monitor the disorder that has shifted so much about the way that I see. If I were to tell that story, I told her, its earliest chapters would be set beside the winterbourne.

For the rest, my letter to her is private.

....

Note:

In thinking about this essay, and writing it, I would like to acknowledge the following works: Thomas Bernhard's memoir *Gathering Evidence*, New York, Knopf, 1985; Cynthia Ozick's wonderful essay 'Mrs Virginia Woolf: A Madwoman and Her Nurse' in *What Henry James Knew and Other Essays on Writers,* London, Jonathan Cape, 1993; and of course Virginia Woolf herself.

The town of Carn and its present inhabitants exist only in my imagination, although there are towns in Wessex and schools in England that are not dissimilar. I was a pupil at one of them.

The
Orchard

*S*tella Bowen never liked London. When she left Ford Madox Ford in 1926, she and her daughter Julie stayed on in Paris. It was only in the jittery thirties with the approach of war and a downwardly spiralling exchange rate, that she returned to London. As a young woman fresh from Adelaide and knowing no better, she felt London to be filled with dazzling possibilities. Returning in her maturity, this time from Paris, and wanting the sustained pleasure of real talk, she was faced as if for the first time with the conversational heaviness of the English. As a girl she'd suffered it meekly, assuming the fault to be hers. As a woman she was still inclined to put her lack of success with *the English idiom* down to being Australian. But one can be born in England and have exactly the same problem. *The knocking about that I have done*, Stella Bowen wrote, *has turned a shy person into a pretty good mixer, but* *maybe it is only in the sense that a New York taxi-driver is a good mixer – he can talk to anyone. But that is not the English way. In the interests of general conversation, you toss off a remark. In Paris or in New York the ball is quickly thrown back. In London, it crashes to the ground where it lies looking like a suet pudding under the cold and silent eyes of the company.*[1]

In pre-war Paris, commissions for portraits had dried up and without them she could not pay the rent. In London where the prams were still pushed as they'd always been pushed *by dawdling women, peering into unattractive, well-fitted shops*, portraits were still being commissioned. Stella Bowen and Julie set up in a studio in Belsize Park. But while Stella Bowen strained to paint groups, or windows, or only a person's hands, she had to rely on portraiture for an income. If it had to be portraits, then she wanted to paint emperors, or at least maharajas, decked out in *ceremonial robes* and surrounded by *fantastic gee-gaws*. As it was she had English burghers who wished to be flattered without drawing attention to themselves. Composition was of no significance, only the facial expression. On these dreary and frustrating commissions, she raised the fees to finish Julie's education.

When the English finally recognised that the dull trough of the channel would not necessarily save them from the events that were rocking Europe, even these miserable commissions ceased. And then, in the summer of 1939 – while Ettie was waiting for her baby to be born – Ford Madox Ford died, closing off another avenue of support. Stella Bowen had taken Julie across the narrow waterway to see Ford in France, on one last visit to the city, and to the country, she'd made home in exile before returning to the exile in exile so many, even those born to it, have known in London. But rather than wait for the bombs in an unprepared city, as Ettie was forced to do, Stella Bowen moved with Julie to a cottage in the country. Unable to paint *ornamental flesh*, she had begun to dream of painting flowers, and that dream had transformed itself into the desire for a garden. An English country garden that she could almost feel patriotic about. The thing about gardens, she wrote from Green End and a cottage that was listed to be used for the wounded in the event of invasion, is that *life certainly goes on*. Even in war. She bottled and jammed, planted and hoed, stored apples in straw in an old tin bathtub. And wrote her memoirs.

. . .

My own desire for a garden, dormant, barely felt, was reawakened more by chance than design, as if I had to be led to it rather than make my own way there. I had no ambition to paint flowers, or to write of gardens; a garden to visit was all I required. So when Louise saw the advertisement for the house across the river, *old orchard, outhouses, fruit cage*, and rang me at Ettie's that time, I was reluctant to get on the train back to Sydney. The future seemed opaque, beyond anything I could imagine, but I went to the station, as eventually one does, and with a dreary heart let the dictates of fate convey me back to the frayed and abandoned threads of my life. As the train carried me away from the sanctuary of that mountain verandah, I had no idea how close I was to the garden that was still, then, buried in a dark corner of once-dreamed-of desires. I could say it was just a matter of chance that Louise saw the advertisement, and that Hal already knew the valley, but as it is I don't entirely believe in chance. The question is not whether life throws up possibilities, but whether we are able to see them, and if we see them, whether we are able to take them. There are patterns in any life, shapes and meanings that rise out of the constantly shifting possibilities of the present. To speak of luck, or of chance, is a response, sometimes envious, sometimes bewildered, made by those who see others take the opportunities they miss. Or it is the self-deprecating response of those who cannot say *yes, it came to me and I risked it, I risked the whole damn thing.* Clara says this is a view of life that leaves a great deal out. Like the circumstances into which we are born; some people, she says, get dealt a mean hand. Louise says we shouldn't forget those chancy moments, those times we throw ourselves into the lap of the gods and everything falters and the gods do not necessarily smile. She says the things we give up can be as important as those we take. And I say there are times when others can see the shape of our lives more clearly than we can ourselves, and then the great act of friendship is to turn us around so that we stand to face that way.

The day after I arrived back in Sydney, Louise and I set off early for the river, driving north out of the city as the commuters drove in, out through the leafy suburbs, now so smart, where Ettie had grown up and the loopy girl had buried her baby, cutting west across the scrubby plains that have been farmed into dust and consigned to chicken and car yards, and down the steep gorge that comes always with the jolt of surprise – vines, lichens, tree-ferns, stately angophoras growing from the rock, abundance once more – down to the dark silty river at the bottom, where Hal was waiting.

As the ferry ploughed slowly through the dark water, breaking up the reflection of the sky and disturbing the ducks, we leaned like figureheads against the railing. Sea gulls and river birds flipped and dipped in air currents none of us could see, belonging as they do to a spectrum that is not visible to our retinas. I stepped back and framed my hands around the two I was travelling with, framed them as if for a photo, floating out above the water, and in the stillness of that moment I felt a surge, like the kick-start of life, as they turned towards me, their eyes meeting mine in the challenge of a recognition that comes unfinished into the present.

On the other side of the river the road winds through farmland and tall stands of bush, sweet scented and elegant. I'd driven there once with Jack; but this time we turned in towards the hills, on a track that dipped and curved along the edge of a creek. When Louise pulled open the old gate at the top of the rise and Hal drove through, we all got out and stood on the ridge looking down into the shallow scoop of the valley. On the far side we could see the creek tucked in under the rocks where the hills tilt up towards the ranges behind. At a bend beneath a sheer lift of rock that shone pink in the morning sun, the creek deepens into a wide pool beside river gums. We could just make out the shape of a shack in the pepper trees where the creek turns back into open pasture. Nearer us, at the edge of the valley where the road winds down and the bush meets clear land, was the roof of the house, its tin rusting out, set in against a smooth wedge-shaped outcrop of rock. The orchard was to the left of the house in an enclosure formed by the rise of the hill on one side, the rocky outcrop, and the creek.

We drove slowly down the track to the house, a plume of dust rising behind us to mark our arrival in the silent valley. A tulip tree was growing through the verandah floorboards, wisteria had lifted its roof, birds were nesting in the eaves. But the timber was solid and the verandah's dimensions generous, shading us from the sun that was already hot on our backs. We walked through empty rooms with sagging floorboards and sooty fireplaces. We followed a path past seeded and weed-choked beds where once flowers had bloomed and vegetables thrived, past a collapsing fruit cage, a disused sheep pen where the grass grew thick and luxurious, and through a gate into the orchard. The air was still, perfumed by the early blossom and a waft of eucalypt from the bush on the hill above us. Almond trees with last year's crop rotting at their base, gnarled quinces, a magnificent greengage. Apricots, stunted apples, varieties of prunus, a single pear tree. At the centre, a huge fig.

'Some of these will have to come down,' Louise said, poking at an apricot that was rotted through.

'It'll give us room to plant more,' I said, and as I did, standing there in the silent valley where no one had lived for years, the future bloomed around me and before we'd so much as turned the first sod of earth, I could see that the garden we would make there would not be to the formal design of Ettie's, or of the gardens I had grown up with in England. There would be no box hedges and gravel paths meeting at sharp angles, no roses growing over arches, no wall to stop the winds and train the espalier pear. Here, protected by the flank of rock, and held in that shallow valley, our garden would blend itself to the shape of the land, with holly-hocks and lupins, if that's what we chose, or Sturt's desert pea and flannel flowers, edging the paths, form-ing banks where the ground rises, fading into shrubs, into herbs, into the shade of the verandah. No one would mistake our garden for a work of art as they do Ettie's with its mannerist certainties; and even if they did, like her I'd almost certainly reply that in gardens where everything is real, control is always temporary: provisional, contingent. Meaning, of course, that it was therefore not a work of art. But secretly I would be disappointed if no one made the mistake, and paid us that compliment, for when the risks of youth become the challenge of age, one learns the provisional nature of all art, and that the existence of every painting, how-ever certain it appears on the canvas, is always contin-gent. Art is created in the tension between that contingency, a necessary instability, and the order, the meaning, the pattern, that graces it. As is a garden. Or a well-lived life.

That morning in the garden that was not yet our garden, when we were still looking for a landscape that would house us all, close but not within sight of each other, we walked on through the orchard following the slope of the ground up towards the rim of the valley, and there, just before the bush begins, we came upon a small clearing hidden from the house by the orchard and the wedge-shaped rock: a secret clearing sur-rounded by trees: on one side bush, on the other side garden. In the grass we could see traces of foundations that must once have been a small building. A summer house perhaps, or a shed. The shades of its occupants were dug peacefully into the ground. It was the perfect place for a studio, and I stretched my arms into the claim I made.

From the orchard we followed the path along the creek bank with its smooth rocks, small sandy beaches, and grassy banks held in place by the roots of the river gums. The shack, when we came to it, looked as though it had once been flooded, but the floor was intact, there was a fireplace in working order, an outside privy, two rooms, and wide windows set into the wall overlooking the river.

'I could just about move in,' Hal said.

And now, almost two years later, he has.

. . .

When Clara came over the crest of the hill one recent weekend when Louise and I were up there planting, I could tell by the smile bursting from her face that a crack had opened in her world and she was going to risk it all and wade in. While I had returned to Australia as if restored to an ancient home, she had come back from New York, where she'd spent another year after London, restless, full of displaced, clashing energies. Living in Ettie's flat without Tom was a relief, she said, though they were getting on well enough; but being there was like returning to a part of herself that had worn thin. For the two months since her return, she had walked the streets of Kings Cross like a prowling cat, sitting in coffee shops, watching the daily trade of pawn-brokers and sex shops. Three days a week she went to her job at the gallery and came home tired and irritable. She wanted more, she said, stretching her arms above her head when I met her for a coffee. 'I feel greedy,' she said. And though she wore it as a secret, I knew that whatever it was that had engaged her during those recent months in Manhattan, or should I say whoever, had brought into a focus a part of her that had sunk back, unmatched since her return. Something had begun, and though she was not saying what that something was, it was easy to see her fear that it might end before it had had the chance of expression. Everything about her was waiting for the opening that would take her into the future, and her heart was heavy with fear that it would not come in time. She was poised for this moment, and that she could take it was due in part to Tom who, as it turned out, realised more than any of us. She'd been offered a job back in New York, part time and temporary, in a small gallery; it was an offer arranged for her by the man whose name she had not yet acknowledged. The pay was low, barely pocket money, but it was a start that would enable the necessary departure.

Take it, Tom said, meaning the job as well as the cheque he offered: the fare, a little over, enough for her insurance, and to get back if she needed to. After all, Tom said, he'd lived with her rent free for all those years, he was earning well and had no one to support: no family, no child. Where once he shone with ambition and the certainty of the future, he now wears his success as a burden he can't save himself from. When I see him with Clara, watching him watching her, it is a tender incomprehension that I see in his face for although he understands better than any of us the form of the events that are taking her from him, he does not comprehend their substance, or meaning; but then men rarely realise why it is that they lose the women whom they think it is sufficient simply to love.

'So,' Clara said, standing there in the valley with the car door open, 'what do you think?'

The surprise in Louise's face exactly matched the shock of apprehension in mine, as Clara's announcement tumbled into the still valley. We left our planting in the orchard and walked down to the creek where Louise and I washed the earth from our hands, and there, under the river gums, we lay on rugs while Clara, taking photos and watching us through the lens of her camera, talked about the rush of preparations: the task of packing up the flat she'd lived in since she'd left Helena's house; the excitement of the work, the life, that lay ahead; the sudden stab of grief when she looked up into the great dome of sky. But when we tried to draw her on the love that was drawing her from us, she became veiled, not evasive so much as wary, as if to protect us from the risk she took as her own, as if she was afraid of destroying the future by naming it too soon, as if a secret had become obscurely necessary.

'There is one thing I want to ask you,' she said. 'A favour.'

'Anything,' Louise said. 'For you, just about anything.'

'It's the paintings,' she said. 'Will you look after them?'

'Sure,' Louise said, 'if that's what you want.'

'I thought you could take Gerhard's portrait,' she said to Louise. 'That cruel neck. Do you mind?'

'I'd love to,' she said.

'And will you take the eye?' she asked, turning to me. 'Ettie's tethered eye.'

'Of course,' I said. 'But it's small. Why don't you take it with you?'

'I don't want to carry anything,' she said. 'I want to leave here free.'

'Is that possible?' I asked. 'Even the most stringent exile carries something.'

'I don't want memories to become a form of blackmail,' she said.

Clara will have to learn for herself the double vision of the exile, the ability to live at once with that which has been left behind and that which is here and now. When she does Louise and I can pack the paintings and take them to her. But despite the modern ease of such arrangements, and despite my own flight across hemispheres and continents, that afternoon I greeted Clara's move with more grief than excitement. When I looked at the house Louise and Akim were reshaping, tipping its roof so that the effect appears oriental while remaining Australian, not quite of the west, not quite of the east, but perfectly complementing the valley, I knew the distance to be travelled before such juxtaposition, such expression of self, could find ease, or elegance of form. The self that is found in exile, deepened by displacement, takes a long time to reach.

Stella Bowen knew this when she painted her self-portrait in Paris in 1929, three years after she had separated from Ford, and ten years before the war. Light strikes her face from the left, and her eyes, shaded not with grief so much as with knowledge, meet us as the challenge of a woman who wears the clothes of her new city with the ease of one born to it. And Artemisia Gentileschi painted *her* great self-portrait in 1630, the year she arrived in Naples, a city she never liked, living there only for the richness of its commissions. It was the beginning of a decade away from her preferred city of Rome, a decade that ended in London where she went late in 1638 to assist her father with the ceiling of the gallery in the Queen's House at Greenwich. It was not a happy visit. Civil war was not far off; London was jittery. Her father, from whom she had been somewhat estranged since the rape trial, was dying; his brief for Henrietta Maria's ceiling was a conservative, lumbering apology for a doomed court: *An allegory of Peace and The Arts under the English Crown.* Yet it was there, in the position of paid artisan to a soon to be decapitated king, that she painted the muse Terpsichore who looks out from a side panel among all that decorative pap, with the startling grace of Artemisia herself.

Her own *Self-Portrait as an Allegory of Painting*, that brilliant statement of a powerful femininity, had already been bought by Charles I and is still today in the Queen's collection at Kensington Palace. That afternoon, when the fates of Artemisia Gentileschi and Stella Bowen, and also of Ettie, seemed somehow linked as each life played out the claims of displacement and creation, the image of Artemisia's self-portrait, left to civil war on her return to Italy, and surviving in the royal collection, seemed at once miraculous and horribly ironic.

And now there is Clara, embarking on a journey from which I long to protect her, even as my heart beats with the pulse of an excitement I understand well.

'What about Jock's portrait of Ettie,' Louise said. 'What are you going to do with that?'

'I'm leaving it in the flat,' she said.

But it would be some time before I understood the irony of her gesture, for that day I didn't yet know who it would be who would next live in the flat that was once Ettie's, in those rooms I hadn't yet slept in but one day would with their windows opening over a shaded street; and I'm not sure that Clara did either. Thinking only of beginnings there was a lot we did not know that afternoon as the future pressed on us with its claims and responsibilities. When I close my eyes I remember Clara slightly flushed and leaning against the great trunk of the fig that is the centrepiece of the orchard. But the photo I took to commemorate the moment was badly composed. A shadow falls across her face casting her expression into the indecipherable grains of the paper; only her hands are illuminated, folded over the slight swell of her belly.

. . .

When Clara left, catching an afternoon flight straight through to New York, Ettie didn't stay in Sydney to see her off. She said she didn't want to burden the girl with her griefs. When Louise and I drove up to see her in the mountains the next day we found her not in the garden, but lying where we usually lie on the verandah bed. Her long proud neck seemed to have shrunk, as if at last it had settled for union with her body. Alec was fussing around her. He said she should take it as a compliment, Clara going off like that. It meant Ettie had done her job, handing her what she needs to take the risk, to grow into her own life.

'True,' Ettie said. 'And she has to go. But allow an old woman her grief.'

'You'll see her again,' Alec said. 'Mark my words.'

'Alec,' Ettie said, 'you'll go to the grave hoping for the best. I will go to mine with reality in my eyes.'

'Dear girl,' Alec said. 'Do buck up.'

But Ettie is not one to buck up. She knows that the rise and fall of emotion will pass and, in the quiet of the house where she has lived since she and Gerhard married after the war that had made refugees of them both, she gives it her due. On the wall above her chair where Jock's portrait hung for so many years, is Clara's pen-and-ink drawing of silver hands, beautiful but macabre. Waiting to hang beside it is Clara's parting gift to Ettie. Painted in the empty flat at Kings Cross when the packing was done and the boxes removed, it is a gouache in which the round orb of an eye lifts up into the sky as if it were a balloon, its tether broken free, drifting up, above the plants and flowers that are growing in the garden below.

. . .

With Clara's departure, this story ends; or if it does not end then it halts, for the life of those of whom I speak will continue even if this account does not. All that is left for me to do is to tell you the story that Ettie told Louise, and that Louise told the mistress as they walked above the harbour at the end of the affair; it is the same story that Ettie told Clara that weekend she arrived in a rage, and that Clara drew for Ettie: the legend of the princess with the silver hands. Ettie told it to me one winter afternoon many years ago now, when I was helping her prune the pear tree. Great drops of rain fell on us, large splats of icy water, and her voice was blown up to me by the wind as I stood on the ladder following her instructions. Ettie herself was told it by her mother the year she turned twelve and her neck grew two inches and the tremble in her arms began. It is the story at the heart of every incident, every story I have told you.

Listen, it is this:

Once upon a time, a maiden was sweeping under the

apple tree at the back of her father's house, when the devil knocked at the front. The girl's father opened the door and the devil offered him great wealth if he gave up all that lay behind his house. As there was only an old apple tree out there, the girl's father thought he had nothing to lose, and eagerly made the bargain.

'Oh husband, husband, how could you do this,' wept his wife, the girl's mother, when the mistake was realised. 'Whatever shall we do?'

When the devil came to collect the girl, she stood inside a chalk circle, protected by the magical substance that rises white through the ground, and the devil couldn't prise her from it. At last, in desperation, he ordered the man, her father, to chop off the maiden's hands so that she would lose strength and he could win her from the chalk. Her father wept, her mother wept, the girl herself wept, but what other choice was there: a bargain was a bargain. So her father took his axe and chopped off his daughter's hands. Her mother bound the stumps in white muslin, and the girl's tears fell on them, protecting them, protecting her; and still the devil couldn't prise her from the circle of chalk within which she stood.

When the devil went away, and it seemed that he had given up, the girl's father promised that, in recompense, he'd keep her in finery, lavishing her with every comfort. But the maiden, prompted by her protecting spirit, the spirit of chalk and tears, knew that such riches would be sterile and that instead she must leave her father's house and take her chances in the wilderness.

This she did, as the injured do, accompanied only by the spirit that walked beside her, a guardian angel perhaps, or that part of herself she had not yet learned to recognise.

One day, after many months of wandering, the maiden came upon a palace surrounded by a wondrous garden in the centre of which was an orchard. As she stood and gazed at trees laden with fruit, the moat parted, and thus the maiden entered the orchard. Pear trees bent their boughs at her approach so that she could take their fruit between her stumps and eat her fill. The next night the king, having seen that his fruit had been eaten, spied on her, and seeing her, fell in love. He fell in love with her handless helplessnesss which, as much as the glowing spirit beside her, made her beautiful to him. In his adoration he promised to care for her all his life; he went down on his knees before her, and married her. And then, when once she was his wife, he arranged for a pair of beautiful hands that would exactly fit her to be manufactured from the finest silver, and the maiden moved into the palace where she lived a happy wifely life, with hands that, all things considered, worked remarkably well. It might almost have been happily ever after.

But in every story there's a point of instability, and in this tale the king, as kings are, was called away to war. He left his wife with her silver hands and a belly ready to deliver their first child. When the child was born, the old queen mother sent a message to the king. But on the journeyings of messengers to and fro, the devil, sore that he had lost the girl, worked his evil way and made sure the king was told not that he was safely delivered of a child, but that his wife had borne a calf. The old queen received in turn the message not that she was to care for the young wife in her time of trouble, which were the king's words, but that she was to kill her and keep her eye and her tongue (those were the devil's instructions) as proof that she had obeyed his kingly command. But this mother, this queenly mother, rather than collude in further strife, helped the young wife and her child escape.

For many years the outcast queen wandered alone in the forest with only her daughter and her spirit for company. During those years of solitude, bit by bit, day by day, her hands grew slowly back: first as buds, then as a little girl's hands, and finally as a woman's hands. And as they did, the spirit moved from outside to within her, and shone from her eyes.

Meanwhile the king, her husband, returned to the palace and discovered the cruel mistake. Weeping and cast low, he set off into the woods to find his beloved wife. Wandering dirty and alone, searching the forest for many years, this abject king did not recognise the beautiful woman and lovely child he came across in a woodsman's cottage. She, the young queen, could recognise him, but without her silver hands, dense king, clinging to the symbols of literality, he could not recognise her. The woodsman, who had taken the queen and the young princess into his care, went to the trunk and produced the discarded silver hands as proof and evidence. Then there was great rejoicing.

The king and the queen returned to the palace where the old queen mother still lived, and there, in a splendid ceremony of exactly the sort Artemisia would have taken in her stride and Stella Bowen would have loved to have painted, they were married again. A hundred guests in glorious robes were invited to feast this second union. A hundred guests bearing jewelled gifts heard the story of the young queen's hands that grew back during those years in the forest. A hundred guests heard the story and went back into the world where they each told a hundred guests of their own.[2]

As you will do, now that I've told you.

....

[1] Stella Bowen, *Drawn From Life*, p. 225

[2] This is the final story, named 'The Handless Maiden', in Clarissa Pinkola Estés, *The Women Who Run With The Wolves*, London, Random House, 1992. The traditional name of this story, which originated in Eastern Europe, is 'The Orchard'. There are various versions of the story. In one version the hands do not grow back slowly, but all of a rush. The queen drops the baby into a well, and with only stumps for hands she cannot rescue her. As she weeps beside the well the spirit urges her, *try, reach in, try*. So the young queen thrusts her hands into the water and lo! her hands grow back and she recovers the child, wet but uninjured. There are some who prefer this order of events, and for those who need to be urged into sudden action, the impetuous risk, it is the best version to tell. But personally I prefer the other.

The Women's Press is Britain's leading women's publishing house. Established in 1978, we publish high-quality fiction and non-fiction from outstanding women writers worldwide. Our exciting and diverse list includes literary fiction, detective novels, biography and autobiography, health, women's studies, handbooks, literary criticism, psychology and self help, the arts, our popular Livewire Books series for young women and the bestselling annual *Women Artists Diary* featuring beautiful colour and black-and-white illustrations from the best in contemporary women's art.

If you would like more information about our books or about our mail order book club, please send an A5 sae for our latest catalogue and complete list to:

The Sales Department
The Women's Press Ltd
34 Great Sutton Street
London EC1V 0DX
Tel: 0171 251 3007
Fax: 0171 608 1938

Also of interest:

Beth Yahp
The Crocodile Fury

Winner of the Premier's Literary Award

In her youth, Grandmother was a famous ghost-hunter. But she is old now and has lost the power of her extra eye. Instead, she relies on her granddaughter to write down her magic, curses, remedies, wisdom and stories. But granddaughter must also discover the secrets of the nuns at the convent where she has been sent to study and to spy . . .

Spanning three generations of women and covering fifty years of history, from the heyday of colonialism to the struggle for independence, *The Crocodile Fury* is a magical, sweeping celebration of women, culture and power – and has been internationally acclaimed as Malaysia's long-awaited successor to *One Hundred Years of Solitude* and *House of the Spirits*.

'Reading *The Crocodile Fury* is like snuggling into the chest of a loving parent at bedtime . . . It engages all the senses. It is rich with colours and rustles, the shrieks of schoolgirls, soft caresses and sharp pinches . . . It is a marvellous read: sad, funny, clever, witty, lyric and joyous. Our literature cannot but be enriched by the addition of writers like Beth Yahp.' *Canberra Times*

'Amy Tan is to Beth Yahp what a lightly seasoned Chinese soup is to a spicy Malaysian curry . . . Fiery, feisty and as complex as her heritage.' *Australian Bookseller*

Fiction £6.99
ISBN 0 7043 4466 1

Stevie Davies
The Web of Belonging

'The woman writes like a dream.'
Marcelle d'Argy Smith, *Independent*

'Jacob is my wall; my rock. I have not encountered the
solidity of this truth until now. Jacob was there, a quality
of my being; a rootedness, a quiet.'

Jess has lived peaceably in Shrewsbury with her husband Jacob for
many years. He is solid, dependable, beautiful to her. She is
contented to be his wife, to look after his elderly mother, aunt
and cousin, to be a pillar of their family and community. Then,
suddenly, everything changes.

Now Jess must question the entire basis on which she has lived
so many years of her life. Must discover whether the identity she
has created has really been so valuable to herself and to those
around her, and whether there is a different – angry, passionate,
fulfillable Jess – waiting to get out.

The Web of Belonging is Stevie Davies' sixth novel – an hilarious,
moving, astute and tender book by one of the most respected
and acclaimed novelists of our time.

'A poignant, funny and luminous story . . . Davies has
written an immensely enjoyable novel, lit by comedy and
wisdom . . . One of the funniest, most poignant novels I
have read this year.' Helen Dunmore, *The Times*

Fiction £6.99
ISBN 0 7043 4519 6

Hiromi Goto
Chorus of Mushrooms

**Winner of the Commonwealth Writers Prize for Best
First Book, Canada and the Caribbean Region**

Chorus of Mushrooms is the exquisite story of three generations of
Japanese women. Naoe, the grandmother, has mourned the loss
of her life in Japan ever since her family left. Keiko, her daughter,
who has changed her name to Kaye and abandoned her Japanese-
ness in order to assimilate. And Murasaki, who longs to reclaim
the heritage her mother threw away and to forge an identity of
her own – to bridge the divide between Naoe and Keiko, while
closing the gaps in herself.

Chorus of Mushrooms is a beautiful and resonant novel, by an
author who has been likened to Jung Chang.

**'In the process of re-telling personal myth, I have taken
tremendous liberties with my grandmother's history.
This novel is a departure from historical "fact" into the
realms of contemporary folk legend. And should (amost)
always be considered a work of fiction.' Hiromi Goto**

**'Hiromi Goto has written a chorus of place and family
and imagination with such clarity and sensitivity that our
tongues rest in awe and our ears feel cleansed.' Fred Wah**

Fiction £6.99
ISBN 0 7043 4518 8

Linda D Cirino
The Egg Woman

'I come from a long line of farmers. And farmers' wives.
There is a picture of a woman farmer on the sack of corn
feed we use that shows the woman just the way I've
always seen most farmers, looking down. I don't know
what she's supposed to be doing on the bag of feed, but
she could be bending her head to some work in the
house or in the field, some mending or cooking, tending
the children. Every once in a while, just to check the
weather, I'll take a look at the sky, see how the setting
sun tells the next day's temperature, see if storm clouds
will come over before the laundry is dry. Mostly, though,
my head is bent over like hers. As far back as anyone can
recollect, we have been working the land.'

It is southwest Germany, 1936. A woman, isolated from the
events of the world, tends her farm. Her husband is away at war;
her children are absorbed in the youth movement. Then she finds
a man – a Jew – hiding in the chicken coop. Instinctively, she
protects him . . .

The Egg Woman is an extraordinary, beautiful and touching novel
about prejudice, integrity, self-knowledge and courage.

Fiction £6.99
ISBN 0 7043 4511 0

Elisabeth Brooke
A February Cuckoo

**Her elegiac new novel of emotional and spiritual
transformation**

London, 1990. Candida survives by reading tarot cards, friendless
save for her familiar, a black panther. Elsie, an ex-dancer, lives
alone but for her memories and a flatful of cats. Bill has worked
all his life as a magician and now, in his sixties, lives in the tunnels
under Waterloo. Here he meets Mark, a young runaway, who
one night is brutally attacked by a group of men.

Candida, Elsie, Bill and Mark join together to hunt down the
attackers. As others are drawn into the search, they each must
come to terms with the tragedy and emotional trauma that
feature in their lives. Through circumstance and choice, all of
them lead lives outside the norm and must struggle to survive in
a hostile and increasingly fragmented world. But they must each
confront their own shortcomings and illusions – and each will be
entirely transformed.

Fiction £6.99
ISBN 0 7043 4516 1

May Sarton
Crucial Conversations

'**Sarton has published over forty books and attracted a
large and devoted following . . . [Her] utter involvement
with life has always been the wellspring of her art.'
Claire Messud,** *Guardian*

On the surface, there was no visible reason for Poppy to leave
Reed. They had shared a robust and lively marriage, full of storms
and passions. They had comfort and money. They seemed
friends. True, she was a frustrated artist in her spare time, but
she had more time to spare now, and Reed had built her a studio.
Yet suddenly she had gone, leaving a cold and angry note. To her
husband and to their closest friend, who had nourished himself
on their marriage, Poppy's act was a selfish, destructive
desertion. But then, in a series of brilliant, searing conversations,
a different truth emerges.

A truth about a woman desperate to exist as an individual. To
discover once and for all whether her art was real, or mere
therapy. To escape from the trap of wifehood, where a woman
can suffocate unless her husband has extraordinary
understanding, which Reed did not.

In this classic, exhilarating and acclaimed novel, May Sarton
reveals the explosive consequences of a growing individual stifled
by a social contract.

'**The finest achievement of Miss Sarton's novel-writing
career . . . A remarkable statement of understanding one
woman's inescapable, inscrutable entirety.' Nancy Hal**

Fiction £6.99
ISBN 0 7043 4524 2

May Sarton
Mrs Stevens Hears the Mermaids Singing

May Sarton is internationally acclaimed for her novels – *The Magnificent Spinster, The Education of Harriet Hatfield, A Reckoning, A Shower of Summer Days, As We Are Now, The Single Hound* and *Kinds of Love* – as well as for her bestselling journals, but this classic and much-loved novel has a special significance both to the author herself and to her readers. It is the first in which May Sarton wrote openly about homosexual love.

Hilary Stevens, a formidable personality and renowned poet, is in her seventies. But her hard-won peace is disrupted first by an angry young poet, Mar, and then by two journalists seeking the source of her inspiration. In the course of her interview with them, and as her relationship with Mar develops, Hilary Stevens finally comes to terms with her own past and her creative muse.

'May Sarton ranks with the very best of distinguished novelists. The reader is compelled to that feeling of awe which the accomplishments of first-rate literary creation inevitably bring forth.' *New York Times Book Review*

Fiction £6.99
ISBN 0 7043 4333 9